SNEAKERS

A Novel by
DEWEY GRAM

Based on a Screenplay by
PHIL ALDEN ROBINSON

W0006674

Ⓞ A SIGNET BOOK

SIGNET
Published by the Penguin Group
Penguin Books USA Inc., 375 Hudson Street,
New York, New York 10014, U.S.A.
Penguin Books Ltd, 27 Wrights Lane,
London W8 5TZ, England
Penguin Books Australia Ltd, Ringwood,
Victoria, Australia
Penguin Books Canada Ltd, 10 Alcorn Avenue,
Toronto, Ontario, Canada M4V 3B2
Penguin Books (N.Z.) Ltd, 182-190 Wairau Road,
Auckland 10, New Zealand

Penguin Books Ltd, Registered Offices:
Harmondsworth, Middlesex, England

First published by Signet, an imprint of New American Library, a division of
Penguin Books USA Inc.

First Printing, September 1992
10 9 8 7 6 5 4 3 2 1

PUBLISHER'S NOTE
This is a work of fiction. Names, characters, places, and incidents either are
the product of the author's imagination or are used fictitiously, and any
resemblance to actual persons, living or dead, events, or locales is entirely
coincidental.

One

A snow day—good news for the school kids of Madison, Wisconsin.

They awoke to drifts as high as their first-floor windows, curtains of snow lashing their yards. They ate their breakfasts, waiting, dressed for school, one eye on the morning news—hoping. At last the word came: a snow day. A no-school day. A day of pure fun.

Good news for government workers used to a few free days of leisure as reward for the long Wisconsin winters. Good news too for cops, booksellers and bartenders as life slowed down and took a turn for the contemplative.

And good news for University of Wisconsin undergrads Martin Bishop and his friend Cosmo; or so they thought when they saw the morning's chilly bounty. In fact, it would be bad news, news of the worst kind. News that would change their lives. But that was still hours away.

By mid-morning, Bishop and Cosmo had slogged their way through howling wind and high drifts to the campus computer lab, figuring they would have the place to themselves all day. A prime chance to perfect a technique they had been working on, and to accomplish some important goals.

The gray stone science hall was locked. Bishop went to work with a lock pick, trying to spring the latch on the ancient wooden doors. No luck. Cosmo fiddled and also failed. They went around to the back doors. Nothing. They tried the heavy casement windows and fared no better. Bishop, frustration mounting, was getting ready to kick in a window, when a janitor made his way slowly up the front walk and let himself in to check the furnace.

Bishop and Cosmo slipped in behind his back and padded up to the computer lab. They left the lights off, locked the door, switched on the mainframe computer and quietly got down to business in the glow of its cathode-ray tube. They were in heaven. They had what they needed: a long uninterrupted time to work.

Big mistake. It gave the other side exactly what it needed: a long uninterrupted time to work.

All day long a faint blue-green glow emanated from the third-story window of the gray stone campus building in Madison, an eerie halo in the swirling snow. Bishop and Cosmo brought out their small stash of munchies. They worked, snacked, didn't budge for hours. They thought they had the thing nailed down several times; they were coming close.

At nightfall the blue-green glow from the mainframe computer's cathode-ray tube continued to cast its faint light on the now dark corner of the campus. They pressed on. No stopping now.

Cosmo—wiry, long slicked-backed hair, big intense dark eyes behind rimless glasses—had rigged wires from the back of the mainframe to a pulled-apart rotary telephone. They had dialed all day long, trying combinations: trunk lines, feeders, back doors, side doors, numbers, letters, symbols, anagrams, and inversions. They got part way in more than once, but never all the way home. Never pay dirt.

Bishop leaned back, tired, put his feet up. He looked every bit the romantic young radical: tight faded jeans, cowboy boots, long hair a brazen two or three inches longer than almost any other guy on campus. Ambling across the quad in his sharp Navy peacoat and raffish scarf, he was the Errol Flynn of Madison in '69. This was a young man you would be hearing from: smart, fearless, unwavering sense of self. His fellow students expected they would someday be looking back and saying, we knew him when.

Bishop, too, looked down the road. It was a great time to be in college. He was part of a special generation. And once out in the world, he was sure, they were destined to soar.

Late in the evening, Cosmo straightened up from the keyboard. "And we are in," he said.

Bishop leaned over his shoulder, reading the screen. He whooped. "Cosmo, you're a genius." He gave the undemonstrative Cosmo an exuberant kiss on the top of his head.

Cosmo allowed himself a faint smile.

Bishop grabbed up an enormous computer printout three inches thick and flipped through it until he found what he was looking for. He read it to Cosmo, "Okay. 46–99402, transfer to 53–01138."

Cosmo typed it in. And added the figure $24,999. "What'd we just do?" he said.

"The Republican Party just made a generous donation to the Black Panthers," Bishop said happily.

Cosmo nodded. "Farm out."

"Right arm," Bishop said.

"Who's next?" Cosmo asked.

"Well, there's a lot of defense contractors in here," Bishop said, turning pages in the printout. "And you know, not one of them gives enough money to radical groups."

"Disgraceful," Cosmo said.

"Disgusting," Bishop agreed.

"Despicable," Cosmo said.

"Dis . . . dis is good," Bishop said, getting a rare laugh out of Cosmo. "How about Northrop, Hughes and Lockheed all give to SDS?" He held up the printout for Cosmo to read. Cosmo typed in three more sets of numbers, each time ending with $24,999.

"Why not an even twenty-five?" Bishop asked, turning the pages of the printout.

"Anything $25,000 and over triggers an audit," Cosmo said. "This way, they will never know."

Bishop thought about that. That was an interesting fact. "So you mean, if the government of South Vietnam, say, put $50,000 into Richard Nixon's personal checking account . . ."

"We could do that." Cosmo smiled that faint smile again.

Bishop showed him the numbers and Cosmo got to work. "He's gonna have a hell of a time explaining this," Bishop exulted.

"We're gonna crack open this rotten system," Cosmo said, bent over his keyboard. Cosmo was so intensely focused and no-nonsense that nobody hearing him would ever doubt he would go to the wall trying.

Bishop flipped more printout pages, looking for the next clay pigeon. "So many targets, so little time," he said.

Cosmo leaned back in his chair and stared at the ceiling, sorting though diabolical ideas. "How about the Society to Legalize Marijuana gives money to Vice President Agnew?" he said.

"How about Spiro Agnew gives money to legalize marijuana?" Bishop came back.

"Better," Cosmo said, jumping back on the keyboard. "How much?"

"He's a generous man," Bishop said. "I'd say all he's got . . ." He showed Cosmo the number.

"Dig it." Cosmo did his twisted magic.

"Solid," Bishop said, rising and stretching his long legs. "Man, we are in the pipeline. I am starved."

"Posit—major premise: The phone company has too much money," Cosmo said.

"Ooh, good one," Bishop said. "Minor premise: They are corrupt."

"Conclusion: The system perpetuates itself at the expense of the people," Cosmo said.

"Consequence," Bishop said. "Ma Bell herself needs to give away some money."

"We're going to change the world, Marty," Cosmo said.

"I just wish we could get course credit for it," Bishop said, peering out the window at the foul weather. "Hey, you want some feed?"

Cosmo scooped up a coin from the table, put it in one hand and held out two fists. "Loser goes," he said.

"I never lose," Bishop said. He whacked Cosmo's left hand. Cosmo opened it: Empty.

"A pepperoni pizza, please," Cosmo said. "Shaken, not stirred."

Bishop headed for the door giving the clenched fist salute. "Power to the people, Cos."

"Power to the people, Marty," Cosmo said, raising his still-clenched right fist.

Marty left. Cosmo slowly opened his right hand. It too was empty. He smiled to himself. "Who do you trust? Always the $64,000 question." Cosmo went back to work, feeling the power.

In Washington, D.C., it was a hushed night. An unusual snowfall gilded the monuments and bare cherry trees. Big flakes settled on the long reflecting pool in front of the Washington Monument and melted, disturbing the surface so slightly that only someone watching closely would see the faint rings spreading out.

The few cars in the streets were virtually crawling. Washingtonians throw up their hands in helplessness at a mere inch or two.

And at this late hour the power brokers were home snug in their beds, sleeping soundly in the knowledge that the U.S. Government had a firm hold on the levers of the free world; that Richard Nixon and his chosen few were standing guard against the red menace abroad and the pinko-rad collaborators shaking their fists on college campuses at home.

Down on Constitution Avenue, the august, white marble Federal Reserve building with its stately columns was as dark as the rest of the bureaucratic strongholds, except for some bright lights on the top floor: the Night Ops Office. There, alarm bells were ringing and shorthaired men in white shirts with pocket protectors ran frantically back and forth answering phones, poring over maps, studying computer screens.

"Wisconsin?!" the balding, sweating night-ops chief screamed into the phone. "That's all you've got for me?— Wisconsin! We've had that for the last hour! *Where* in Wisconsin . . . ?!" He listened for a moment, plucking at his remaining hair compulsively. "Well then, how many channels, how many lines coming out of Wisconsin? Come on! This—is—a—major—conspiracy, man. Get it through your head. They're hitting a shitload of federal facilities! What the hell kind of setup can they be using? How big an organization we dealing with?"

"It's Madison!" shouted a grim-faced young operative, looking up and gesturing from another phone. "The phone company has the trace. They say it's a single line."

"Bullshit! A single line," shouted the night-ops officer in rage. "Those incompetent asses!"

"That's what they say," the young agent said. "They're giving it to the FBI right now."

"About bloody time they gave 'em something!" the night-ops chief spat into the phone. "Now that half the cows in the federal system are out of the barn!" He slammed the phone down, wiped his clammy pate with a handkerchief. "Communists running amok in Madison, Wisconsin. I never thought I'd see the day."

In the Department of Justice, a tall gray granite building on Pennsylvania Avenue, at the headquarters of the Federal Bureau of Investigation, one lit upper floor was alive with activity. FBI Special Agent in Charge of Infrastructure, Ray Hutcherson, in shirt-sleeves and shoulder holster, spoke into a red phone while ripping a dispatch off a teletype. "University of Wisconsin, Madison, sir . . . A small but extremely sophisticated and well-planned operation. Very professional, almost certainly a trained provocateur cell . . . Yes, this could be the one we've been waiting for . . . Yes, sir! Sorry we had to wake you, sir.'' He grimaced at the response. ''You bet we will, sir . . . No chance of that, sir.'' He hung up, turned to the other phone he was holding and barked, ''University Computer Center. Go!''

Inside the computer lab in Madison, Cosmo bent over the console, referring from time to time to the printout, punching in more numbers. And singing Berry Gordy's ''Money.'' ''Oh, the best things in life are free, when you rip 'em off the bourgeoisie—''

He stopped when he heard a sound. He looked up. ''Marty?''

Bishop, bearing his burden of pizzas, plodded through the darkened snowdrift covered campus, bucolic and peaceful now with large flakes falling straight down. He came up the rise toward the computer lab, humming ''Do You Want to Know a Secret,'' lately from the Beatles. He was a few steps from turning up the front walk when he noticed the strobe of flashing red lights on both sides of the building.

Upstairs, Cosmo heard another sound. He pushed back from the CRT and walked over to the door. ''Marty?''

Out front, Bishop's thoughts filled with dread. He took a dozen quiet steps past the entrance walk and checked out the situation, just an innocent student on a late-night errand. In the parking lot were several marked and unmarked police cars. A dozen heavily armed men were moving quickly to surround the building. A half dozen more police vehicles came churning up the hill throwing up clouds of snow. They charged in the driveway, no sirens but red lights flashing, just missing Bishop by a few feet.

Upstairs, Cosmo heard the crackle of a two-way radio from outside the window. A bit concerned, he walked to the window and looked out. He saw Bishop, standing alone in the snow, looking up at him. The rotating glow of red lights played across Marty's face. Cosmo was puzzled. ''Marty?'' he said.

Behind Cosmo, the door burst open and burly, helmeted policemen with weapons drawn charged across the room and grabbed him.

Now, Cosmo felt betrayed. "Marty!" he cried out in a mixture of rage and fear.

Bishop, half-hidden in the shadows behind the snow-drifts, took a few halting steps backward, then dropped the pizzas in the snow, turned and fled.

In the computer room, Cosmo struggled but was easily overpowered. As the shock troops handcuffed the wide-eyed radical and pulled him from the room, the lieutenant in charge barked an order: "Alright, fan out. Let's find 'Marty.' "

Outside, all that was left of Marty were desperate, running footprints in the virgin snow.

Two

San Francisco—1992

"Marty . . . Hey, Marty . . ." A man's voice called to the dozing Bishop.

Bishop awoke. Twenty years can make more of a difference in a man's eyes than in his face. Bishop still had the buccaneer's handsomeness, weathered and a little hardened by time. But now a questioning seriousness vied with a maverick gleam for command of his eyes. No doubt that twenty-year road had been marked by more than one regret. Had it also been punctuated by lesser triumphs, fewer grand accomplishments than the ebullient world-changer of the sixties foresaw?

The Marty Bishop who now shook himself awake in the back of a van had not straightened out and grown up into a captain of industry, a high-powered lawyer, a respected cancer researcher, or a mergers-and-acquisitions million-aire. Nor had he gone the other route some campus radicals traveled: Nader-esque citizen advocate or new-breed poli-tician gadflying the system from within.

No. This Marty Bishop—dressed down in a black turtle-neck, funky corduroy jacket, jeans—was catching a snooze in the back of a nondescript, faded-red van packed with a hodgepodge of tools and electronic gear. He looked like nothing so much as an out-of-work high school biology teacher or failed golf pro.

The black man who called him awake from the driver's seat was straight-looking, serious of mien and much better dressed than Bishop. He was wearing a well-cut business suit: Donald Crease, late forties. "So . . . how much do you want?" he said. "Let's make a deposit."

While Bishop tried to smooth the wrinkles from his corduroy jacket and comb his hair into a presentable state of semi-chaos with his fingers, Crease watched an armed guard unlocking the heavy glass doors of the bank across the street.

Centurion Savings and Loan was opening for another day of trade. About a dozen customers filed in, all of them respectably dressed business types . . . followed a few minutes later by Bishop and Crease.

Crease stood in the teller line for a few moments, looking casually around, taking in the layout of the bank and the tone of the place. He raised his brows. Gravity in the personnel seemed to be valued over congeniality.

Crease noted the ceiling-mounted video cameras which monitored the customers, most of whom appeared to be wealthy older people. He took a last look at the layout, checked his watch, nodded to Bishop and hurried out.

Bishop's casually careless attire had immediately drawn the attention of the hefty bank guard. The guard watched him as he shrugged his rumpled coat straight on his shoulders and headed for the customer-service window.

Bishop put on his smile. He was still, despite the flight of years, what women who like a little danger in their lives would call dashing. And he knew it—and knew he could trade on it to advantage.

"Hi," he said to a middle-aged female bank officer. "I need to open a safe-deposit—"

"One of the tellers can help you," she said, barely looking up. She walked away.

"Oh," Bishop said. He stepped over to a young female teller who was counting receipts. "Excuse me," he said. "I'd like to—"

The young woman gestured to the NEXT WINDOW PLEASE sign in front of her, then pointed Bishop to the now-lengthy line of customers queued up to see a teller. She continued counting her receipts.

Bishop looked around. He spotted a sleek, blond, mid-twentyish bank officer sitting at her desk doing absolutely nothing. He walked over to her—MS. EMERSON her name plate said.

"Hi," Bishop said with his best half-smile. "Are you busy?"

"Not at all," Ms. Emerson said with a dazzling smile. "Can I help you?" She was a knockout, expensively coiffed, dressed in a designer power suit that must have cost half a month's salary. This was clearly a woman on her way up, and one who just as clearly liked the attention of men—or so Bishop sensed.

"Yes, thank you," Bishop said, relieved. "My name's Marty Bishop, and I need to open a safe-deposit box, but everybody else seems to be—"

"I am sorry, Mr. Bishop," Ms. Emerson said, "but I don't do that." She smiled at him, then went back to doing what she had been doing before he came over: nothing.

Bishop couldn't believe this. "What do you do?" he asked.

"I'm a vice president," Ms. Emerson said.

"Ah, that accounts for why you're so busy," Bishop said.

"Customer service," Ms. Emerson said icily, and turned her carefully made-up profile to him.

"Customer service!" Bishop exploded. "Why she just . . ." He calmed himself down. He leaned halfway across the desk and looked the startled Ms. Emerson in the eye. "Ms. Emerson," he said. "It's nice to be important, but it's also important to be nice, don't you think?"

She just stared up at him.

"You have gorgeous green eyes, Ms. Em," Bishop said.

She made no response. Then she laughed. "You really think you're something, don't you?" she said.

"You do have time for the 'little' customers, don't you?" he asked.

"Some of them," she said. "Joy Emerson, Mr. Bishop." She stood, offered her hand for Bishop to shake. "Follow me," she said. She gave him the once over and led him across the floor of the bank.

They approached the vault. "I haven't seen you here before, Mr. Bishop," Ms. Emerson said. "Are you new here?"

"My work keeps me away a lot," Bishop said.

"And what is it you do, Mr. Bishop?" she asked, as they entered the safe-deposit area.

"I'm a bank robber," he said.

This time she just shook her head. "You're a little boy who needs to grow up," she said. She unlocked a safe-deposit box, pulled it out and placed it on the counter for him. She turned her back to give him some privacy.

Bishop opened his briefcase and withdrew a small device the size of a hand grenade. On its face was a timer, which he set for 1:00 A.M. He casually laid the device into the safe-deposit box, closed and locked the lid and shut his briefcase. Ms. Emerson listened to these last sounds and spoke to him without turning around. "All set?" she asked.

"Yes, it's set," he said. He smiled his boyish smile as Ms. Emerson put his safe-deposit box back in its niche and locked it. She handed Bishop his key and they walked out of the vault together.

"Thanks, Ms. Emerson," Bishop said as they approached her desk. "I'll try to grow up."

"Joy," she said. "Next time come around noon and maybe I'll let you take me to lunch. I'll teach you about table manners."

Bishop laughed, gave her a friendly smile and sauntered across the lobby past the narrow-eyed guard.

"How 'bout them Giants?" he said to the guard with a wink. And strolled out into the morning air.

Three

Bishop walked for half a block and stopped at the first telephone kiosk. He dialed a number. "Hello, Mother?" he said.

Halfway across town, in a subbasement recording studio, a cacophonous hip-hop band was just finishing up a session on the other side of the glass. At the rear of the chaotic, less-than-chrome-plated but nevertheless technically advanced control room, Mother had the phone to his ear. Mother was a harried, overweight, ponytailed ex-hippie with patch cords around his neck. He and Whistler ran this place, now and then at a profit.

"Yeah," Mother said, nodding seriously. "Right." He

hung up and called to the lean, dark-haired guy in shades tweeking knobs at the master console. "Hey, Whistler," he said. "We're on for tonight."

"I know," Whistler said without turning his head. "I heard him." Whistler was blind, but he had ears like a spy-satellite's microphone's. He was one of few people who could listen in on a phone call from across the room. He hit the talk-back button to open a mike to the band members. "Fellas, that bass sounds like crap," he said.

"Thanks, man," said the anorexic bass player. "I really worked hard to get that."

"In that case," Whistler said, shrugging, "everything's cool."

At the phone, Mother was dialing.

In one of the big ballrooms of the Grand Hyatt Hotel off Union Square in San Francisco, the International Security Systems annual trade fair was underway. The hall was filled to capacity with booths, and teeming with prospective customers ranging from button-down corporate straight arrows to *Soldier-of-Fortune* mercenaries in camouflage jumpsuits.

A prominent central bay featured the offerings of PROTEC SPECIAL SYSTEMS LABORATORY according to the large but tasteful sign overhead.

Leading some South American businessmen through this supermarket of security gadgets—alarms, electric eyes, Kevlar bullet-proof body stockings, disguised weaponry, miniature surveillance cameras and much, much more—was Donald Crease, Bishop's associate.

He guided the businessmen away from the armored limo with signs all over it pointing to its rocket-proof glass, gun ports and undeflatable solid rubber tires. He stopped before a beefy, rednecked security guard standing at attention, shotgun athwart, casting his eyes around for the enemy.

"We are forced to spend millions developing new security technologies every year," Crease said to the South Americans. "And why? Because of this man." He gestured to the blue-shirted security man. "Undereducated, underpaid, occasionally sociopathic," Crease said. "Never without egregious failings—*never*, it's safe to say, one hundred percent reliable. In fact, not worth the uniform on his back."

The businessmen exchanged embarrassed glances.

Crease, undeterred, went up to the guard and gave him a vicious slap across the face. Crease's hand passed magically through the guard's head. The businessmen laughed in surprise.

"Holographic," Crease said. "Saves manpower, training and cleaning bills. Requires no health insurance or other benefits. Will never sue you for wrongful termination. Takes no religious holidays and scares the shit out of an intruder."

A voice came over the Protec PA: "Mr. Crease, line two please."

"Excuse me," Crease said to the South Americans, who were now taking their own pokes at the beefy guard. He walked to a nearby desk and picked up the phone. "Crease," he said. And then, "Good." He hung up and dialed a new number.

In a noisy and grimy high-school metal shop in Oakland, a student messenger, a nerdy teacher's-pet sort sent down from the school principal's office, came loping into the class and looked around as though at a zoo. It was a zoo of sorts—a continuing-ed class for motley dropouts trying halfheartedly to scrape together a degree. A few of the students were in their forties—there was one grandmother—but most of the enrollees were disgruntled late-teens who would rather be anywhere else and acted it.

The messenger handed the shop teacher a note and beat it. The hairy-armed teacher made his way across the shop, passing students working desultorily on metal shelf building, pipe welding, electrical wiring projects—things that ought to be useful in the real world. He came up behind a lean, floppy-haired kid who was so eagerly and intensely tied up in his work that he jumped nervously when the teacher said, "Carl, what the hell is that?"

"That" was a miniature elongated motor-driven device that looked like the innards of an electric toothbrush, and yet far too complicated.

"Oh," Carl said, "it's a . . . it's an electric gum-massager, you know . . ." He turned it on. The end vibrated. The teacher looked skeptical. Carl, bad at lying, tried to make it more believable. "For my dog."

The teacher gave him a sardonic look. "Why don't you work on something that might make you a buck someday?" he said. He handed Carl the note and walked away.

Carl read the note: "Your father called. Bring your sneakers home tonight."

Carl looked up and saw the muscular spike-haired girl at the next bench watching him. He smiled secretively, crumpled the note, put it in his mouth and swallowed it, secret-agent style.

He hurriedly packed his device and his tools in his gym bag, waited until the teacher with his back turned was occupied at the front of the room and slipped out the back door. The spike-haired girl shook her head and went back to her own project, which appeared to be haircutting scissors with a mirror attached on a stalk for cutting the back of your own hair.

Four

A full moon was out. A dry wind scattered leaves and papers along the deserted sidewalk in front of Centurion Savings and Loan and past the locked and iron-gated stores to either side of it. Light but steady late-night traffic trickled by. A patrolling squad car slowed in front of the bank. The officers cast a look into the bank, saw nothing amiss and continued on their rounds.

The faded red van had returned to the scene and was parked catty-corner across the adjacent intersection with a sight line to the front door of the bank. The van now had a "Department of Public Works" logo on its doors. Its one-way black-glass side wall faced the bank. The Sneakers were hard at work.

Inside the van, Donald Crease, dressed in dark jogging sweats, had a binocular-eye view of the young guard sitting at the security console in the bank lobby. The guard's station rested between the bank's entrance and the curtain-covered glass wall separating him from the bank proper behind him. He had his feet up and was watching music videos on a tiny portable TV set.

"We're in," Crease whispered, nudging Bishop who was once again sprawled, eyes closed, in the back of the van.

Bishop roused himself quickly. He sat up and listened to

Whistler at the front of the van, talking softly with someone over a pencil-thin headset. "Okay, Mother, try the leads coming off the blue trunk."

A low tone came over the headset. "No . . ." Whistler said. Another, slightly higher tone. "No . . ." he said again. "Try the white trunk, Mother. These don't sound right."

In the street just south of Centurion Savings and Loan was an open manhole. Over it was a sign: DANGER: HIGH VOLTAGE.

Down in the cable vault—swarming with pipes, wires and cables—worked Mother, sweating and swearing. Mother wore a similar pencil-thin headset and a miner's lighted hardhat with the stencil MOTHER on the back. He hooked a pair of alligator clips to wires from the white trunk in the panel box. A tone sounded. Again Whistler's voice came over the headset: "No . . ."

"They even got pictures of the guy actually leaving the embassy," Mother said into the headset. "Hey, Crease, you there?"

"Yeah, I hear you," Crease said, keeping an eye on the bank as Whistler sorted through the tones from Mother's patches.

"Were you still in the CIA in '72," Mother said, moving his clips to another wire.

"Yeah. Why?" Crease said.

"No . . ." Whistler said, after another tone.

Mother picked out another wire and clamped it. "Did you know," he said, "the deputy director for planning was in Managua, Nicaragua, *the day before the earthquake*?"

Whistler was listening intently to this last tone.

"Now what are you saying?" Crease said. "The CIA caused the Managua earthquake?"

"Well, I can't prove it," Mother said. "Hey, I can't prove the moonwalks were faked in a film studio, either. It'll all come out someday."

Crease snorted in disgust. Bishop placed a calming hand on Crease's arm without taking his eyes off the bank.

Mother changed wires again, generating another tone. Whistler's voice came over his headset: "Wait a second. Go back one." Mother repatched the previous wire.

Whistler nodded with certainty. "That's the one." Whistler had been blind since age nine, but since then he had developed a poet's touch for Braille and a Rhodes-scholar hearing in all aural wavelengths, including, his teammates were sure, the bat ranges.

Down in the hole, Mother attached a second alligator clip to the same line, then cut the line with a wirecutters between the two clips.

Twenty-five blocks away, in the Westguard Security offices, three uniformed hire cops sat at the central station, playing three-handed poker at a large console. Above them, a map of the Bay Area showed the location of Westguard's customers, Centurian S&L among them.

Meters on the console, all displaying green lights, ticked off the flow of current that ran through the various clients' alarm lines. One of the officers glanced up. No problems anywhere. Just as he looked back down at his cards, the current sputtered and blanked on the Centurian S&L meter, the green light turning red for an instant. The officer glanced up again. But by the time he did, the light was back to green, the flow normalized. He watched it for a few moments: nothing. The card game went on uninterrupted.

Bishop and Crease exited the van. They waited for the light and crossed the street. Staying close to the adjacent building, they stayed out of the lobby guard's sight and trotted along the side of the bank building.

In the shadowy alley next to the S&L, hyperactive Carl waited, dressed all in black, nervously affixing and reaffixing two big suction cups with an attached handle to the glass door of the bank's emergency exit.

Bishop and Crease approached. They both reacted when Carl turned. He had outdone himself this time. He had grease-painted himself in blackface. Crease just looked at him and shook his head. Bishop smiled.

Crease peered through the glass door. "Where is it?"

"Safe-deposit box, main vault," Bishop said, checking his watch. "The hardest part was getting those snobs to believe I might have anything of value to put in a bank."

"We're going to have to buy you a suit, Martin," Crease said. "You don't dress for success."

The seconds ticked off to 1:00 A.M.

In the safe-deposit vault there was a quiet ticking. Then— in the wall of boxes in which Bishop's treasure snuggled— a muffled pop. Heavy white smoke began to pour out, gradually rising to the smoke detector on the ceiling. A fire alarm wailed. A red alarm-light bathed the room.

Electronic deadbolts automatically slid back in the glass firedoor.

"Banking hours," Carl said, pulling it open. Bishop and Crease slipped into the darkened bank and Carl followed them.

The night guard in the main lobby leapt up at the sound of the alarm, knocking over the portable TV with his feet. He started running toward the curtained-off main floor of the bank building, stopped, came back to his guard console and pulled out a manual.

Behind the curtained glass wall, Bishop, Carl and Crease scuttled across the bank floor. Carl vaulted over the tellers' counter. Bishop followed, but halfway through his leap, he caught his foot on a divider and crashed to the floor. Crease helped him up. "We're getting too old for this," Bishop said.

From inside the tellers' area, Carl clicked a latch and opened a gate for the two older men. Bishop and Crease walked through into the inner area, scowling at Carl, who kept an absolutely straight face.

The guard in the lobby frantically read the manual: "Do not leave post in an emergency. Call Westguard for instructions." He found the proper phone number in the manual and laboriously punched it in one digit at a time, to get it right. This was an emergency.

"Westguard Security," came the response.

"I got a fire at Centurian Savings," the guard reported.

"Yeah, we got the alarm," the Westguard voice said. "Any secondary indications?"

"Whadaya mean?"

"Any smoke?" the Westguard voice barked. "Any flames or smoke? Do you smell anything, sir?"

The guard raised his nose. "Uh, nope."

"Probably a false alarm," Westguard said. "We been getting them in your area all night. Power surges. See if it resets."

"Oh man, I don't know," the guard said nervously. The alarm continued to ring unabated.

"It should reset inside of two minutes," Westguard said. "Don't panic, man."

Inside the bank, Bishop and Crease stopped at a computer

terminal and turned it on. Carl raced by and ran down a corridor, opening doors. Xerox room. Bathroom. Utility room. That was the one he wanted.

He slipped in and went straight to a row of junction boxes. Locked. He pulled out his chrome-plated electronic "doggy gum massager"—actually his own version of a Cobra pick. He inserted it in the lock and pulled the trigger; it vibrated a few seconds and the lock opened. Carl pulled open the cabinet, searched amid the tangle of wires and circuit breakers inside. He found the wire he wanted—a green one—and was about to snip it with a wire cutter when Bishop came in to check what was holding him up.

"Whoa whoa whoa!" Bishop said. "You know which one to cut?"

"Yeah, the alarm's always the green one," Carl said. He confidently cut the wire—and plunged the bank into total darkness. The alarm kept ringing.

"Oh, Carl," Bishop said.

"—except sometimes it's the yellow one," Carl said.

The guard in the lobby was now fully freaked at the sudden darkness and the blaring alarm. "Hey, man," he bleated into the phone, "I'm calling the fire depart—"

At that moment, the alarm went dead. Soothing silence. The guard looked around. "Oh. It, uh . . . it stopped. Sorry."

"No problem," Westguard came back. "And son?"

"Sir?" the guard said.

Outside, down the street in the faded-red van, Whistler, speaking authoritatively into his headset, finished the sentence: "Good work," he said.

"Thank you, sir," the relieved bank guard answered.

Whistler smiled as he unplugged his line; then replugged into a different jack. "All yours, Bish," he said.

Inside, Bishop nodded at Crease who was poised at the computer terminal. Crease hit select keys, and waited. The screen lit up with: "PRIVILEGED ACCESS."

"So," Crease said, "how much do you want?"

Bishop thought for moment, and came up with a nice round number.

Five

At noon, the next day it was busy banking hours at Centurian S&L. Bishop, wearing a suit and tie that Crease had shamed him into borrowing, waited patiently while a very polite bank officer placed neatly wrapped bundles of cash in his briefcase. "Ninety-eight . . . Ninety-nine . . . One hundred thousand," the bank officer said, lifting the briefcase and handing it to Bishop.

Bishop looked inside. "I just had an awful feeling my money wasn't safe here."

The bank officer sighed and looked pained, but kept his own counsel.

"Not your fault, Mac," Bishop said, shaking the officer's hand. Bishop snapped the briefcase closed and walked off through the carpeted bank with the self-satisfaction that only a really clean bank job can bestow.

But instead of going out the front door, Bishop turned down a hallway and walked toward a door marked CONFER-ENCE ROOM.

He opened the door. Inside the plush conference room, swiveling toward him, were all eight of the bank's top offi-cers: seven men including the hulking, dour bank president at the head of the table, and the attractive Ms. Emerson, who looked at Bishop a little sheepishly. Present also was the bank's bull-necked chief security officer, Hugh Ayns-worth.

"Let's have it, Bishop," said the bank president.

"Your communication lines are vulnerable," Bishop said, walking to the other end of the table and tipping his brief-case over on it. Tens of thousands of dollars spilled out. "Your fire exits should be monitored, your computers are far too user-friendly, your rent-a-cops have the IQ of"—He remembered Aynsworth was there—"They're just a tad un-dertrained."

Joy Emerson whistled. Very impressed.

Wrong move. The rest of the executive board glowered at

her. She resumed a serious expression, studying the face of this intriguing man, Bishop.

"Once the bank was isolated from the response force," Bishop said, "entry and access were child's play."

The bank president looked over at Aynsworth, whose face was turning purple. "Would our security department like to respond to that?" the bank president said.

"Goddamn right I would," Aynsworth blurted. "I thought we were hiring a consulting firm. I thought a bunch of pencil-heads were gonna look over our security setup and write recommendations." He was squeezing the edge of the table so hard he cracked his knuckles. "Nobody told me some two-bit cowboy was gonna blow off bombs and play some asinine cops and robbers game in the damn place!"

"Mr. Aynsworth," Bishop said coolly, "whether you're working for a bank, a department store or muffin shop, it's axiomatic in my business that the best way to test a client's security is to break in."

"Not to mention the most memorable," the bank president said, still staring torch holes through Aynsworth.

"And the most fun," Bishop said with a smile at Ms. Emerson.

"Well, I'm not impressed," Aynsworth said, taking the offensive. "I'd like to point out, gentlemen, that Mr. Bishop was *not* able to get into the vault. He didn't even get into the goddamn cash drawers."

"Excuse me, pal," Bishop said, "I don't think you understand what happened here. Who cares about your cash drawers? That's chump change. Once I accessed your computer, I *owned* this bank." He picked a last packet of hundreds out of his briefcase and tossed it down.

Ms. Emerson chuckled audibly. Again the other executives turned to look at her. She cleared her throat and tried to regain her cool.

"I don't care what this clown says," Aynsworth said. "If we weren't secure against any *reasonable* threat, I wouldn't keep *my* account here, now would I?"

Bishop walked over and pulled Aynsworth to a standing position by his tie. "First off, try not to call me a clown," Bishop said to the man's face. "And secondly, you used to have an account here. I closed it out last night. Your life savings are there on the table." He let the big man fall back into his seat and returned to the head of the table.

"You'll be getting our full analysis and recommendations in a few days," Bishop said, snapping his briefcase shut. He smiled at the group. "So . . . who's got my check?"

"Uh . . . I do," Ms. Emerson said, rising quickly. The sour-faced president pushed himself up slowly, a storm gathering in his face. As Bishop and Ms. Emerson walked out and closed the door, thunder rolled inside.

At her vice-president's desk out front, Ms. Emerson hunt-and-pecked Bishop's check on her typewriter, while he casually watched the workings of the bank, storing information for future professional use.

"So this is incredible," Ms. Emerson said, shaking her head. "People hire you to break into their places to make sure no one can break into their places?"

"It's a living," Bishop said.

She pulled the check out of her typewriter, signed it with a flourish and examined it before handing it over apologetically to him. "Not a great one," she said, rising.

"Times are tough," he said.

She walked him toward the door. "Tell me the truth," she said. "Once you've broken into a place, don't you ever think about . . . really taking something?"

"No. I have this strange aversion to jail," Bishop said. "Besides, there are plenty of people willing to pay me for it. Like the bozo who owns your bank."

Ms. Emerson laughed.

"How about you?" Bishop said. "You ever think of dipping into the till?"

"Constantly," she said. "It's all I can do to stop myself. And I'd do it, too, except my uncle'd kill me."

"What is he, a cop?" Bishop said.

"He's the bozo who owns this bank," she said, stopping by the door. "The lunch I suggested? You're an interesting man, Mr. Bishop. But not interesting enough to overcome that paycheck. Good luck." She shook his hand, turned on her heel and strode back toward her desk.

Bishop looked after her, unsure whether he should feel stabbed or tickled. He tried stabbed; it felt lousy. He laughed and it felt better. He walked out.

From outside the bank, there was a clear view through the bank's broad front window of the spot where Bishop and

Ms. Emerson had sat talking. In a late-model blue Plymouth two conservatively dressed men wielding binoculars, had been watching the conversation. As Bishop walked out and along the street, one of the men glanced down at a photo he held in his lap, then back up at Bishop. "Come to me, baby," he said.

"We're gonna give him a big hug," the other man said.

Six

In a mixed commercial-industrial neighborhood in Oakland, the wider avenues were a dispiriting array of discount clothes and furniture stores, pawnshops, run-down laundromats, nail salons, convenience stores, a few ethnic delis and many empty storefronts. Even among the auto repair businesses, motorcycle shops and auto upholstery shops, which always seemed to have enough business, were many dead enterprises.

The cross streets were lined with stretches of squat, graffiti-scarred cinderblock buildings housing anonymous warehouses and God-knows-what-they-really-make businesses like Syntech Imports, Allied Manufacturing, Amercorp Products and a good many empty shells of abandoned small manufacturers. It was a whole bleak world of erratic economic struggle and loss.

On one of the still-alive commercial blocks was The Oakland, a now-abandoned, once-ornate Deco movie palace, its long-extinguished neon marquee still rising majestically up the front of the three-story building. An attempt to convert the space to shops and offices had flopped. The Oakland was occasionally home to squatters.

But on the top floor was a going concern, of sorts: M. Bishop & Assoc. - Security Consultants. Its front windows looked out across the Bay toward San Francisco— toward a fancier, more monied world than industrial Oakland could ever deliver.

The late-model blue Plymouth from the bank was now parked across the street and down a few buildings from the Oakland Theater. The same two gray suits sat inside.

The driver hung up his portable phone, and nodded to the other man. They got out, crossed the street and walked back to the defunct theater.

They found M. BISHOP & ASSOC. on the ruined directory board with its broken front glass, and missing letters. The men got on the elevator and punched 3. It groaned upward.

In the Sneakers' reception area, mushroom-haired Carl paced back and forth in front of a telephone service man disconnecting the Centrex-type telephone station. "But we just got paid, man," he pleaded with the guy. "The check's in the mail. I swear it!"

"And when it arrives, I'll bring this back," the phone company man said. "I swear it."

As the elevator doors opened and the two suits from the Plymouth emerged, the telephone man yanked the cord from the wall, hefted the unit and headed for the elevator.

Carl took one look at the two men, guessed at who they probably were and did some fast thinking. It was not a good moment for their phone to be repo'ed. "And don't bring it back this time until it works!" he called after the phone guy.

The phone guy gave him a what-drug-are-you-on-kid look and disappeared inside the elevator.

"Huh! Junk," Carl said, and turned to the two men. "Can I help you boys?" he said.

"Gordon and Wallace," the younger, preppy suit said. He had a friendly reddish mustache. "Is Mr. Bishop in?"

Carl, conscientious security-operative-in-training, gave a suspicious once-over to the men, who stood there looking as pleasantly harmless as they could.

"We have a job we'd like to discuss with him," said Wallace, a fleshy older man who had a face like Broderick Crawford locked in a fish cannery.

Carl liked the sound of what the man said. "Really?" he blurted. "I mean . . . yeah, he's here. I mean, he might be here. Let me call back and see." He turned to grab the phone, but it was no longer on the desk. "Hey, you know what?" he said. "Why don't I just go back and see? It'll be a lot quicker." And at the last second he remembered: He glanced at their shoes. Then back at their faces. "Don't go away," he said. He went through a door into the back.

The Sneakers' Lair lay behind the reception area. The rest of the top floor was an open loft, windows wrapping around three sides. Bishop's modest apartment occupied one corner at the back: a bed, a bureau, some weights, an electric guitar and amp and a Bob Dylan "Don't Look Back" poster on the bathroom door.

In an open kitchen area there was a stove, a sink, a refrigerator, an eating table and chairs. Nearby were a couple of overstuffed chairs and a reading lamp. The minimum necessary to sustain life.

And the rest of the loft was toyland. From one end to the other, high-tech gadgetry, tools, sound systems, the latest tape and video machines, workbenches full of electronics in various stages of testing and development, stacks of CDs, books, magazines, piles of sport shoes, a bag of basketballs and a motorcycle under repair.

The loft was divided into separate areas of turf, each with its own variety of techno-junk surrounding it like asteroidal debris around suns.

Whistler, in the middle, had a large U-shaped table set up with digital audio tape machines, shotgun mikes, amps, Braille boxes attached to PCs, a torn-apart but functioning telephone, racks of old stereo music albums, speakers of all sizes and shapes, two constantly spinning turntables, a TEAC mixing panel and a synthesizer.

Mother's area at one end was stacked with powerful scanners, radar and sonar devices, lock-pick oscillators, portable electrical transformers, power surge boosters, long lens cameras disguised as tote bags and miniature cameras. It was a mess with barely enough room to sit down. In the middle of it all was an Exercycle and a mat for doing calisthenics.

Crease's area along the eastern wall was anally neat, with a straight-backed chair, glass-front bookcases and an orderly desk with locked drawers. There was even a small oriental rug fronting his area, with chairs and a sofa.

Carl, in his niche along the opposite wall, was in charge of and inundated by phone books—local and national—and as many other city, county and state directories as he could lay his hands on. His modest workbench displayed a variety of break-in devices he was working on, along with his Cobra pick. The keystone of his domain was his boom box with a sizeable tape collection and earphones.

Bishop's area on the west end by the kitchen had three different computers; books on politics, computer programming, security, cryptography; some ledgers and record books; three telephones, all with tape recorder jacks attached; and several large filing cabinets.

These guys were serious snoops, by all appearances, with ample hi-tech equipment to play the game like pros.

Bishop leaned back at his desk eyeing the blue-shirted security guard armed with a shotgun standing next to Crease.

"He'd be perfect for that export company," Crease said. "What do you think?"

Mother stopped to sneer at the holograph guard. "Him? He's garbage," he said.

"Look who's talking," Crease said. "Eight thousand bucks isn't garbage."

"If our clients could afford that, they wouldn't hire us," Bishop said skeptically.

"We're getting forty percent off from the manufacturer," Crease said. "We sell five of them to Sheeser Imports, mark 'em up twenty percent, we make eight-grand profit. Sheeser cuts down on his break-ins, plus he saves on salary, benefits and dry cleaning."

"Lemme think about it," Bishop said. "Who's got the report for the bank sneak?" he asked. The rest of the team was slouched nearby like college fraternity vegetables. The Sneakers were holding what passed for a business meeting.

"I'm going to type it up later," Mother said.

"*You* are?" Bishop asked.

"We haven't paid the typist since January," Mother said. "It's either me or Whistler."

Whistler knocked over his diet cola, to remind everybody he was blind.

"Better Whistler," Crease said. Mother shot him a hurt look.

Feeling around on the floor for his cola can, Whistler came up with a big plastic bag. From it he pulled two extra-fat, four-foot-long foam baseball bats in red and yellow. "Let me guess," he said, feeling the bats. "Cue tips for elephants."

"Those are mine," Crease said testily. "Put 'em down."

"The right tool for the right job," Mother said, grabbing one of the bats and taking vicious swings at the holograph guard. The bat swished harmlessly through the figure's head. Crease took the bat from him.

"What are those for?" Carl asked, trotting up to the circle.

"Never mind," Crease said, stuffing the bats back in the bag and pushing it behind his desk.

"Aggression therapy," Whistler said, pulling it out of the air. "Conflict resolution devices. You and your wife"—

"Really?" Bishop said. "You and Caroline bash each other with those things?"

—"And scream and release primal emotions," Whistler said helpfully. "It's very healthy shit." The other Sneakers chuckled.

"Maybe we do and maybe we don't," Crease said irritably. "It's not my idea."

"That's like a totally retro-seventies thing to do," Mother said. "Can I borrow them when you're done? I know this girl—"

The other Sneakers hooted him down.

Carl remembered why he had come in. "Hey, Bish, customers outside," he said. "Real ones." That got everyone's attention. Customers at the door were not so rare as a total eclipse of the sun, but almost.

"Shoes?" Bishop said.

"Expensive," Carl dutifully reported.

Bishop quickly grabbed a jacket and tie and strode briskly across the loft, calling behind him, "Look busy, guys. Mother, have you done your sit-ups and push-ups?"

Mother groaned and dragged his feet toward his calisthenics mat like a sullen eight-year-old.

Crease walked out with Bishop. Carl scrambled to keep up.

"What about the law firm on Powell?" Bishop said to Crease.

"They accepted our bid," Crease said.

"I'm gonna sweep for bugs and install some scramblers," Carl said.

"Is this going to cost us more than they're paying us?" Bishop asked.

"Not by much," Crease said, shrugging.

"Good," Bishop said as they entered the hallway to the front. Crease went left; Bishop continued toward the reception area with Carl trailing close. "Do something with your

hair," Bishop said to Carl, who quickly tried to finger comb
it.

The two suits rose as Bishop and Carl entered. "Mr.
Bishop—Dick Gordon," said the friendly preppy fellow with
the reddish mustache, shaking Bishop's hand. "Bud Wallace," he said, introducing the surly older man. "We've
heard a lot of great things about you," Gordon went on.

"They're all true," Bishop said. The two men smiled
politely. Carl laughed a little too loudly.

"Thank you, Carl," Bishop said, arching an eyebrow.
"Gentlemen, why don't we go to the conference room, and
you can tell us how we can help you." Bishop held open
the door as the two men walked through. Carl started to
follow. Bishop shook his head.

"Come on, Bish, when are you going to let me sit in on
meetings?" Carl pleaded.

"As soon as you start to shave."

Seven

Wallace and Gordon sat across from Bishop with several file folders before them. Through the glass windows of
the conference room, the visitors could see the Sneakers in
the loft, all convincingly at work.

"Before we begin, there's something we'd like to clear
up," Gordon said. "Most firms of this kind, so-called Tiger
Teams or Black Hatters, are staffed by ex-law-enforcement
types. But your team is—"

"Kind of different," Bishop said.

"Yes, you are," Gordon said.

Wallace opened one of the file folders and pulled out photographs and fact sheets. "Irwin Emery, aka 'Whistler,' "
Wallace said, looking around, locating the rail-thin Whistler
out on the floor.

Whistler was practicing with a customized Navy sonar,
trying to identify objects in the room from their echoes.

Wallace said, "Nine counts of fraudulently obtained telephone service."

"He was eleven years old at the time," Bishop said. "He's an absolute genius at that stuff."

"Pickpocketing charge when he was seventeen?" Wallace asked.

"He was just practicing and he gave it back," Bishop said. "His father made him learn manual dexterity after he went blind—sleight-of-hand magic, jazz piano."

"Worked for JPL for a while, then for IBM as a programmer and designer but got fired," Wallace said.

"He kept ragging them to join forces with Apple," Bishop said. "He insisted they'd save billions a few years down the line. At IBM, that was subversive. They were sure he was actually working for Apple."

Gordon opened a second file. "Darryl Roskow, aka 'Mother,' " he said.

Mother could be heard grunting out in the loft, engaged in the one hundred push-ups, one hundred sit-ups per day regimen decreed by Bishop as the condition for Mother's remaining part of the team.

"Felony conviction: eighteen months at Dannemora for breaking and entering a federal installation," Gordon said.

"He was framed," Bishop said. "But he's got the best hands in the business—any lock, any safe—electronic or old-fashioned."

"Uh-huh," Wallace said.

"The other guy later admitted the frame. Is that in there?" Bishop asked. "Or that he's a college graduate."

Gordon looked out at the scruffy, animalistic Mother. "That guy?" he asked in disbelief.

"It took him a few years," Bishop said. "In between, he got involved in some personal drug research. A lot of different drugs. It kinda left its mark. But that's all in the past."

"Carl Arbogast," Wallace said, "age nineteen, did a half year in the Pritchess Honor Ranch for tapping into government data bases." Carl, out in the loft, could be seen trying to reassemble in working order an $8,000 high-definition television he had, to everyone's horror, disassembled out of curiosity.

"Oh, come on," Bishop said. "He was fourteen at the time."

"And—" Wallace began.

"Yeah, yeah, yeah, he broke into his school's computer and changed his grades," Bishop said.

"He gave himself a scholarship," Gordon said.

"And all the other hard-up kids in his class who wanted to go to college. Okay," Bishop said, altering his tack. "You want law enforcement? Donald Crease, twelve-year veteran of the CIA."

"Donald Crease, twenty-two-year veteran of the CIA," Wallace said, finding Crease with his eyes.

Crease was sitting at his tidy desk halfway across the loft, doing absolutely nothing but staring at the visitors in the glass-walled room as if reading their minds.

"Terminated in 1986," Wallace added. "Why was that?"

Bishop was no longer liking the drift. A slight edge rose in his voice. "I think it was a personality conflict. Who are you guys?"

"Relax, Marty," Gordon said. "We have to check on these things, and it's just that everyone on your team's had some sort of problem in their past."

"And then there's Martin Bishop," Wallace said. He looked at Bishop evenly, opening the final folder labeled with Bishop's name. It was empty. "He doesn't seem to have a past," Wallace said.

The mood at the table turned decidedly chilly. Bishop looked at the empty file on the table, and eyeballed the two men stonily. He figured it out. He stood.

"I'm sorry to have wasted your time, gentlemen," he said, "but I don't work for the government."

"We know," Gordon said matter-of-factly.

Wallace held out both his and Gordon's leather identification holders. "National Security Agency," he said, looking back at Bishop just as stonily.

"Ah, you're the guys I hear breathing on the other end of my phone," Bishop said.

"No, that's the FBI," Gordon said. "We're not chartered for domestic surveillance."

"Oh, right," Bishop said. "You just overthrow governments and set up friendly dictators."

"No," Gordon said, smiling. "That's the CIA. The NSA protects our government's electronic communications, and tries to break the other fellow's codes. We're the good guys, Marty."

Bishop remained standing. "Gee, I can't tell you what a

relief that is . . . Dick," he said. "But even as we speak, I'm remembering too much of what I've read about the NSA's capabilities—and propensities—to make me comfortable. Sorry." He opened the conference-room door. "If you like," he said, "I'll give you a long list of my competitors who probably don't care." He waited for them to get up.

Wallace gave Gordon a look, gathered his file folders and shoved back his chair. "All right, let's go," he said. He gave a last narrow-eyed scan of the Sneakers in their lair and walked out of the room.

Gordon sighed, pulled an envelope out of his pocket and wrote something on it. He walked out the door and Bishop accompanied him to the elevator.

Carl watched curiously from the receptionist's desk as Wallace sourly pushed the "down" button. Gordon handed Bishop the envelope he had written on. "If you change your mind," he said, "you can call us at this number, Mr. Brice." The elevator door opened.

Bishop turned pale at the mention of that name. He froze, the envelope clutched in his hand, waiting for what came next. But Gordon and Wallace stepped into the elevator without looking back and the doors closed.

Bishop looked down at the envelope. He opened it, withdrew a one-sheet FBI WANTED notice dated 1969 with his picture. Except the name listed was "Martin Brice."

"Why'd he call you Brice?" Carl asked.

Bishop didn't answer. He just stood there.

Eight

Bishop walked out of the Lair by himself. He walked around the corner and kept going. He came to the edge of a Chinese neighborhood and pushed open the door of the first bar he came to: Red's Dragon.

He entered the smokey dive, waited for his eyes to adjust, and sat down on a wooden stool at the bar. He checked out the eclectic decor: Chinese calligraphy art, rice-paper fans, fishing nets and conch shells, a South Sea Island mural with palms and hula girls, a floor-to-ceiling Easter Island sculpture and a three-tiered fern fountain behind the bar. Something for everybody.

"What you want, friend?" the bartender said with a small crinkly smile that disappeared as fast as it came. The bartender—presumably "Red"—was Chinese, round-faced, tired-looking and bald.

"I want a life," Bishop said. Then rolled his eyes at his own pathetic bleat. Not at all his style. He was a man who protected his privacy and kept his emotions on an even keel at all costs. And he tried to keep himself so busy he didn't have time to reflect. He rarely allowed himself the slack to look back across his life since college and the Days of Rage.

"Sorry," he said to the bartender. "Give me a . . ." He looked up at the daily specials listed on the blackboard menu above the bar. ". . . a Singapore sling," he said.

The bartender nodded and walked away. Bishop couldn't remember exactly what a Singapore sling was, but he was sure it was lethal and easy to drink. What the doctor ordered: anesthetic.

He looked around the bar. Most of the dozen or so other patrons—afternoon drinkers, probably from the rolls of the unemployed and unemployable, thought Bishop—were gathered around the gambling tables in the back playing a game with dice and cards unfamiliar to Bishop. They were all of Chinese origin, jabbering and joking, caught up in their world.

"Here. You feel better," the bartender said with his quick smile as he put down Bishop's drink.

Bishop gave the off-color potion the fish eye, and drank it down.

The bartender looked at him for a moment, taking in his morose expression. He pulled up a stool on the other side of the bar and sat down. He sat sideways to Bishop, not looking at him, watching the men at the back. He said nothing.

Bishop stared at the man peevishly. He looked up at the blackboard and ordered again. "A foghorn," he said. He had no idea what that was.

The bartender made it, brought it back, puttered for a moment and sat down, again not looking at Bishop.

Bishop drank his foghorn, not quite so fast as the sling.

The outside door banged open and a fourteen-year-old

boy breezed in. He was of Chinese descent, dressed in American ripped-knee jeans and had a floppy haircut like Carl's. He walked up and leaned on the bar next to Bishop. "Dad, can I have ten dollars?" he said to Red. "We're going to a movie."

"Where?" the bartender said.

"Where?" the boy repeated. "At the West Bank."

"That's $4.50 for matinee," his father said, getting up and going to the cash register. He handed his son a bill. "Here five dollars."

"Thanks, Dad," the kid said with a grin and breezed out.

The bartender sat back down, facing west.

Bishop returned to his bleak thoughts. His life had been shaped *for* him, by a single youthful escapade that denied him free choice thereafter. He had lived in the negative, not daring to do this, forced to do that, running like a thief in the dark from the other. Not a bad life, by certain lights. He was able to use his quick mind and enjoy the exercise of his talents. He had the material necessities and the sustaining pleasures of good friends and associates. He *seemed* free.

But, behind the easy-going mask, Bishop felt chained in a banal gulag that shut him off from all but the most modest possibilities. A jail that shut off prospects for the other Sneakers as well. The jobs, the career chances that Bishop had turned down to protect his own anonymity—he couldn't even tell them about. He couldn't seek absolution from them or anyone else.

Periodically he would try this—a blow-out—though it almost never worked. In the past he had gotten down four or five drinks and gone home sick, feeling worse than when he had started.

"A volcano," he said to the bartender, who sat there Buddha-like in profile.

The bartender got up and made a drink that involved brandy, liqueurs, lime juice and flame. He placed a stone crock that spit fire in front of Bishop, blew it out and sat back down.

"A man and his conscience . . ." the bartender began, still facing west.

Bishop looked at him incredulously.

"You know story of Lao Tzu and Killer Tiger?" the bartender asked.

Bishop just looked at him.

"Tiger killed sheep and goats and even children," the bartender said. "Big trouble. Lao Tzu, help us, villagers say. Make long story short: Lao Tzu say, you do not understand this old fellow. Lao Tzu take lamb to tiger lair, put lamb in tiger bed. Tiger return—"

The street door swung open again and two teenaged girls walked in, one Chinese, the other Caucasian. The Chinese girl, the taller and prettier of the two, came and leaned on the bar. "Hi, Dad," she said. "Can I buy some roller blades?"

The Chinese man looked at her. "Are you nuts?" he said.

"Da-ad," she said. "I can get them for under one hundred dollars at Target."

"No," her father said.

"They're for the AIDS Skate-in," she said. "Geez, Pop, AIDS you know, we gotta do our part."

Her father gave her a gimme-a-break look and turned to the cash register. He pulled out two twenties and a ten and held them out to his daughter. "Matching funds," he said. "You get half from Arby paycheck."

"Oh, Dad," she groaned.

"And you bring home dinner tonight," her father said. "I want curly fries."

"Do I have to?" she whined. "My paycheck will be so small!"

"It hard out there for everybody," the bartender said.

"Thanks, Dad," the girl said somewhat dejectedly. She leaned over and kissed him. Bishop watched her turn and start for the door—and give her waiting girlfriend a secret look of triumph. "Wow, he's tough," the other girl said as they sailed out.

"So . . ." the bartender said, "Tiger come home with fresh killed deer in mouth and find lamb in bed. He lick lamb like own kitten. They play, they lie down, sleep together. As long as tiger and lamb live together, say Lao Tzu, all well in village. End of story." He smiled his quick smile. "What next?" he asked, picking up Bishop's empty crock.

Bishop checked the list over the bar. "Sidecar," he said. "You forgot the part about the tiger turning into a half-man and saving the baby from the snake."

The bartender looked at him in surprise. "You come here before?" he said.

"No, man," Bishop said with an ironic half-smile. "I read Lao Tzu in college. How many other kids you got?"

Nine

The old Federal building in San Francisco was *old:* a neoclassical ruin that looked habitable only in comparison to the rest of the neighborhood. Bishop walked past an abandoned newsstand and through some scaffolding and construction materials blocking the front of the building. A derelict in tattered clothes sat on the Federal building's front steps.

"Spare a quarter?" the old boy asked. "The government's taking away my home. Help me out?" Bishop handed him some coins, took a deep breath and entered the building.

Gordon was waiting for Bishop in the lobby, standing beneath the official portrait of George Bush on the begrimed wall. Workmen pushed dollies stacked with old office equipment past them out the door. Gordon, in his shirt sleeves— white shirt, narrow tie—extended his hand.

"How are you?" he said to Bishop, leading the way to the elevators. "Sorry for the mess. This place has been set for immediate renovation for three years." He pushed the "up" button. "Finally getting around to repairing what the quake did to us," he said. "Probably just in time for the next one, huh? Anyway, thanks for coming."

Bishop was hungover. He couldn't care less what the place looked or smelled like. "This isn't exactly a voluntary visit," he said. They entered the elevator.

Gordon punched a floor button. The elevator car started up. He leaned back against the wall and looked sympathetically at the visibly out-of-sorts Bishop. "Marty, let me reassure you about something," he said. "We don't want to bust you; we want to hire you." Bishop looked at him blankly. Gordon gave his affable smile. "We routinely perform background checks on potential contractors. The fact that yours turned out to be a little more colorful than we expected is not a problem.''

The elevator stopped, they got off. "In fact," Gordon said, "it sort of helps." Gordon stopped just outside the elevator. "Look," he said, "before we get to my partner, I just want to say I admire what you did back then.''

"Oh?" Bishop said.

"See, I was in the ROTC while you and your pal Cosmo were tapping computers and getting people draft deferments," Gordon said. "I was sucking up to corporate recruiters and you guys were ripping off Dow Chemical to fund the Black Panthers.''

"Are we here to talk about your guilt or mine?" Bishop said.

Gordon chuckled self-deprecatingly. They started walking toward an office. "Hey," he said. "This is just my roundabout way of saying that your attitude about the government . . . well, it's just not accurate anymore. Fifteen years ago, yeah. But it's different now." He stopped and turned to Bishop. "*We're* the government now." He crossed the corridor and opened a door marked RESOURCE ALLOCATION SERVICES ADMINISTRATION.

Wallace, sitting at his desk in his shirt sleeves, was sorting through Bishop's criminal past strewn out before him: the wanted poster, copies of warrants and indictments, newspaper articles with headlines like RADICAL NEST RAIDED: ONE STILL SOUGHT and WAR PROTESTER GIVEN STIFF PRISON TERM.

Wallace stood, smiling smugly. "Well, if it isn't Robin Hood," he said, picking up the rap sheet. "Let's see: fraud by wire, grand larceny, conspiracy. How many years you think you'll get? Five? Seven?" He pushed a photo across the desk. It was a blowup of Bishop and Cosmo in college, smiling as they took apart a telephone.

Bishop picked it up and looked at it: a snapshot of history, of the friendship of youth, of ancient ideals. "Add flight to evade prosecution," Wallace said. "Five more years right there.''

Bishop smiled back at him, but it was a dangerous smile. He hadn't liked this guy to begin with. "You know, I kinda wanted to join the NSA, but they found out my parents were married," he said.

Wallace lost his smile. Gordon immediately stepped between the two and made a "time out" sign with his hands. "Okay, okay," he said. "Peace. We're all friends now. You want a beer, some coffee?" he asked Bishop.

Bishop shook his head no. "Let's get it over with," he said.

"Okay," Gordon said, walking around behind his desk. He took a file folder out of the drawer. From it he pulled a photograph of a man, placed it on the desk in front of Bishop. "This is a young mathematician named Gunter Janek, Dr. Gunter Janek," he said, as Bishop picked up the photo and studied it. "He's a full tenured professor at UC. He also works at a think tank called the Coolidge Institute," Gordon went on. "He specializes in large number theory, prime numbers and factoring."

"Yeah, cryptography," Bishop muttered.

"Very good," Wallace said.

"He teaches a few advanced seminars, does some re search, publishes a paper now and then," Gordon said. "He had a fast start in his early twenties, lit up the sky in his field. Recently, nothing startling. In fact his career appeared to be on the wane. Until last month. Suddenly the good Dr. Janek gets a grant for $380,000." He raised his brows "Way out of profile for a guy like that—*we* thought. From a foundation no one ever heard of. It's our job to be curious, so we traced the money. Guess where it comes from?"

"I haven't the foggiest. I *know* you're not going to say Russia," Bishop said.

Gordon and Wallace both nodded.

Bishop laughed. "Gimme a break," he said.

"It came from a numbered account in Zurich," Gordon said.

"A lot of people keep their money in Zurich," Bishop said. He was neither impressed nor intrigued. Nor convinced they were telling him anything like a true story. His hangover headache was making him woozy.

"It's a longtime KGB hard-currency account," Wallace said. "We monitor a number of them in Switzerland."

"I got some startling news for you guys," Bishop said. "They gave up. We won. It's been in a few papers. Yeltsin disbanded the KGB last year. You didn't hear?"

"And we still spy on them, and they still spy on us," Gordon said. "Don't be fooled by the headlines, Marty. They're there to reassure the people. You think a professional corps of tens of thousands of trained career agents is going to evaporate overnight? Go home and get a job down at the factory and be happy? Spies spy. They may change their names or their targets, but they don't just turn into barbers and shoemakers.''

Wallace pulled another document from the file and laid it on the table under Bishop's eyes. It was a badly reproduced schematic diagram of a small rectangular electronic device unlike any other piece of electronics Bishop was familiar with, foreign or domestic, and his knowledge was extensive.

"We intercepted a fax last week," Gordon said. "Janek seems to be making a 'box' of some kind. A little black box.'' He pointed to a legend along the side: SETEC ASTRONOMY. "This is what they call the project, Setec Astronomy," he said. "We don't know what the 'Setec' stands for. And we haven't a clue about the 'Astronomy' part.''

"Security technology," Bishop mused. He was intrigued despite himself. He turned the schematic this way and that.

"Sensor techniques? Whatever," Gordon said. "Now maybe it's nothing or maybe it's something. But we think an airline reservation in his name to Brussels in the middle of the week might mean something. We think that's the delivery time and place for the box. But even if we're wrong and he's intending to bring it back, that box is too vulnerable to a snatch by the other side once it's out of the country.''

"We gotta get our hands on it before it leaves the U.S.,'' Wallace said.

"Your job is to find out all about Setec Astronomy," Gordon said. "What it is, who's involved, what are they up to with this black box? And we need to examine the box and make a judgment about it before somebody takes it home to Boris.''

"We figure it's in a vault," Wallace said, "either at his house or the Institute. Somewhere he can get at it to work on it.''

"It's not going to be easy, he's probably pretty careful with it,'' Gordon said. "But you can take my word this is important—highest priority national security.''

"Three days," Wallace said.

Bishop looked at the two government agents. "No way,''

he said. "You guys did all that homework. You know this is not the sort of thing I do."

"I'm sorry, Marty," Gordon said gently, "but we don't have a lot of choice here. Or time."

"Do it yourselves if it's that big a national-security deal," Bishop said. "You're big boys. Do your own dirty work."

"NSA is not allowed or equipped to perform this kind of operation," Wallace said. "We don't have black-bag operatives."

Bishop didn't get it. They weren't telling him the whole story. "So use the FBI," he said.

"Yeah, right," Wallace snorted. "They'd still be generating the forms three weeks from now."

"You wouldn't believe the channels we have to go through to get authorized for a surreptitious entry," Gordon said. "You wanna hear? First we have to go to G Group—they're responsible for Russia. The chief of G Group has to meet with the chief of W Group, who do intercept operations. The proposal then has to work its way up the chain of command to the deputy director for Operations, the deputy director of NSA and then to the NSA General Counsel."

Bishop shook his head in annoyance. He didn't want to know.

"Ha. I'm just beginning," Gordon said. "The NSA General Counsel takes the application to the NSA Director, the Secretary of Defense and the Justice Department's Office of Intelligence Policy and Review—I shouldn't even be telling you this stuff. Then, if the U.S. Attorney General puts his little stamp on the documents, the Foreign Intelligence Surveillance Court—which is a secret court you're not supposed to know exists—is called into session to hear the merits of the case. If they give us the nod, then we get to ask the FBI. Can you believe it?"

Bishop's head was hurting. He got lost back at W Group and he didn't care.

"Then!" Wallace said, taking over, "the FBI can't work for us without official approval from *their* Congressional oversight committee. Well, it so happens the chairman of that goddamned committee is fly-fishing in New Zealand! The subchairman has the balls of a sea slug. We're not going to get him to get off his ass unless we can show that a fully armed hydrogen bomb is being towed on a raft from Havana."

Bishop could see Gordon was actually pained by all this—probably more emotion than the guy had felt since he earned his first scout merit badge.

"If this Janek thing turns out to be something of value," Gordon said, "you can bet your last dollar it's our hide that'll hang out for skeet. We're up against it, period."

"Still leaves me asking, why me?" Bishop said.

"Frankly, it's because it *is* illegal," Gordon said. "There are plenty of classier private outfits out there—I'm sorry to have to say that. But you've managed to stay underground for twenty years. That's a hell of an accomplishment, given the price the feds had on your head. That tells us you know how to work both sides of the street, and, more importantly, that you know how not to get caught."

"And that you can keep your mouth shut," Wallace said. Charming as always.

"All we're asking from you is to do what you do for a living," Gordon said. "Not a bad way to repay your debt to society."

Bishop watched the men's faces, trying to read what they weren't telling him. So far he'd heard nothing to make him want to jump in—nothing but a bad job for the usual lousy reasons.

"Marty, I have to tell you this," Gordon said. "If you do get caught, we don't know you, and we can't help you."

That did it. *The hell with this gig,* Bishop thought. "I'd have to be out of my mind," he said.

"The job pays $175,000," Gordon said. "Payable on delivery."

"You can distribute it among the poor, if you like," Wallace said.

Bishop looked at them, stood up and shook his head. "Pass," he said.

Gordon came around his desk. "We also clean up your record," he said. "And quash the outstanding warrant for your arrest."

Bishop looked at him. The light was beginning to dawn. He waited for the other shoe to drop.

"Your pal Cosmo got twelve years, and that was *without* flight to evade prosecution," Wallace said.

"And we all know what happened to him in there," Gordon said.

Bishop heart sank. "And if I say no?" He already knew the answer.

"Don't say no," Wallace said.

"What good would you do anybody in prison?" Gordon said, trying to soften it.

Ten

A cold San Francisco Bay fog was rolling in over Oakland. Up in the muddy Berkeley Hills where the big fire had swept away the city's toniest residential neighborhood, a few people worked late at their dogged rebuilding. Off to the south, traffic was sparse and a chill breeze blew loose newspapers against the buildings in the bay front industrial section. Lights burned on the top floor of the defunct Oakland Theater building.

"I don't believe this. You lied to us all these years?" Crease said. He was standing, and the other Sneakers sat on the threadbare couches and chairs of the living area watching Bishop pace. They were not happy; they were stunned, let down. "You even lied to us about your name?" Crease said. Crease was a man who hated lies with a strangely personal vengeance.

"Jesus, Marty," Mother said. "Why didn't you ever tell us?"

"Fellas, I'm sorry, okay?" Bishop said evenly. "But when you're wanted by the Feds you don't go around telling everybody about it."

"We're not 'everybody,' Martin," Crease said. "We're your partners. You tell *us*!"

"Fine," Bishop said, standing in front of Crease. "And exactly why is it you had to leave the agency?"

No response from Crease, just a hard stare. Finally: "I'm legally bound," he said. "You know that."

Bishop shrugged. "We all have our little secrets, don't we?" he said. He looked from face to face ruefully. He knew all along this moment would come, but he was sick just the same.

"How come you didn't get nailed at the time?" Mother
said.

"When they raided the computer lab, I was out getting
pizza," Bishop said. "Then I went to Canada."

"Did you have to burn off your fingerprints? Did you have
plastic surgery?" Carl asked, fascinated.

"Carl, the men are talking," Whistler said.

Carl sank back in his seat.

The light went on in Mother's head. "We've been playing
in the bush leagues this whole time because of that?" he
said. "Because you're on the lam?" Mother looked like his
already large head was ready to blow up.

"I regret it," Bishop said.

"Not me!" Mother said. "It's like somebody said, 'Your
real father is the king.' I am born again."

Right. There was that brighter side of the coin. A moment
of silence as it sank in. It didn't help. They'd still been
duped. And by Marty Bishop himself.

"Look, you guys gotta make a decision now," Bishop
said. He got up and walked out to the edge of the circle,
facing the empty work area. "This is not a test. The pene-
tration is live, the target is unaware. If we get caught, it
could be big trouble."

"Sneaking a foreign intelligence service that might kill
us to keep us out is not what we do," Crease said.

"The probable level of security is very low," Bishop said.
"But if anybody doesn't want to risk it just to keep me out
of jail . . . I understand."

The team was sober and silent. Bishop waited. The core
of this team had been together almost a decade. It seemed
forever to Bishop—a way of life. A ragtag pack of eccentrics
who had drifted together not always for the best of reasons
and found camaraderie, a challenging sport, a grown-up
kids' treehouse with state-of-the-art toys. It was too good
to last.

"I can't speak for the others, Bish," Whistler said, "but
hey, what do I care about you going to jail?" He held a
spinning servo-mechanism from a retractable Maserati
headlamp up to his ear and memorized its hum, then turned
his head toward where he knew Bishop was standing,
cloaked in doom. "I'm in it for the money."

"Me, too," Carl chimed in. "I'm in."

Bishop tried not to smile.

"Uh, Bish," Mother said, "can we go back to the 'They might kill us' part?"

"Mother," Bishop said, "if I thought that was going to happen, I wouldn't bring this to you. But there is a risk."

"You bet your ass there's a risk," Crease said. "Do any of you *boys* know a damn thing about the NSA, for Christ's sake?!"

"Electronic spying," Mother said. "Telecommunications, spy satellites and stuff. They're supposed to protect ours and break into theirs."

"That's their stated mission," Crease said. "Their charter is secret. They're a fucking octopus. Unlike the CIA and FBI, they've got nothing reining them in. No effective laws on the books, no congressional oversight, no watchdog of any kind. In practice, they've got a license to do pretty much what they want."

"Like what?" Carl said.

"Like eavesdropping on your telephone, telex, fax, microwave relay, computer networks, electronic data bases. Like making postal employees spy for them if they want. Like secretly manipulating FCC business—telephone company operations, radio frequency usage, civilian communications satellites. You name it. They *own* our mass communications."

"Big Brother is listening to us,' Mother said. "I coulda told you."

"Privacy is *the* dirty word to the NSA," Crease said. "Except about themselves. They're secretive to the point of insanity: 'No Such Agency,' we used to call 'em at the CIA. Funding in the billions, totally secret, buried in the Pentagon budget. Unlimited technical eavesdropping capacity—a worldwide electronic vacuum cleaner. Who knows what they know about you and me?"

"Or what they do with it," Mother said.

"So we encode things," Carl said. "Why get all hyper?"

"Carl," Crease said, shaking his head, "these guys invented the game. They've got the biggest computer complex in the world at Ft. Meade. Acres. There's no code they can't break, no data base they don't own, no facility they can't penetrate."

"So why would they care about some little electronic box Janek makes?" Mother said.

"*Any* little electronic box is their business," Crease said.

"They quietly got laws passed that make it illegal to develop or market any electronic device having to do with communications that they don't approve first. If they don't like what you make, they're all over you with a secrecy order—you even discuss your own device, you go to jail."

"Come on," Carl said.

"The only devices they want consumers to use," Crease said, "are ones they themselves have the 'keys' to, that they can read at will, for obvious reasons. The NSA's potential for violating your privacy as an American citizen should make your skin crawl."

"Man, you accuse me of being a paranoid conspiracy nut," Mother said. "You scare me, Crease."

"Good," Crease said. "It's better to be scared about something real than that fantasy shit floating around in your brain, Mother. What'd'ya think," he said, looking from face to face. "You still want to be in bed with these boys?"

A long silence.

"It pays $175,000," Whistler said.

Mother agonized, looked around at the others. "Better to be on their side than against them, maybe, huh?" he said. "Maybe just this once."

All eyes turned to Crease. Crease looked sour. He looked down at his hands. "You guys never learn," he said quietly. "You'll be chalk outlines without me. What do we need?"

Now Bishop let out his breath and smiled. But not too much. Not in front of these twisted dudes.

"Let's start with real light surveillance," he said. "Level three. First sign of baby sitters, we back off. He's lecturing at UC tomorrow afternoon. I'm going to check him out." He looked around at the team. "Any questions?"

The Sneakers looked at each other. Routine. They would all know what to do. They had done it hundreds of times, even if the stakes were a little different this time. They had no questions.

Except Crease. "For the lecture," he said. "You want to take Whistler, or should I go with you?"

"Oh, that's okay," Bishop said. "I thought . . . you know . . . I'll probably . . . ask Liz."

Everyone froze in their tracks and the Lair became instantly silent. It was as if he said, "My broker is E. F. Hutton."

Eleven

Bishop entered the leafy, manicured campus of the private St. Regis academy and walked the length of the oak-lined entrance drive passing uniformed students leaving for the day. Girls in plaid skirts and white blouses, boys in blue pants and white shirts, dragging book bags, sports bags. The kids were laughing and horsing around as primary schoolers anywhere do, but all within pretty decorous bounds. No guns or graffiti or foul mouthing on this campus. No mugging other kids for their one-hundred-dollar pump-up sneakers. This was above all a breeding ground for "nice" boys and girls, where extravagant tuition paid for such amenities as lectures on manners in morning chapel, afterschool ballet classes, weekly instruction in madrigal singing. This was where the enfranchised of America invested in the future of the culture as they preferred it to be. This was not a place that blew with every wind of change. At St. Regis they still required classes in Latin.

Bishop stopped a smiling, crisply confident woman in a white blouse with a big white bow. The smiling woman, who identified herself as Mrs. Izzy, the principal, pointed Bishop toward a gothic red-brick building halfway down the quad.

Bishop walked up the stone stairs into the old building and started down the hallway. The sounds of live classical piano playing emanated from the far end of the corridor—a difficult Schubert piece, being played with virtuosity. Quite remarkable, thought Bishop, who had a fair amateur's ear for good music.

He stopped, took a breath and peered through the glass window of the music room door. The sunlight angling through the tall casement windows fell on Liz, a lovely woman in her late thirties who sat facing him at a grand piano, tall sheet music propped up before her. Her eyes were closed in concentration, her head moving slightly with the music. The slanting afternoon light picked up gold-red highlights in her short, stylishly swept-back auburn hair and warmed the entire scene in a romantic glow. Stirred by the music, by the anachronistic charm of the picture, Bishop stopped, unwilling to push open the door and end it.

Liz opened her eyes and saw Bishop watching her. She looked surprised, then managed a wry, well-look-who's-here smile.

Bishop grinned and entered the music room. As he approached the piano, he saw that it wasn't Liz playing. Sitting next to her and hidden behind the tall sheet music was the actual pianist—a six-year-old prodigy, a slim little girl with long blond hair pulled back in a high ponytail. The girl saw Bishop and stopped playing, annoyed.

"Who's this person?" she said with a serious scowl.

"Sort of an old friend," Liz said. "Margaret, this is Martin Bishop." She closed up the sheet music. "You need to work on the D-minor section. There's way too much rubato."

"I like the rubato," the girl said.

"The victory of charm over content, Margaret," Liz said with a smile, first for her protégée, then a slightly more sardonic version for Bishop.

Bishop put on his most innocent look. "I'm against that," he said.

Liz held his look. It was clear there once was something between these two, and not at all clear there still wasn't.

The little girl saw plainly that she had been usurped and looked up sourly at Liz.

Liz stroked an imaginary beard. "Practice, practice, practice," she said solemnly.

Margaret giggled, took her sheet music and bounded out, like any other little kid.

"You look terrific," Bishop said.

"Thanks. You too," Liz said. "We're not getting back together." She stayed seated at the piano.

"I know," Bishop said. "This is business."

"Oh, Bishop," Liz said. "You don't have a business, you have a club. A boys' club. You have your little clubhouse, you probably have a secret handshake." She said this not disdainfully, but wistfully.

"I need your help, Liz," Bishop said.

"A new approach," she said. "You're not without resource, Bishop."

"I seriously need your help," he said.

"I seriously will not be dragged back into your adolescent, reality-avoiding world," she said. "I have a new group of gifted children now, and I like the fact that they are under thirty. And that they may grow into gifted adults."

"There's a mathematician named Gunter Janek," Bishop said. "Do you know him?"

"I've read him," she said. "Now go away." It was said kindly but unjokingly.

"He's giving a master lecture at five-thirty," Bishop said. "I'll buy you dinner after."

"I am *not* going out with you!" Liz said, standing and walking away from the piano.

"It's not a date, dummy," Bishop said. "I need someone to explain it to me!"

"Read a book!" Liz said, walking to the far windows.

"Liz, they found me," Bishop said quietly.

"Oh my God," she said. She turned toward him. As luck would have it, Bishop was momentarily firelit by the afternoon sun, bathed in a golden corona that obscured the actual man and brought back to Liz some taste of what haunted her about this guy in the first place—his incompleteness, his yearning.

"They offered me a deal," he said. "I do this job, they clear my record. I can get my name back. I can stop running."

She was touched by his admission, and felt herself swayed against every logical bone in her body. She turned away again and looked out across the serene and pretty campus. "Bishop," she said, steeling herself, "I will help you, if you genuinely need my help." She turned back to him. "You will thank me. I will say you're welcome, we'll exchange cards at Christmas. But you and I are not getting together again."

"Hey, don't flatter yourself," Bishop said in his best what-me-worry? manner that fooled neither of them.

"Pick me up at five," she said, not budging toward him an inch.

Bishop nodded gratefully and headed out the door. Striding down the creaking hardwood hallway toward the sunlight, he allowed himself a tiny, "Yes."

Twelve

Bishop had grown up in New York City, in a household of old-fashioned pre-World-War-Two lefties. His parents moved in a vociferous West Side crowd who believed in Roosevelt's New Deal and the urgency of social reform, who cried aloud against the evils of the Joe McCarthy witch hunt and the wrongness of the Rosenberg executions. They were people of principle who believed in standing up publicly for their beliefs.

To high-schooler Marty Bishop and to his family, John Kennedy's assassination was a serious emotional blow. Here at last was a president who seemed to represent the coming of age of enlightened American democracy—a smart, urbane leftie who never forgot his underdog Irish roots and carried it all off with ironic wit. From the hero-hungry teenager's point of view, here finally was a national figure with an acceptable sense of cool, smoothly elbowing aside the gray-jowled zombies of the establishment.

Without quite realizing it was so, Bishop loved Kennedy, loved him for giving guys like him a role model. He wept in front of the TV. It was a deep personal insult and it hardened his cynicism and sharpened his resolve.

In college he was always the first in line to carry posters and help organize marches against the by-then out-of-control war machine. He had inherited a genuine idealist's commitment to making a personal difference, not a personal name. He didn't make speeches himself; he worked behind the scenes. And he worked as if it mattered. You weren't authentic if you didn't lay it on the line in a way that rearranged some furniture.

His effort with Cosmo to throw monkey wrenches into the military-industrial juggernaut came as naturally as eating bagels and knishes at Zabar's. He didn't think deeply about it beforehand. Whatever your talent, both he and Cosmo thought if you didn't get out there and use it on the side of the angels in a time of crisis, you were as good as contributing to evil.

They went about their marauding with light spirits, happy in the rightness of their cause, naive to consequences. Unaware that when you tear the web of society—any society—it will turn like an enraged spider to kill the intruder and patch up the damage. Bishop was shocked at the explosion over their deeds. His parents may have approved of his social protest and his flight to Canada, they may have honored him as a martyred hero, but he couldn't even call them for the first five years. He couldn't go home for Christmas. He was lonely and lost. He saw them only once again before they died, and then only briefly.

There was nothing of honor in running, he knew, it was just running. Nothing you could ever tell your children about, if you could ever justify having children. He was dying for an excuse to stand and fight.

"He's just a kid," Bishop said in amazement.

"Sure he's young," Liz said as they stopped at the notice board outside Mathematics Hall on the university campus. Bishop stared at the photograph under the heading UC FORUM - 5:30 P.M.—DR. GUNTER JANEK ON LARGE NUMBER THEORY.

"No older mathematician would be capable of doing the kind of juicy work that'll draw this kind of crowd," Liz said. "It's a kid's game. The brain changes, loses its intuitive snap. Sad but true."

Bishop looked around at the bustling tweed-and-corduroy crowd filing eagerly into the imposing Georgian building. These people appeared to be the extreme end of the spectrum—academics' academics—brainy-looking women in sensible sexless shoes; lean, spectacled young men carrying pocket computers, scratch pads and pipes calculated to give them weightiness.

"You think this guy'll put on quite a show?" Bishop asked. They walked in between the tall white columns.

"Number theory is one of the oldest branches of mathematics," Liz said as they made their way toward the auditorium. "Goes back to the ancient Greeks and Chinese. Pretty deadly to the uninitiated, though, Bishop. You know—primes and tests for primality and all that. As I'm sure you remember," she said, giving Bishop a sidelong look, "I did my doctoral thesis on Fermat's Little Theorem and how to get around its probabilistic nature by using algebraic number fields instead of ordinary numbers."

"Oh yeah," Bishop said. "I remember." Blessedly, they just then passed into the auditorium and had to busy themselves with finding seats.

Pacing back and forth on the stage, gesturing theatrically with a short pointer, was the impressive Dr. Gunter Janek. With strikingly long flowing hair, a boyish face, a rakishly tailored cream-colored suit on an athletic body, he looked more like an eccentric European rock star than a renowned mathematican. Behind him was a floor-to-ceiling overhead-projection screen filled with giant numbers and impossible-looking equations. Janek walked in and out of the shadows, talking exuberantly into his lapel mike.

"With three linear equations in three unknowns," he said, "we proceed analogously by multiplying the first with a21/all and subtracting it from the second. Multiply with a31/all and subtract it from the third. This reduces the algorithm to a system of two equations in two unknowns."

He was coming to the climax, the audience rapt at his every word. In the back of the room, Liz leaned over to Bishop. "This hasn't been about large number theory, by the way," she whispered. "It's about cryptography."

Bishop raised his brows as if this were news to him. "Really?" he said. "You mean, like codes?"

"I mean like *unbreakable* codes," she said.

That *was* news to Bishop.

At the front of the room, Janek continued being brilliant. He wrote ten to the hundredth power on the board.

"See that?" Janek said. "That's more than the number of atoms in the whole wack universe. Let's say I could find a shortcut hidden in the numbers, finding primes would be the least of the things I could do with it. This hypothetical shortcut would allow me to do manipulations that would make your eyes water. I'm talking about a Picasso, the leaves turning in Vermont, a beautiful girl on the beach at Rio who can't find her top." He laughed his eccentric laugh. "But that's for another time," he said. "Thanks for coming." He dropped his pointer and walked off. The crowd was on its feet applauding, buzzing feverishly about that last tantalizing bit.

* * *

The reception afterward, in a low-ceilinged classroom with third-degree-bright fluorescent lights, was in Bishop's eyes even deadlier than the lecture. A refreshment table heavy with raw carrots, turnips and runny tofu dip was encircled by paunchy, nearsighted balding party goers—the women, that is. The men were mostly descended from either Uriah Heep or Ichabod Crane. And at the center of it all, expatiating to a small circle of admirers, was the intriguing Dr. Janek.

". . . No!" he was saying. "The numbers are so unbelievably large that mere computer power is nowhere near enough, even parallel processing. All the computers in the world could not break them down. But as I said, maybe—perhaps!—there is a shortcut."

Bishop made sure he and Liz were close enough to the small group of acolytes to hear, for what it might be worth.

"I'll bet you anything he's found it," Liz whispered to Bishop. "And if he has, I really don't think you want to be getting involved in this. I'm going to get my coat."

Bishop stopped her. "What do you mean?"

"No mathematician can do cryptographic work without having the government all over his back," Liz whispered. "As soon as you do anything the least bit interesting, the feds move in and try to classify it. They're serious. And they're dangerously nuts." Liz walked off to find her coat.

Bishop stayed to listen.

". . . a hitherto unimagined—call it an operation or a constant or a universal—hidden in the numbers," Janek said, "that could unlock all the wonderful mysteries of these numbers. Hidden right before our eyes."

"Dr. Janek," said an enthralled undergraduate with a delicate Modigliani face, wire-rimmed glasses and long jet-black hair, "you say so far it's all speculation, but are you going to give us a hint of the directions of your speculations? I mean, why else would you bring it up?"

Dr. Janek, taken with the girl's chutzpah, was flashing his rock-star smile, touching her lightly with his eyes, when a man's voice made Bishop jump.

"Martin!" the man called out in a cultured voice. "Martin, how wonderful to see you."

Bishop turned to find a tall, handsome man in an expensive double-breasted suit bearing down on him, arms extended.

"Hello, Greg," Bishop said, surprised and slightly annoyed.

"Is it not fabulous?" asked Greg in a Russian accent. He linked arms with Bishop, steering him a few steps away from Janek's group under the guise of reaching for a passing refreshment tray. Bishop clearly didn't want to stray from Janek's side, but this man was a professional. He skillfully gave him no choice.

"Today, I can in public come to learn your scientists' new secrets," Greg said. "Alas, I did not understand one bit what this man Janek talks about. But at least I cannot understand without skulking about anymore. Oh, goodness!" he said dramatically. "Can it be Elizabeth?!"

Liz joined them. She rolled her eyes and indulged Greg's having to Slavicly kiss her on both cheeks. "Hello, Greg," she said.

"Elizabeth and Martin!" Greg said. "My heart leaps like a gazelle to see you back together again."

"Tell it to stop leaping," Liz said. "We're *not* back together."

"What a pity," Greg said. "If ever there were two lovers. Wait! I have a smashing idea." He took two tickets—and his business card—from his breast pocket. "I have extra tickets to the Bolshoi for Saturday night. One of the few Russian institutions that remains unshakable, at least this week." He laughed urbanely. "You will be my guests. Take advantage. Next week, who knows, maybe it will be eleven separate little ballet companies." He gave another charming self-deprecating laugh.

Bishop still had one eye on Janek's little circle. "Oh, really, Greg. I wouldn't know how to repay you," he said automatically—far more interested in the middle-aged woman who had come up behind Janek. She was a busty woman, with her hair pulled back severely in a bun. She whispered discreetly in Janek's ear.

"Perhaps someday soon, Martin," Greg said, "now that our countries are such good friends, perhaps you will finally be able to do the occasional favor for me." He folded the tickets, along with the business card, into Bishop's hand. "I'm in a whole different business now," he said with an open face.

"Gregor," Liz said, "you are shameless."

"I see you Saturday night," he said with a slight, debonair declining of his head.

Bishop gave him a skeptical look, pulled out the business card and read it. "Cultural attaché," he said. "Greg, you *always* had the title 'Cultural Attaché.' ''

"Ah, but now," Greg said, "it is my actual job! In part." He chuckled.

"Unbelievable," Bishop said.

"Last two years has been very confusing for people in my work," Greg said. He winked and walked off.

Liz watched after him. "I don't care what anybody says about Glasnost and the new Russia," she said, "I wouldn't trust that guy."

Bishop was busy watching Janek. "Oh, Greg's okay," he said distractedly. "He's harmless."

"Bishop, listen to me," Liz said, taking his arm. "If I'm right about what Janek is into, it's no accident Greg is here, and you're in over your head."

"Yeah," Bishop said, not listening. He was watching the dark-eyed bun-woman whisper something else to Janek, who now appeared uncomfortable. Janek moved abruptly to take his leave from his admirers.

"Uh, I *must* finish some important work tonight," Bishop heard him say. "It's due in a matter of hours. Excuse me, please." Janek extricated himself and headed for the back door, leaving the bun-woman behind.

Bishop straightened up and scanned the room. He made eye contact with a black man standing by the front entrance—a properly academic-looking fellow in nubby tweed jacket with elbow patches and sporting eyeglasses and a pipe. It was Crease. Bishop figured he would show up. Bishop nodded urgently toward the departing mathematician. Crease started moving quickly through the room.

"Crease is here," Liz said with an I-should-have-known expression. "You're going to follow Janek, aren't you?"

Bishop turned to her. She knew him too well for him to deny it. "I'm sorry. I—"

"It's okay," Liz said shortly. "I'll get a cab." She put on her coat and started toward the door.

"Can I call you?" Bishop said.

"Just be careful," she said, and walked out.

Bishop looked after her thoughtfully, then hurried and caught up with Crease waiting in the hallway.

"Janek's trying to 'finish some important work' tonight," Bishop said in a low voice.

Crease nodded. "The van's in the back," he said. They moved quickly down the hallway. "I'll wager the bloke's going to try to subdivide the Maxwell minimals into subzero integers," Crease said with mock gravity, puffing his pipe. "Or maybe go for some inverse factoring of binomials."

Bishop looked at him dumbfounded. A joke from Crease was very rare. Something about this case must be giving him great pleasure, Bishop thought.

Whistler and Carl were waiting for them in the van.

"Call Mother," Bishop said. "Get him in place. Sixth floor."

Thirteen

The faded-red van kept a discreet distance from Janek's classic old Jaguar. The mathematician drove as fast and unpredictably as his nimble mind worked, turning corners unexpectedly, taking shortcuts through shopping centers and alleys. As they'd hoped, he was heading toward the Coolidge Institute. He covered the three miles in a record few minutes, severely testing Crease's tailing skills. The Sneakers' van pulled up across from the glass-wall highrise in time to see the black Jaguar disappear into the underground parking garage.

"Mother, he just drove in the building," Bishop said into the intercom. "Are you in position?"

"Am I in position?!" Mother growled over the headset. "Does this look like Spiderman?"

Looking out from the van, they could see a windowwasher's platform creeping slowly down the face of the highrise toward the sixth floor.

Crease swung the van into the parking structure across the street and sped up to the fifth and top floor. He parked the van at the front of the structure with a view—angling slightly upward—of the windows of Janek's office, now dark.

"How we doing with audio," Bishop said.

"Good," Whistler said. "Mother's pretty close."

Through the binoculars, Bishop could see Mother, hanging over the edge of the window-washer's platform just above Janek's window. He was hanging on for dear life, extending a shotgun mike downward to the edge of the window.

"He's only got *four* safety belts on this time," Bishop said.

"What, no parachute?" Whistler said.

Crease and Carl were busily unloading electronic gear. They hefted it, sprinted to the stairwell at the side of the parking structure and climbed upward.

On the roof, Crease stuck his nose out the fire door, looked around, then quietly walked out. Carl followed, carrying the video camera and tripod. They moved over to the parapet and checked out the angle. Still not quite high enough to see what they needed to see in Janek's office.

Crease scoped out the giant billboard that topped the parking garage. There was a ladder up one of the thick stanchions. He signaled Carl to climb up.

Carl did not look happy—there was a gusty wind. But without a word, he clambered up to the catwalk underneath the sign. Crease handed up the equipment. Carl quickly set up his camera on the small platform, and lay down behind it, trying to make himself invisible. He focused through the viewfinder. The angle was good. Luckily, Janek's office across the street had wall-to-wall windows.

So far so good, Crease thought. No obstacles, a heavily clouded sky shrouding the moon, no one on the roofs nearby. It felt like a standard gig. He relaxed a little as Carl turned on his equipment and started sending a signal down to the boys in the van on the floor below.

But even standard gigs have problems. At that moment on top of the next building, the roof-access door cracked open. A skinheaded young guy dressed in gray maintenance coveralls peered out, then slipped out the door, turned and pulled somebody after him. A pretty, dark-haired girl, dressed in the same style gray coveralls—the kind of thing night cleaning crews wear.

Carl, humming to himself, fussed with the focus on his long lens, aiming at objects like Janek's desk in the dim reflected light in the office. "You picking up anything?" he said quietly into his headset.

Neither he nor Crease had noticed they had neighbors.

Below in the van, Bishop tuned the picture on his video screen as Whistler monitored audio. Bishop could make out filing cabinets, an erasable whiteboard, a drafting table, a workbench and shelves of books.

At that moment, the office door swung open, light flooded in from the hallway and a figure walked in.

"Okay," Bishop said into his mike. "Entry! And lights on. We're in there just in time."

"Get out of there!" said a girl's voice, seemingly at Carl's and Crease's elbows. They both spun around, hearts pounding.

The young skinhead next door had his hand in the side slit of the girl's coveralls as they necked against the stairwell shack. "How'm I gonna maul your oochie if you lock the door?" the guy said, zipping open her coveralls and massaging her breasts.

"You're not gonna maul nothing," she said, putting her tongue well down his throat.

The lovers obviously hadn't seen Carl and Crease. Crease looked up at Carl and the exposed camera. The kids were sure to spot them.

Carl gaped at the performers, forgetting all about the surveillance.

"He's got the desk light on," Bishop said in the headset.

"Describe the place," Whistler said.

"It's more like a workroom than an office," Bishop said. "What d'ya think, Crease?"

"Delay!" Crease whispered hoarsely into his headset.

Bishop hesitated a moment, listening in alarm. "You want me up there?" he said.

"Negative!" whispered Crease.

Bishop waited again. "What is it?" he asked quietly. "Crease?" No answer. Bishop debated about running upstairs. But the video camera was sending its picture uninterrupted. The screen showed Janek entering his office, taking off his jacket, reading through a pile of phone message slips, checking his fax machine and doing other housekeeping chores.

On the roof, Crease looked around frantically, trying to figure a way out. The girl was completely out of her coveralls now, naked in the chill night air, leaning back on a ledge. The guy was struggling out of his coveralls . . . when static erupted from his walkie-talkie, startling him. "Proctor, Labelle—where the hell are you two?'' came a harsh voice. ''I find you humpin' again on company time, you're dog meat.''

On the headset, Bishop quietly narrated to Whistler, ''A bench with a soldering gun, two spools of wire, a magnifying lamp . . .''

''He's doing more than math in there,'' Whistler said.

The kid on the next roof snatched up his walkie-talkie and spoke into it, ''I'm right here, Chief.'' He kept clicking the on-off button to cause interference. ''Don't know where Lanie is.''

''*Where* the hell are you?!'' the harsh voice on the walkie-talkie said. The kid just clicked his button, causing more static.

Crease watched them hopefully. Now they would surely dress and get back to their cleaning-crew chores.

Instead, the kid dropped the walkie-talkie, stripped naked and moved between the girl's legs. She wrapped him in tight and they started to move and make the sounds of love.

Carl, riveted on the action, was going out of his mind, not seeing a thing happening in Janek's office.

''. . . then on the desk—telephone, fax machine,'' Bishop's voice droned over the headset, ''. . . lamp, answering machine, jar of pencils. Nothing mysterioso—no little black box.''

Suddenly the girl stopped her movements. ''Hey!'' she said. ''What you lookin' at?'' She was looking right at Crease. She hadn't seen Carl perched above on the catwalk.

The shaved-headed kid turned. ''Aw, shit!'' he said. His manhood wilted. He grabbed at his pants.

Crease walked directly toward them, putting on his most menacing stone face. He stopped at the edge of the roof, folded his arms and glared—searching desperately for a usable tack. The girl stared back sullenly, making no effort to hide her body or get dressed.

Crease reached into his coat, pulled out his wallet and flipped it open to his P.I.'s license. ''Private investigator,'' he said. Then glowered some more.

''Alonzo hired you to spy on us?!'' the kid said. ''Man, is he sick. What's a little boning to him?'' he said. ''Jesus! What a freak.''

''Every other night on the company nickel?'' Crease said evenly.

"Not every other night!" the kid said. "Who told you that?!" The girl sneered at Crease in disgust.

"It doesn't matter," Crease said. "Look, you get back to work right away, he doesn't have to know."

The kid grumbled and pulled on his coveralls. The girl still leaned there naked, staring malevolently at Crease. The kid grabbed the girl's hand and dragged her toward the stairwell.

"Pervert!" the girl hissed at Crease.

"Shut up, Lanie!" the kid said, pulling her inside.

"We've lost the picture completely," Bishop said on Crease's headset. "What's going on up there?"

Crease wiped the sweat off his face and went back to his post. "All clear up here," he said into his lapel mike. He looked up. Carl was still transfixed on the spot where the young lovers had performed, his mouth open, breathing hard.

"Carl!" Crease barked. "Back to work."

"That was *so* great! Why did they have to stop?" he said, heartbroken. "I *hate* it when that happens." He turned back reluctantly to his duties. He repointed the camera at the correct office windows.

Across the street, Janek sat down at his desk, and flipped a switch.

"He's logging on to his computer," Bishop said for Whistler's benefit.

Janek punched some keys. His computer screen greeted him with a request for his password.

"Oh, this is good," Bishop said. "This is perfect. Show me your password and I'll have all your computer files before morning."

Dr. Janek was just about to type when Mother's shotgun mike picked up a knock at his door. Janek got up, crossed the room, opened his door. It was the buxom middle-aged bun-woman from the reception.

"Oh, Dr. Ryzhkov, good evening," Janek said. His voice was muffled through the shotgun mike, but understandable.

"Excuse me," the bun-toting Dr. Ryzhkov said with a Slavic accent. "Do you have moment?"

"Yes, of course," Dr. Janek said politely. "Please come in."

Dr. Ryzhkov entered; Janek closed the door.

"Let's get an ID on Ryzhkov," Bishop said into his headset. "She was at the lecture today. She told him something, and then he got all—"

The chunky Dr. Ryzhkov circled Dr. Janek. She reached back, released her hair from the bun and shook it out. A thick wavy mane fell halfway down her back. She took off her glasses. Suddenly she looked a lot more desirable, her body quite zaftig.

Janek had his hands up, protesting. "Elena," he said. "Elena, I have to do this work." He backed up as she started to close on him. "Now, Elena!" Janek said, almost in alarm. "Honest to God, I've got to—"

She was on him, kissing him passionately. He kissed her back. They writhed together. Then Janek broke away, breathless. "I'm sorry," he blurted, and turned back to his computer and sat down.

"Oh, Gunter," Ryzhkov said, panting.

Bishop, Whistler and Crease broke up. "Oh, Gunter!" "Oh yes!" "You stud!" "Don't stop now!" they cried.

Carl put his chin in his hand and watched in disbelief.

Mother, stretched out like a rock lizard on the platform above the window, couldn't see what was going on, but he could hear. "A little professionalism, you guys," He whispered in his mike.

"Let's do what we did in Mexico City," Ryzhkov purred, coming behind Janek and kissing his neck. "We must."

"I didn't know you could *do* that in Mexico City," Bishop said.

"Get real, dorks," Mother said.

"Carl shouldn't be seeing this without a note from his mother," Bishop said into his mike.

Crease chuckled. "You don't know the half of it."

"We're taping this, aren't we?" Carl said in a high voice.

"Carl!" Bishop said.

"Grow up," Crease said with a laugh.

"Elena, really," Janek said, panting, "My work . . . My deadline."

"Genius has always a deadline, *n'est-ce pas?*" the aroused Elena said. She moved around beside him and began rubbing her bosom against the side of his face. "Think of your health. A man works better when he is . . . relaxed." She kissed his lips, his neck.

Janek tried to stand firm, smiling but not encouraging her. "Elena," he said again, gently separating from her,

trying to get back to his computer. Ryzhkov straightened
her blouse.

"He's getting rid of her," Crease said.

"He's doing the right thing," Bishop said, leaning forward eagerly. "Alright, Studley, show me your password."

Janek was in the act of typing his password when Ryzhkov
moved in front of him, sat on the desk and began unbutton-
ing her blouse. Janek started groaning through his teeth.

"Get out of the way, you fleshpot!" Bishop shouted.

"Sex, sex, sex," muttered Mother on the headset.
"Doesn't anybody just work anymore?"

As though he heard, Janek got hold of himself, and tried
to ignore Elena's display.

"Alright, here comes our password," Bishop said.

The phone in Janek's office rang. He leaned over to answer it, partly exposing the screen to view. Ryzhkov reached
over and stopped him.

"I leave messages here on service, but you do not call
me," she said huskily. "That is why we have service here.
You should never have to handle a phone call, Gunter." She
swivelled his chair toward her. She hiked her skirt up her
thighs and straddled his legs, easing down on his lap. "You
have bigger things to handle." She unbuttoned her blouse
all the way, exposing large handsome breasts with no bra.
"I leave messages with your service," she said. "But you
do not call me." She slowly straightened her back, pulling
her blouse loose from her skirt, flaunting her attributes before his eyes.

"I'm sorry, I simply have to work . . ." Janek protested
unconvincingly.

"I give you this to work, baby," Ryzhkov said, pulling
his face into her naked breasts.

"I don't believe this," Bishop said, leaning back from
the monitor.

The Sneakers whooped for joy. Even Mother on the platform above let out a snort of laughter.

Suddenly they stopped short. Janek had lost the battle.
"Alright," he said. "But just for a little while." Ryzhkov
rose up off Janek's lap, reached for the window and pulled
the blinds.

"No!" "Don't do it!" "No!" they cried out. They
looked at each other in frustration.

"I *hate* it when that happens," Carl said.

Crease reached up and patted Carl's foot consolingly as if to say "There, there."

Janek, having evidently followed Elena to the window, was now on her. They fell against the blinds and set to, broadcasting their lovemaking in rhythmic pulses of light and sound escaping through the straining blinds.

"I can't stand this," Carl said, burying his head on his arm.

Fourteen

The scene in Janek's office spooled out in full video-taped glory on a large HDTV monitor at the Sneakers' Lair. Janek was just starting to type in his password, the phone rang, he reached for it, Elena stopped him from answering. "I leave messages here on service, but you do not call me," her voice repeated. "That is why we have a service here. *You* should never have to handle a phone call, Gunter. You have bigger things to handle."

Bishop backed up the tape and replayed from the phone ringing and Janek leaning forward. Mother and Carl studied the images too, while Whistler listened. Bishop replayed the tape and froze it at the spot where Janek leaned forward. He moved forward a frame at a time until Elena's wide form began to eclipse the picture.

"There might be a frame or two where she doesn't block it," Mother said, fiddling with some patch cords. "Lemme blow it up."

"Gentlemen," Crease said, coming in the door and walking across toward them.

"Hey. So who's Ryzhkov?" Bishop said.

"Visiting professor from Czechoslovakia," Crease said. "Senior Research Fellow in . . . Astrophysics."

"Bingo," Bishop said.

"Setec Astronomy," Crease said. "Whatever that is."

"I don't get it," Carl said. "Why does the National Security Agency give a shit about astronomy?"

The other Sneakers gave him heavy-eyed looks.

"Keep your eye on the money, Carl," Bishop said.

"Somebody paid Janek $380,000 from a Zurich bank account."

"You don't pay that kind of covert dough for a better look at the man in the moon," Crease said.

"Yeah?" Carl said, even more confused.

"Setec Astronomy is a code name," Bishop said.

"So who is Ryzhkov?" Mother said to Crease. "Is she the broker, do we think? She lines up an Eastern European buyer for the mysterious little black box, she gets a piece while Janek's getting his piece."

Bishop and Crease groaned.

Crease recited from his notes: "Brilliant theoretical astronomer. Career stalled because she wouldn't join the Communist Party. She got to be a Senior Research Fellow only after Havel came in. Born and raised in Prague, sophisticated well-to-do parents who managed to steer clear of politics and the secret police. Both now deceased. No brothers or sisters. Educated at the Sorbonne, doctorate Cambridge. She married late, then supposedly divorced her husband when she found out he was secretly a party member."

"None of this screams KGB agent or intermediary," Bishop said, puzzled.

"Right about that," Crease said. "In fact, her file indicates she's apolitical, thinks politics is a dirty business, something an honest person wouldn't get involved in."

"Maybe she's got nothing to do with the little black box," Carl said. "Maybe she likes his body."

The other Sneakers gave him the Carl-the-men-are-talking look.

"Impossible to tell what makes the Czechs tick," Crease said. "They don't know how to follow ordinary rules—look who they elected president."

"She's doing it for money," Mother said. "A person will do anything for money." Now everyone gave Mother a look. "Well?" he said.

Mother turned back to the VCR, ran the tape again and enlarged the image at the point where Janek began to type on his computer keyboard.

"There!" Bishop said.

Mother froze the enlarged image of Janek's terminal. They could barely make out some fuzzy letters.

" 'L' . . . 'O' . . ." Bishop read.

"I think the next one's an 'N,' " Carl said.

"Let's see where his fingers are on the keyboard," Bishop said. He rewound the tape and replayed it while Mother enlarged the image of Janek's fingers on the keyboard.

"Let the service pick it up . . ." Ryzhkov's voice repeated. Bishop froze the tape.

"Definitely 'L,' 'O' . . . Maybe 'H?' " Mother said, squinting, tilting his head to alter the angle of the light.

Bishop rewound, played and stopped the tape again. Again Ryzhkov intoned, "I leave messages here on service, but you do not call me." Crease, Bishop and Mother shook their heads in frustration. They were realizing they would never be able to figure out what keys Janek was typing.

"She's in the way," Bishop said with finality. They sat there frustrated.

"So Plan B," Mother said. "We get the guy where he lives."

Fifteen

Dr. Gunter Janek lived at the north end of the Berkeley Hills, in a tiny, rustic redwood-and-glass house perched on a steep slope, looking across San Francisco Bay at the fishing wharves and the Golden Gate Bridge.

The red van with the black-glass side window was parked inconspicuously on the shoulder of a winding street above the house. Bishop sat in the back of the van with his binoculars trained on the window of Dr. Janek's den, focusing on the mathematician's home computer. There was no sign of Janek.

"Come on, Doc," Bishop said. "Get to work."

Carl manned his video camera, waiting, bored. Crease lay back with his eyes closed.

"Hey, Bish," Mother's voice came over the headset.

"Yeah?" Bishop said.

"I don't think he's gonna log on tonight," Mother said, trying not to whine. He was crouched ankle-deep in cold water at the bottom of an underground phone vault in the street below Janek's house. He was freezing. "Whaddyasay we go home, huh?"

"Let's give him a little more time, okay?" Bishop said sympathetically.

"Movement," Carl said, peering through the eyepiece of the video camera.

Bishop snapped his binoculars up in time to see a door across the hall from the den open, and a silhouetted figure appear. A light was turned on. A girl walked out. She was slim, with long black hair and long coltish legs—about twenty. She was tucking her blouse into her skirt. She pulled wire-rimmed glasses out of her skirt pocket and put them on. Now Bishop recognized her.

Janek appeared behind her, stylishly accoutered in nothing but a short Japanese-style bathrobe with a fiery serpent embroidered on the back.

"Why Gunter, you devil," Bishop said. "I had no idea higher math was such a turn-on."

"Elena's there again?" Crease said, taking Carl's video camera. Carl looked at him dismayed.

"Oh, no," said Mother, down in the hole. "What are they doing?"

"Another candidate altogether," Bishop said. "She was at the lecture. Undergrad. Asked a provocative question."

"It's over now, she's leaving." Crease said. "Well, maybe not."

Janek's student had her hands inside his kimono, and Janek had his nose buried in her long black tresses. They kissed—more a prelude than a goodbye kiss.

"Doc, damn it! You got homework to do," Bishop said. "How many women've you got?"

Bishop handed the binoculars to an appreciative Carl. He checked out the girl and chuckled.

"Man, the square root of power is power, I guess," Crease said.

"What's that mean?" Carl asked, glued to his binocs. "Ooh, he's taking her to the door. Don't go!"

The front door opened, the girl gave Janek another wet kiss and sauntered out, slipping on a studded leather jacket. She climbed into an open-topped jeep and roared off down the hill.

Janek appeared back in his den. He punched the air, as though that last tryst was a particularly memorable one. He walked over to his computer and leaned on the back of the chair, clearly debating whether he had enough energy left to do some work.

"Do it, Doc," Bishop said. "Belgium on Thursday."

Janek must have heard. He pulled out the chair, sat down and turned his terminal on. He reached for the phone and placed it in the computer/telephone modem.

"Alright!" Bishop said. "Whistler, you're on. Mother, here we go."

"Locked in and ready," Mother said from underground. "For the record, my feet went numb fifteen minutes ago."

Whistler listened carefully to the rising and falling beeps as Janek's modem automatically dialed. He heard the phone ring twice. It was answered by a single high-pitched tone. Whistler smiled. "208-7648," he said.

Carl excitedly scribbled the number down in his small black notebook and wrote after it, "Coolidge Institute Computer." That number joined hundreds of other sensitive industry, science and government phone numbers in Carl's book. "I love this job," he said. "It's so educational."

"Go, Crease," Bishop said.

Crease, sitting in the back of the van at a dual computer setup, dialed the same 208-7648 on his own telephone modem. He watched the screen as the Coolidge Institute computer 'answered' its phone. He got the same connect tone—the single high-pitched beep. At the bottom of the screen, a log line spelled out: "ENTER PASSWORD."

Crease quickly copied the Coolidge message—the beep-tone and the request for password onto the memory of the second computer.

Bishop, taking his cue from Crease, spoke into his head-set mike: "Okay, Mother, yank him."

Underground, Mother pulled a wire from its connection.

In Janek's den, the screen went blank. Janek looked surprised. He picked up his telephone from the modem and listened. He clicked the button a couple of times, held it down, then listened again. He stuck the telephone back in the computer modem and hit the auto-dial command.

Bishop, watching all this through binoculars, said to Mother: "And . . . now."

Mother swiftly reconnected Janek's phone line, but not to the telephone company trunk line. Instead he connected it to a cable that ran up out of the vault onto the street, through a backyard, up a short steep hill and into the red van. "Done," Mother said.

"And now he calls *us*," Bishop said.

The telephone on Crease's modem rang twice, his "Coolidgized" computer answered and the screen came to life. The long high tone . . . then the "ENTER PASSWORD" command.

"Greetings, Dr. Janek," Bishop murmured. "What's the magic word?"

Obligingly, Janek entered some characters and they appeared in rapid succession across the bottom of the screen: "*l-o-v-e p-u-m-p*,"

Four of the five Sneakers screamed at once, "Love pump?!!"

"You're not serious?" Whistler said.

"Disgusting," Bishop said. "Okay, let's lose him," he said into the headset.

Down in the vault, Mother pulled apart the two wires. "Bye-bye," he said.

Janek, facing another blank screen, slumped back tiredly. Bishop, watching, saw his lips form, "What the fuck?"

"Thanks, Doc," he said. "You can have your phone back."

"Now can we go home?" came Mother's weary voice through the headset. "I got third-degree exposure."

Bishop, watching Janek dial yet again, and get the real Coolidge Institute this time, said, "We're just waiting for you, Mother."

Sixteen

Mother practiced an earnest but lumbering version of tai chi in the middle of the Lair. Carl, watching this strange performance, saw nothing but a kind of lame, slow-motion karate.

"Man, that is useless," he said. "Guys will just move out of the way. You're going too slow."

"Carl," Mother said with forced patience, "it's a meditational exercise. Control. Physical discipline. Balance. I am developing a sense of harmonious well-being in concert with the rest of the universe.''

Bishop, sitting with Crease at a computer terminal, spoke without looking up. "How's your sense of flab well-being, Mother?" he said. "Do your hundreds yet?"

Mother groaned, got down on the floor and started doing loudly painful push-ups.

At the computer, Crease dialed, got on-line with the Coolidge Institute network and typed in "LOVE PUMP." A few seconds and a Dr. Janek menu appeared—a complete list of his working files.

"Ladies and gentlemen," Bishop said to the room at large, "Dr. Janek's secret files."

"Setec Astronomy," Crease said, scanning down. " 'D.' " Crease selected "D"—full name: "PROJECT SETEC ASTRONOMY." The computer searched and produced the file. It was garbled and indecipherable.

"Shit," Crease said. "It's encrypted." He tried several other "PROJECT FILES." All encrypted. Frustrated, Crease and Bishop stared at the screen.

Carl, walking by, glanced briefly over Crease's shoulder at the screen. "Try expenses," he said.

"It's all gonna be encrypted," Crease grumbled. But he tried accessing the "EXPENSES" file. It was not encrypted. Crease looked sourly over at Carl, as if to say, "Aren't you Mr. Wonderful?" But Carl, oblivious, was walking back to his workstation.

Bishop gave Crease a consoling pat on the back. "Beginner's luck," he said. "What do we got?"

Under a subhead, "SETEC ASTRONOMY/EXPENSES," Crease read, "Lunch with Dr. Healy . . . Two airplane tickets to Mexico City symposium, himself and Dr. Ryzhkov. Yeah, I'll bet it was a symposium. Bought a new super-fast computer modem, a new answering machine, some four-bit microprocessors and controller chips . . . more office materials.''

"What's he doing with four-bit mics?" Mother said, leaning over watching.

"He's programming a chip," said Whistler who'd been listening from his central workstation.

"This gets us nowhere," Crease said. "We're blockaded.''

"Forget the computer, that's not where you'll find any-thing," Whistler said.

They all just turned and stared at him.

"What's the date on the four-bit mics entry?" Whistler said.

"Uh, last week," Bishop said, reading down to it. "Why?"

"This guy is building something right now," Whistler said. "We know he's working night and day, or whenever the women let him, I guess. And he's impulsive—not the type to want to be handing over his project to some central lockup, then having to ask for it back whenever he wants to work on it. So—"

"So what?" Crease said.

"So I think Whistler is trying to tell us the little black box is in Janek's office," Bishop said.

"Does he have a safe in there?" Whistler asked.

"Not that we could see," Bishop said. "But that doesn't mean anything. There are two ways to protect something. One is you lock it in a safe, build lots of walls around it and post an armed guard. It's hard to get to but everybody knows right where it is. The other way is you just put it in the corner and don't draw any attention to it."

"Give me a close-up look at that room and I know I'll see it," Whistler said.

"Whistler," Mother said, "I don't know how to tell you this, but . . . you're blind."

"We just haven't been smart enough to see it," Whistler said.

Bishop got up. "Okay," he said. "Well, you know the old saying . . ."

They all looked at him.

"The old saying is," he said with a smile, "If you can't get it with your brains—"

"—go in like the fucking Marines.' " Mother said.

"Close enough," Bishop said.

Seventeen

A messenger boy in jeans and a dark green satin uniform jacket argued with the guard in the lobby of the Coolidge Institute. The kid didn't have the right paperwork for the delivery he wanted to make—several large cartons destined for the maintenance department.

"No invoice, no entry," the guard said.

"Well, just wait," the messenger kid said, aggravated. "I've got the damn invoice here somewhere." He banged his clipboard down on his boxes and searched his pockets. He took off his slightly too-large hat and searched it. His hair flopped out—it was Carl. He made a perfect discombobulated delivery boy.

It was late in the day. Several exiting employees stopped by the guard station and opened their briefcases and attaché cases for inspection, then headed out of the building.

Two of the employees, Young Republican think-tank reseachers with laminated ID badges and attaché cases, made their way toward the exit slowly, talking. They took no notice of a man just inside the door, pacing, checking his watch.

"I don't get it," the shorter one said. "What do you get from damming up the Amazon?"

"Create a ton of energy for development, for one," said the other man, who sported a tiny risque ponytail with his clean-cut suit. "Two, create hundreds of miles of valuable waterfront property. And three, do away with the Indian problem."

"Jeez, sounds cold, Rob," the first researcher said. "The Indians' burial mounds, ancestral hunting grounds, all that shit."

"Got that covered, man," the second guy said. "I was talking to a guy: In Vietnam they had what they called the Strategic Hamlet program—moved whole villages to better places. The natives loved it. Like moving Cleveland to Arizona. It's a win-win."

The shorter guy began to nod understandingly as they passed the pacing figure and walked out the door.

The figure—Bishop—turned and stared after the two post-Vietnam yuppies in disbelief. Bishop was looking very Ivy League: blue Oxford button-down shirt, club tie, herringbone suit. He had his hair slicked back and wore wire glasses. He checked his watch again, and strode back to the guard station, passing Carl still ransacking his pockets for his invoice.

Bishop read the guard's name tag as he approached. "Anne Spencer call, by any chance, Dave? My wife?" Bishop said. "She was supposed to drop a cake off at your station."

"What cake?" the guard said. "There's no cake been left here. No, sir." While they talked, several more employees stopped at the guard's desk, submitted to inspection and left for the day.

"Damn it. We've got this surprise party going for Betsy on the fourth floor," Bishop said. "You know her? Kinda new, cross between Doris Day and Madonna? Sweet."

A honking was heard outside—a Volvo station wagon with what appeared to be a suburban housewife with long blond hair at the wheel.

"There she is," Bishop said. "Late as usual." He bounded out the door.

It was Carl's turn to make a move. He flattened out a crumpled up invoice and thrust it at the guard. "Okay," he said. "It says right here I'm supposed to deliver 136 boxes of Liquid Drāno to this address. Guess you people spend a lotta time on the can, heeyuh-heeyuh-heeyuh!"

The guard gave Carl a sarcastic sneer as he studied the invoice. "This is not Coolidge Institute letterhead," the guard said. "You gotta have one says Coolidge Institute right at the top. Or you gotta be on my list. You're not on the list, you're not getting in."

Out at the station wagon, Bishop yanked open the door and the blond housewife turned to him—it was Mother in drag. He handed Bishop a very large flat cake box with a dozen helium balloons attached.

"Do you have your lock-picker, dear?" Mother said, batting his eyes, tossing his golden tresses.

"Yes, darling. Thank you," Bishop said. "Wear that frilly

little Frederick's thing tonight, will you?" Balancing the box, he kicked the car door closed.

Mother called after him: "Now don't get home late, dear. I made a brisket."

Bishop grinned and headed back inside.

Carl was still throwing a tantrum. "C'mon, man," he said. "I could lose my job. What's it to you? You don't wanna make me drive back downtown."

"Not my problem, kid," the guard said. "Now beat it."

Bishop approached, virtually camouflaged by all the balloons, both hands occupied by the big cake, his briefcase, a raincoat. "Sorry," he said to the guard. "I can't reach my card."

Carl moved to up the ante. "How about I just dump this damn Drāno in your lousy lobby!" he yelled at the guard, pushing his unconvincing invoice under the man's nose again.

"Stop buggin me, man!" the guard said. "I'm gonna mail your fuggin ass outa here."

"Can you just pop the buzzer for me," Bishop said patiently, giving the guy an understanding look.

The guard hit the buzzer, and Bishop walked through the door. "Thanks," he said to the guard. "I'll send you down a piece of cake." Bishop walked across the lobby and into the elevator feeling very pleased.

Carl kicked his boxes in anger, horsed his dolly around and headed for the exit.

In the elevator, Bishop punched "4." Entering behind him were two workmen with a dolly stacked up with small cartons, and another security guard. The security guard punched "5," and the doors closed.

"Cake, huh?" one of the workmen said.

"Yep," Bishop said. He smiled cordially. Then eyed the cartons. "What's that?" he said.

"We're installing new locks on all the offices," the workman said.

Bishop's antennae went up. "Oh?" he said. "What's up? I didn't realize we had problems. Somebody walking off with our computers?"

"No problems," the security guard said. "A precaution. The old locks you could pick with a tool. These are state of the art: electronic keypads. No way in without the combination. All the new buildings have them."

"Oh, those," Bishop said. "The last place I worked, the boss couldn't remember the combination, so he wrote it on the wall outside his office." He laughed pleasantly. The other men laughed with him.

The doors opened on the fourth floor. "See you," Bishop said as he exited.

"See ya," one of the workmen said.

Bishop walked down the corridor looking ill. He dropped the cake box and balloons into a trash can and hurried toward Janek's office at the front of the building. He whispered into his lapel mike, "Anybody know how to beat an electronic keypad?"

Crease, waiting patiently across the street in the van, sat up. "Don't even joke about that, Martin," he said. "Those things are impossible."

Bishop, kneeling in front of Janek's door, was examining a doorknob with no keyhole. To his right, next to the doorframe, was a shiny new electronic keypad. "Does it sound like I'm joking," he whispered. "They just put 'em in . . . goddammit."

"Okay," Crease's voice said in Bishop's earpiece, "as long as it's not from Protek, there are ways around it."

Bishop leaned over and squinted at the keypad's logo. "We've had it," he whispered to Crease. "Protek." Bishop banged his head. "There's gotta be a way around these things, Crease. Come on! We're professionals. This is what we're supposed to be professional at!"

In the van, Crease was thinking and did not look optimistic. "Okay," he said finally, "this *might* work."

Upstairs, Bishop listened on his earpiece, nodding at the lengthy instructions. "Uh huh . . . uh huh . . . yeah . . . above the? . . . uh huh . . . yeah . . . right." He sighed. "Okay," he said. "I'll give it a shot."

He straightened up, looked up and down the hall. A young woman researcher was just leaving her office five doors down. Bishop turned partly away from her and pretended to be laboriously punching his number into the unfamiliar electronic keypad. The researcher glanced his way, then headed for the elevator.

Bishop waited until she had rounded the corner. Then he took a deep breath and gave the doorknob a mighty kick. It broke off cleanly. The door opened. "That worked," he said into his mike. He scrambled after the doorknob and reattached it. He entered the office and closed the door behind him.

Eighteen

Bishop flipped on the lights in Janek's office, then went straight to the broad front window and opened the blinds.

"Gotcha from here," Carl said into Bishop's earpiece. He was perched with his video camera on the same roost he had earlier, the catwalk of the billboard across the street. In the van, once again parked one floor below, Crease now had a good video view of Janek's office on his monitor.

"Walk us through the place," said Whistler, listening to Bishop on his headset. "Give me some details."

"Yeah, well," Bishop said, crossing to the desk, "one thing I sure as hell don't see is any little black box." He scrutinized the workbench, the desktop. "Same stuff," he said. ". . . soldering gun, wire, cardboard boxes of thirty-two bit and four-bit microchips, pieces of circuit board, pliers, set of screwdrivers . . . bag of no-cholesterol sourdough pretzels . . . big comfortable sofa—guess you'd call it a loveseat."

"Keep going," Whistler said.

"What's the box on the desk by the phone?" Crease said.

"Answering machine," Bishop said, pointing to it.

"No, the other one," Crease said. "Next to that."

"Rolodex," Bishop said. He flipped open the plastic-topped rolodex box—inside, nothing but cards. He went on. "Lamp, pencil jar, Post-It notepad."

He tested the desk drawers; they were all unlocked. He went through them. "Papers, envelopes, pens . . . rice crackers . . . package of condoms, hmmm. Toothpaste, deodorant, vanity mirror . . . one of those little doohickeys for clipping your nose hair . . . and *Penthouse*. I'm getting a whole different picture of mathematics as a profession," he said. "That's it for the desk. Any ideas from the cheaper seats?"

"I'm getting the feeling," Crease said, "that he's already taken the thing for a walk."

Bishop moved over to the wall of bookshelves. "Texts on higher mathematics, Boulian algebra. Book on fractals, one on chaos theory, one on *The Dynamics and Stabilics of Large Array Antennae and Other Very Large Objects in Space.*"

"Something's wrong here," Whistler suddenly piped up from the van. "I'm just missing something, I know it. Bish, go back to the desk and—Oh, lord love a duck, that's it! I'll be damned! Sorry, guys. Been asleep at the wheel. There it is right there."

"What?!" Bishop said. "Talk, man."

"Right in front of us, hidden right before our eyes, like he said in his speech," Whistler said.

"I'm dying to know," Bishop said through his teeth. "Come on, man."

"Janek's little black box," Whistler said, "is on his desk, between the pencil jar and the lamp."

"I can't see anything from here," Mother said.

"Me either, Whistler," Bishop said, returning to the desk. "Where you coming from?"

"From my ears, where else?" Whistler said. "We heard Ryzhkov on the tape. Over and over we heard her say, 'Let the service pick it up.' Remember? So use your eyes, you guys. If he's got an answering *service,* why's he need—"

"—an answering *machine,*" Bishop said. "Ah, Whistler." Bishop shook his head appreciatively as he picked up Janek's answering machine. He turned it over, examining it. He got a screwdriver out of his pocket, wedged the blade under the facing, started to pry it off—

—When the knob on Janek's door rattled sharply, followed by a thump and an expletive from the hallway.

Bishop nearly jumped out of his skin. He froze. "Well?" Whistler said eagerly in his ear.

"Trouble!" Bishop whispered hoarsely in his lapel mike. He replaced the answering machine and hustled to the door.

Bishop yanked open the door. He found himself face to face with Elena Ryzhkov picking herself off the floor, bun and all, doorknob in her hand.

She recoiled in fright. She opened her mouth to cry out in alarm, but Bishop was faster. In one motion, he clamped a hand over her mouth, hauled her inside the office and closed the door.

Elena looked up at him, terrified.

"Okay," Bishop said in his most reassuring tones, "I'm going to remove my hand now. Please do not scream. I promise nothing will happen to you. Okay?"

She nodded. Bishop carefully removed a hand from her mouth and moved back, acting as nonthreatening as he could while still staying within grabbing distance just in case.

"Who . . . who are you?" Elena managed. She was shaking. Inwardly, so was Bishop. He was desperately trying to dredge up a plausible story from an empty well.

So were Crease and Whistler in the van. "He's a P.I.?" Crease said to Whistler.

"You're a private investigator!" Whistler blurted into his headset.

"I'm a private investigator," Bishop said coolly to Elena. He didn't volunteer any more details—for the simple reason that his mind was blank.

"But . . . why?" Elena said, wringing her hands nervously. "Who hired you? Why are you in Gunter's office?"

Bishop raised his head and looked at her narrowly for a long moment as though assessing her credibility. At last an idea flew into his head. "*Mrs.* Janek," he said with conviction.

Elena looked outraged and suspicious. "There *is* no Mrs. Janek!" she said. "What is this all about?"

In the van, Crease winced at the bad news. Whistler shook his head helplessly. "You got us stumped, Bish," he whispered. "You're on your own there."

Bishop was beginning to cook, however. He hadn't remained an FBI fugitive-at-large for twenty years by not being able to think on his feet. "Yeah?" he snorted cockily. "Who do you think paid for your little love jaunt . . . to *Mexico City*?"

That got her. Elena blanched and sank onto the couch. She put her hand to her breast to try to calm her fluttering heart.

Crease and Whistler were impressed. "That was good," Whistler said to Crease.

Finally Elena squeaked, "Why? Why would she . . . do that?"

"Why?" Bishop said, opening his hands incredulously, as though the why was as plain as the nose on her face. He had no idea why. As his gaze flicked out the window in mock exasperation, his eye fell on the huge real-estate com-

pany billboard across the street. "Velma Janek lives in
Montreal where she manages her family's real-estate hold-
ings," Bishop vamped. "She supports Gunter, of course.
She's a wealthy woman, but she suspected he was cheating
on her. That's when she hired me."

Whistler and Crease both nodded in appreciation. This
was good.

"Dirty, two-timing bastard liar!" she blurted. "I'll kill
him! I'll find him right now and kill him and expose him!"
She was up and moving toward the door, beside herself with
rage.

Whistler and Crease stiffened. This was bad. "Oh shit,"
they both said.

Bishop stopped Elena gently but firmly. "No!" he said.
"Stop it! Get a hold of yourself, Dr. Ryzhkov!" He shook
her and looked deep in her eyes, trying to will her to calm
down. The wild look in her eyes began to fade just slightly.

"You must never tell him you know. Never!" Bishop said.
"I never should have told you. You weren't here. We didn't
talk. You know nothing about Velma."

"Ha!" she said. "Give me one good reason why I should
aid and abet his sneaky little charade. The pig."

"Alright! Alright," Bishop said desperately. "I'll give
you one." Oh God, what? he thought. "I'll give you a very
good reason." He walked away from her, frowning as
though weighing heavy matters, taking care to keep himself
between her and the door.

"It's just what *she* would want!" Crease hissed in his
earpiece.

Bishop turned. "It's just what she would want you to do,"
he said calmly.

"I don't understand," Elena said.

"Yeah, sometimes I don't either," Bishop said, searching
wildly for a line of reasoning. Then one came to him, a tiny
random blessing. "Look, I could lose my license for this,
but . . . my client is a bitter, vindictive woman," Bishop
said confidentially. "She's withheld her marital favors from
Gunter for many years. Now she's out to ruin him. Not let
him go, just ruin him."

Elena looks thoroughly confused.

"She's using you to get to her," Whistler's voice said in
his ear.

"Yes," Bishop said knowingly. "She's using y—me to

get to her—you! I know it's confusing, but don't you see, Elena, you and me, we're just pawns in this ugly little game?''

Elena looked buffeted by conflicting winds. Bishop sensing an opening, moved in. He took her hands, looked in her eyes with sympathetic rue. "Elena, if you love him," he said softly, "if you *really* love him, just keep loving him. And never let him know. He can never know that you know what he thinks you don't know you know. You know?''

Elena gave it up to tears, and stopped trying to figure it out rationally. She just listened to Bishop's soothing patter.

"Give him head whenever he wants," Whistler whispered in Bishop's ear.

"Give—uh''— Bishop's eyes bulged. He put a hand over his mouth in an effort to keep a straight face. "Be a . . . beacon in his tortured imprisoned life," Bishop managed to blurt without breaking up. "Will you do that for Gunter?'' he said soulfully. "I've gotten to care about him. I know it's unprofessional.''

"I will," she said, very moved. "Yes, I will.''

Bishop squeezed her hand. "Good," he said with a sad smile. Then, putting the tough-guy persona back on with effort: "Go on now. Get out of here.''

Elena fished a tissue from her suit and wiped her eyes. She kissed Bishop on the cheek, walked out the door and down the hall.

Bishop closed the door, and allowed himself a giant sigh of relief. He snarled into his lapel mike: "Give him head?!''

Whistler and Crease were hysterical with laughter. "Be a *beacon*!'' Whistler said.

Bishop, shaking his head, walked back to the desk. He was about to snatch up the answering machine when Elena opened the door and breezed back in.

"No," she said. "I should call him right away." She hurried to Janek's desk, picked up the phone and dialed. "And tell him I love him.''

"Good! Good plan," Bishop said, not knowing whether to laugh or cry.

"Gunter?'' Elena said into the phone after a moment. "I want you to know I am with you. Whatever happens, my love is unbreakable. Yes, Gunter. At your office, I came in to see you. Why, yes, right here by the phone.'' She picked up the answering machine.

Bishop gave a start, almost jumped to grab it from her.

"Yes, I can bring it to you," she said to Janek, turning over the machine, looking at it.

A ripple of panic crossed Bishop's face.

"Well, no I was not coming directly," Elena said. "I must go home and feed my animals, and change to something fresh for you. I want you will have a pretty picture to take to Brussels."

Bishop was in agony, frozen like a statue behind her. She was going to walk off with the box. A life of freedom and $175,000 were going to walk out the door.

"Oh no, Gunter," Elena said, "it is a very little thing to do for you. Yes, about eleven—and for the whole night, I was thinking. Oh, discretion be hanged. Alright, then I leave the machine here. *À bientôt, mon petit.*"

She hung up the phone, placed the answering machine back on the desk and turned to Bishop with a smile. "You're a wise man," she said. "You were so much right." She gave Bishop's hand a squeeze and hurried toward the door.

"God bless you!" Bishop blurted as she walked out and closed the door.

Bishop steadied himself on the desk, took a few long breaths. "I don't know if you guys heard that," he said into his mike. "I almost died."

"You handled that well, Martin," Crease said. "Now why don't you lock the door."

Bishop leapt over and relocked it. He moved back to the desk, picked up the answering machine and got out his screwdriver. "Here we go again, Whistler," he said.

"Come on, baby," Whistler said. "Now we *know* you're in there. You know I know we all know you're in there—"

Bam! Bam! at the office door. Bishop juggled the answering machine, dropped his screwdriver, and whirled around, a petrified look on his face.

"Cleaning man," came a man's voice with an Hispanic accent.

"Uh, not tonight . . . working late," Bishop called out. "Thanks."

"You got broken doorknob here," the cleaning man said helpfully.

"I already reported it," Bishop called. "Don't worry about it. Goodnight."

The cleaning cart rumbled away. Bishop quickly slipped

his screwdriver blade under the facing of the answering machine and pried. Pop!—the front came off. And inside, miraculous to say, was a black box, with sinister-looking ridges. Bishop slid it out. "We got it!" he whispered into his lapel mike. To muffled cheers in his ear, he carefully placed the box back in the answering machine and the whole thing in his briefcase. "God knows what the hell it is," he said, folding a newspaper over the top of it.

"Maybe we don't want to know," Crease said.

Bishop stepped out of the elevator into the Coolidge Institute lobby. Briefcase at his side, he walked past the guard. "G'night Dave," he said, preoccupied, and kept walking.

"Excuse me!" the guard called, getting up. "Your briefcase?"

Bishop stopped. "I'm sorry?" as if it hadn't really registered.

"Open the briefcase," the guard said, coming forward.

Bishop turned, placed the briefcase on the table and opened it.

The guard peered in and saw some legal pads, loose papers, manila files, a folded newspaper. The guard peeked under the fold of the newspaper. Nothing. Certainly nothing that looked like a black box.

"Any outgoing, Dave?" a mailroom guy said, wheeling a large canvas mail cart toward the guard's station from the elevators.

"Not tonight," Dave said, waving the mail cart to come forward. "Okay, thanks," he said to Bishop, handing him the briefcase and returning to his post to give a cursory look to the mail cart.

Bishop closed the briefcase and turned toward the door to the street.

"Hold it," the guard said.

Bishop turned back toward him in alarm.

The guard pointed at Bishop's face. "That Betsy musta been all over you," he said. "Lipstick."

"Oh!" Bishop said with a laugh. With the back of his hand he wiped Elena's kiss from his cheek. "Thanks, pal," he said. He stood aside and watched the mail cart roll through the guard post and past him. On top of the other mail was a Federal Express mailer addressed to: "Martin Bishop."

Bishop followed the cart to the door, then out onto the
street, one happy Sneaker. He whispered into his lapel mike;
"When it absolutely, positively has to be there overnight."

Nineteen

Liz, crossing the quad, fit perfectly within the setting
of shady live oak trees and staunch old Greek Revival buildings on the campus of her private school. In her warm,
nubby Irish sweater, long tartan kilt, she looked serene and
comfortable and properly woodsy for the brisk, sunny afternoon. She greeted passing students with a smile—then
her face stiffened as Trouble hove into view.

It was Bishop again, in his leather-sleeved baseball jacket
and khakis and tousled hair, leaning against a bench. A
boy-man whose smile could too easily light up the air around
her. She put up her guard.

"There's a party. You're invited," Bishop said.

"Go away, Bishop," she said, and tried to walk blithely
on with the stream of students.

"Come on," Bishop said, falling in step with her. "I
want to make it up to you for last night. That was no kind
of date."

"There's nothing to make up," she said. "That was not
a date, we are not seeing each other. I did you a professional
favor for old time's sake and that's it. Bye." She turned up
a path to a classroom building.

He jogged after her, caught her at the foot of the steps.
"Liz," he said, "you'll be surprised how much I've—"

She stopped him with a hand over his mouth. "Marty,"
she said, "at this stage in my life, I don't need surprises in
a man. I don't need disappearing acts and intriguing reap-
pearances. Oh yes, I want spontaneity and fun and laughs.
But I also want dependability. Normality. An adult mind in
a sound body. And in most of those latter categories it is
clear you are deficient to the tune of one."

"And I want all those things for you, too," Bishop said.
He grinned. Absolutely irresistible. "But first, I know you
love a party."

"No," Liz said simply. "No. No. And finally, no." She went up the steps and into work.

Twenty

It was definitely somebody's idea of a party: streamers, balloons, a table laden with Chinese takeout and champagne. The Sneakers' Lair was transformed. None of the usual tools or equipment all over the floor. Mother's stripped-down hog motorcycle had been pushed into one corner. The mascot statue of the rampant Indian love god had been draped with a towel. Only one thirty-six-inch TV was on, without the sound—not the usual five televisions airing different sporting events or CNN, MTV or movie videos in five different parts of the Lair. The place was dressed for company. In the background, the lights of San Francisco and the Bay Bridge twinkled invitingly.

Crease entered with his wife, Caroline, a slim handsome woman who let Crease get away with very little, and their five-year-old daughter, Christine. Crease and Caroline were holding hands and Crease was smiling docilely. The other Sneakers watched, dumbfounded. They stared at Caroline, wondering at her powers. Had she beat him into submission with the foam bat?

Bishop and the other Sneakers turned again at the sound of the elevator bell and door clanking open.

In walked Liz, stunning in a knee-length black dress and pearls. For the other Sneakers she had warm greetings and laughter; but for Bishop, not a smile. She hadn't thawed a bit. It was as if she had Bishop-proofed herself with Scotch-gard.

"Oh, Liz!" Mother said, hugging her. "We are so glad you two are getting back together again."

Bishop winced.

"We are not getting back together again!" Bishop and Liz said simultaneously.

"Here we are in never-never land again," she said to Caroline, woman-to-woman, "where the normal rules don't apply.'' She kissed Caroline, and hugged Carl. "Carl, you have Tinker Bell in a closet over there?"

Bishop laughed, then jumped toward the elevator as the downstairs' doorbell rang.

Bishop was waiting when the elevator door opened to reveal a Federal Express messenger holding a clipboard and a wrapped parcel.

"Federal Express for Martin Bishop," the messenger said.

Bishop scribbled his signature and took the package. "Gosh, my two-way wrist radio," he said. As the messenger went down, Bishop walked back in the Lair and held up the prized package. "Jackpot!" he called out.

Whistler, wearing a tall, Lincolnesque stovepipe hat, a black dustcoat and round opaque white glasses and looking like nothing so much as a cartoon, launched into a weird Star-Wars Cantina anthem at major decibels on his synthesizer. A howl of a cheer went up from the other Sneakers. This was big time, big money. The $175,000 pigeon had come home to roost. A payday the likes of which they'd never had, of which they'd never even dared dream.

Mother danced manically across the furniture, much to the amusement of little Christine. Crease popped open the champagne and poured. Carl accompanied Whistler on air guitar, tossing his hair and prancing around like Little Richard.

Bishop placed the black box in a place of honor on Whistler's well-lit workbench. Liz shook her head. She had no idea what this antic eruption was all about.

"So what're you guys going to do with your share of the money?" Bishop said, digging into the Chinese food, urging Liz to follow suit.

Crease put his arm around Caroline. "We've never been to Europe together," he said. "We're going to go to Paris, in the springtime. London—"

"Lisbon, Athens," Caroline said.

"And Tahiti," Crease said.

Hearty chuckles from the lads. Mother stopped doing the funky chicken long enough to grab some moo goo gai pan. "I've never had a really decent place or a really decent ride," he said. "In all my young life. I'm gonna have both. I'm gonna buy me a Winnebago. With everything. Big kitchen, a waterbed, a big kitchen." More laughs.

"Carl?" Bishop said.

"I want deep romantic love," Carl said, "with a beautiful woman who will crave me the first time our eyes meet." He sighed.

"We're not getting paid *that* much, Carl," Bishop said, to the great glee of the whole group. More merriment than these guys had had in years.

"Someone like Liz," Carl said.

"We're definitely not getting that much," Bishop said, with a friendly look toward Liz. It bounced off her Scotchgard. She gave him a neutral look in return.

"Whistler," Mother said. "What do you want most?"

Whistler did a blues riff on his synthesizer. "Peace on earth. Good will toward men," he said.

"Hear, hear," Bishop said. They all raised their glasses in a toast. Whistler bowed and played his synthesizer rendition of Lou Reed's "Dirty Boulevard," complete with vocals.

Mother caught sight of Christine picking up Janek's box. He leapt and rescued it from the five-year-old. "Whoa, sweetie," he said gently, "really bad idea." Then, in his best Mr. Rogers: "Can you say 'KGB'?" He carried her back to Crease and Caroline.

Christine, taken by surprise by the hulking Mother and a little scared, was about to cry. Bishop stepped in. "I almost forgot, Christine," he said, pulling a large sack from behind his desk. "This wouldn't be a party without presents." He sat near Christine and held out the bulging paper sack. "These things all jumped into my hands the other day when I was in Chinatown."

Christine tore into the package. It was her turn for a jackpot. She pulled out a stream of gifts: a dragon kite, a book of punch-out paper masks, a Build-a-Pagoda kit, a Build-a-Junk kit, a book of children's stories from China and Tibet, a stuffed tiger and her cub, an assortment of tiny Chinese lanterns, parasols, fans and other kid stuff.

Christine was in heaven. She kissed and hugged Bishop, and waded into her toys.

"Why, Martin," Caroline said, touched and impressed, "how did you know the right things to buy for a five-year-old?"

"I consulted with a man named Red," Bishop said. "He's

got six kids and knows where to find bargains for every age.''

He picked up the pagoda and junk kits. ''These are for your age group, pal,'' he said, handing them to Crease. ''Red said it's a matter of honor for fathers in his neighborhood to make flawless models for their kids. Good luck.''

Amid general laughter, Crease looked the model kits over in terror. ''You're coming over next weekend,'' he said with a raised brow.

Liz watched the pleasure Bishop took in Christine's happiness.

''I talked to an FBI buddy today,'' Crease said to Bishop at the drink table. ''He said he's still assigned to the Russian detail. According to him, the KGB external affairs boys are still in business, their paychecks just have a different country's name on them. And they've still got cash to spend. They're out there buying as usual.''

''So Janek's $380,000 might really be from our new best friends and allies,'' Bishop said.

''Hell,'' Mother said, ''the KGB's gonna outlast the next twelve incarnations of the Soviet Union. They still want what we got.''

''Only now it's our credit cards not our souls,'' Whistler said as he passed by and sat down with his dim sum next to Liz.

''I bet you guys all sleep with one eye open,'' Liz said. ''Or one ear,'' she added, remembering Whistler and patting him on the leg. Everybody chuckled but Bishop. He was looking uneasily at the $380,000 box.

Twenty-one

The party had evolved into a quieter mode. Crease and Caroline were playing Scrabble, Christine asleep on the couch between them. Liz and Bishop were dancing to McCartney's melancholy ''Yesterday.'' They were dancing quite close. Liz's resolve had softened.

''Once, Cosmo and I broke into the draft board's computer," Bishop said. "Started giving people deferments. Gave out over a hundred before they changed the number."

"Maybe you saved some lives," Liz said.

"Maybe," Bishop said. "I think we did with our Pentagon work."

"What was that?" Liz said.

"No one had ever gotten into the Pentagon's computer system," Bishop said. "The best hackers had given up trying. But we did it briefly. Cosmo was the best of the best."

"What'd you find out?" Liz said.

"The army was falsifying body counts to make it look like they were winning the war," Bishop said. "There were also secret reports about the side effects of Agent Orange. And other pretty smelly things. We sent copies to every paper in the world that would print it."

"You made a good team," Liz said. "Cosmo the brainy technician, Bishop the philosopher-gadfly, the engagé warrior. Sartre and Camus would have loved you both."

A disparaging laugh from Bishop. "It was a good way to meet girls."

"You never told me how come only Cosmo got caught," she said.

Bishop shook his head. "We flipped a coin. I went out for food," he said. "I was just lucky. Cosmo wasn't. I swore to him we wouldn't get in trouble."

"How'd the Feds catch on to you guys?" Liz said.

"It was a snow day in Madison," Bishop said. "We had the computer room all to ourselves. We broke the first rule of what we used to call 'Black-wire engineering': We used the same phone line uninterrupted all day long. We thought we were bullet-proof. We were kids."

"Did he ever forgive you," Liz said.

"I hope so," Bishop said. "He died in prison."

They moved in time to the music for a while. Then Bishop said, "I got in touch with Cosmo before I copped out. He sent word back there was no point us both rotting. I always wonder, if I'd gone in too . . ."

"Marty," Liz said, glimpsing again, as she sometimes had before, an ugly shadow beating its wings over him, "I think it's time you put the sixties to bed."

Bishop nodded mechanically. "I'm sorry, Liz." He dredged up a smile and a change of direction: "So Paul McCartney was in a group before Wings, I hear?"

Liz laughed.

At his workbench, Whistler was prying the top off Janek's box, exposing the insides. He felt around and found an input jack.

"What does it say here?" he asked Carl.

Carl turned on the lamp. " 'System Out,' " he read on the face of the box.

"Guys," Crease said, looking up from his Scrabble game, "I really think you ought to leave that thing alone."

"Yeah," Whistler said, "I just want to see something." He poked farther inside, feeling the topography of the instrument.

"Setec," Carl mused, "Special, Extra-Terrestrial . . ."

"Earthling Convertor," Mother said helpfully. "Wait a minute—Season Ticket Counterfeiter, Astronomical Moneymaker!—That's it," the ponytailed comedian crowed. "A ticket scalper's wet dream! I'll be rich!" He cackled like a mad scientist.

"What you gonna buy with *this* fortune, Mother?" Crease said with a half-laugh.

"Two Winnebagos!" Mother said. "Solar-yellow and thermonuclear-red, the colors of the gods."

Liz, dancing close with Bishop, watched Mother out of the corner of her eye: he *was* mad. Now Bishop started mumbling distractedly in her ear. "What?" she said.

"Setec Astronomy," he said distantly.

"I love it when a man says that to me," she said. "You guys are all nuts."

" 'Setec' doesn't mean anything," Bishop said with absolute conviction. Liz looked at him, waiting for some explanation. Bishop simply walked away from her, straight over to the Creases' Scrabble game.

"Excuse me," he said to them, and started pawing urgently through the Scrabble tiles. He spelled out "Setec Astronomy." Liz and Crease looked at each other and shrugged.

Whistler grabbed Carl's sleeve and motioned him toward the supply bay. "Get me some cable and i-o interface," he said. Carl hopped to do it.

Bishop rearranged the Scrabble letters to form "Montereys Coast." " 'Monterey's coast' mean anything to you guys?" he called out. A chorus of nos came back. Bishop shuffled the letters again.

"Carl, get the Diagnostics," Whistler commanded. "Mother?"

"Yo," Mother said. He sniffed at some now cold Chinese food, put it down and joined Whistler and Carl.

Liz tried her hand. "How about 'My Socrates Notes,' " she said, pointing to her composition. Everyone grumbled no.

Bishop tried again: "Cootys rat semen." Liz looked at him. They both shook their heads.

The Lair was now strangely quiet and tense. Whistler hooked Janek's box up to a small computer. He and Mother bent over the opened device as Mother attached a probe to different parts of it. At each move of the probe, a different page of data appeared on the screen. Whistler, with his left hand inserted in an electronic Braille box, "read" what appeared on the screen.

Mother moved the probe to another component. "Holy cow," Whistler said. "Do that again."

Mother touched the probe to a chip that looked different from the others. It was large, black and shiny. Whistler read the Braille printout. He sat back and thought, looking deeply alarmed.

At the same moment, Bishop clicked the Scrabble tiles down in a new order and straightened up abruptly. The message he'd spelled out this time was: "too many secrets." He muttered the phrase aloud. It made sense.

And Whistler's super-sensitive hearing picked it up. He raised his head. Two ideas suddenly arced together in his brain and became one. "I think you'd better come here, Bish," he said.

Bishop, Liz and Crease got up and went to Whistler's workbench, disturbed by his tone.

"Carl, you got your little book?" Whistler said.

"Yeah," Carl said, producing his small loose-leaf address book.

"Give me the number for something impossible to access," Whistler said. "Top security, one of the biggies."

"What're you doing?" Crease said. He was starting to get an inkling, and it disturbed the hell out of him. Bishop was sensing it too and moved in close to Whistler.

"I've got the Federal Reserve Transfer Node in Culpepper, Virginia," Carl said excitedly. "Nine hundred billion dollars a day goes through there."

"That'll do," Whistler said. "Dial."

Carl punched the number into the computer modem. "You won't get in," Carl predicted. "It's encrypted."

The modem beeped through its scale of tones . . . and connected. The computer screen came to life with pages full of garbled, encrypted letters, numbers and symbols.

"See?" Carl said. The others gathered at the screen to watch. Even Caroline got up and came over.

"Mother," Whistler said, "that last contact."

Mother touched the probe to the shiny black chip in Janek's mysterious box. The screen's garbled characters began flashing through thousands of permutations in seconds; characters, numbers, symbols changing into other characters, numbers and symbols, so fast it was just a blur, as though the machine had gone insane.

"What the heck is it doing?" Caroline said. "Going through the history of mathematics?"

Whistler, with his hand in the box, feeling just a fraction of the chaotic passing stream but getting the whole picture intuitively, nodded. "That's what any normal computer would try to do," he said. "Not this thing. It's doing something else."

Some of the racing characters stopped changing and gradually formed recognizable combinations of letters. Then some complete words. Then more. Soon, most of the screen was decrypted. Two final groupings kept changing, letters and numbers flipping over, searching. One of them finished. Then the other. The log line at the bottom of the entirely decrypted screen said: "ENTRY CONFIRMED. PLEASE STATE YOUR REQUEST."

"Anybody want to shut down the Federal Reserve?" Whistler asked quietly.

An awed silence. Finally Liz spoke. "My God. You're not serious?" she said.

"National Air Traffic Control System," Whistler said to Carl. Carl flipped through his book and punched in the numbers.

"What are you doing? Don't screw around with this, guys," Crease said, beginning to sweat. There was fear in his voice. He had his wife and child here.

A garbled screen from the National Air Traffic Control System computer network appeared on Whistler's computer.

Mother touched the chip, made the connection. The garbled information slowly but steadily de-garbled.

"Anybody want to crash a couple of passenger jets?" Whistler said, tilting his head, listening for reactions. "Re-route all planes from Chicago-O'Hare to the Moline County Airport?"

"Turn it off," Crease said, low and with urgency.

"National Power Grid?" Whistler said to Carl. Carl found the number, dialed it.

"How does it do that?" Liz asked, vaguely aware of the momentousness of what she was witnessing.

"Cryptography systems," Whistler said, "are based on mathematical problems so complex they can't be solved without a key."

"That much I know," Liz said. "Remember, I'm a math PhD."

The Power Grid connection appeared, another garbled entry.

"Janek must have discovered a way to solve those problems without the key," Whistler said, "and he hardwired it into a chip. That chip." He pointed at the box.

Once again, the screen de-garbled.

Crease stepped forward and put his hand on it. "Alright, turn it off," he said. "Fun's over."

"Anybody want to black out North America?" Whistler said blithely, feeling the unscrambled Power Grid access code with his fingers in the Braille box.

"I said: Turn it off," Crease commanded.

Finally, Mother acquiesced, giving Crease a look. "Well, excuse us," he said sarcastically.

Mother and everyone else looked at Janek's black box with deep respect for its powers.

"So it's a code-breaker," Carl said

"No. It's *the* code-breaker," Bishop said.

"No more secrets," Whistler said. "I think maybe this Janek guy has horns and a barbed tail."

"Yeah," several Sneakers agreed.

"Why do you say that?" Carl said.

"It's only the computer-science equvalent of 'E equals MC squared,' that's all," Whistler said. "Better. It's big time. A universal Rosetta stone. You gotta believe me no one man could do this without Satanic help." He laughed a crazy, nervous laugh.

Crease turned abruptly to Caroline and gave her his car keys. "Honey, you and Christine go home."

Caroline eyed him sharply. She did not take kindly to being ordered around.

"Now!" Crease said.

"What about you?" she said.

"Don't even ask," he said evenly. "And don't answer the door or make any unnecessary trips outside. I'll call you."

Caroline, a former CIA wife, was used to the drill, much as she didn't like it. She shrugged, took the keys, marched over and picked up her sleeping daughter.

"Good night, everybody," she said. She kissed Crease. "Don't get killed," she said. "We already paid for six more therapy sessions, and I'm not giving up any turns at beating on you." She gave him a small shove and strode away with her light burden.

The Sneakers watched his reaction, always delighted at Caroline's ability to face down the lion in Crease.

Crease managed a half smile. He began moving around the Lair, locking windows and pulling down shades.

"Crease, we're on the third floor!" Mother said.

"Yeah, right below the roof," Crease grumbled, making sure the fire door was locked. When his wife and daughter had gone down in the elevator, he went out and locked it off for the night. He came back in the Lair. "What time's the hand-off," he said to Bishop.

"Nine A.M.," Bishop said. "You okay?"

"Well, between now and then," Crease said, "we're going to institute some security around here." He rattled the grates over the old-fashioned airducts to make sure they were bolted tight. And opening his locker, he withdrew a revolver and loaded it.

At the sight of the gun, Liz got her purse and turned to Bishop. "This is where I get off, Bishop," she said. "I'm going home."

Crease stepped in front of her. "Don't take this personally, Liz," he said, "but you were the only one who knew Martin's secret. And somebody talked."

Liz looked at him confused.

"To the Feds," Crease said. "The Feds know all about him and all about each of us. Somebody talked. So make yourself comfortable. We're all staying right here tonight."

"What?!" Liz said, looking from him to Bishop to the other strange ducks standing around her. "Come on, Crease," she said. "Chill out."

"Uh, yeah," Mother said. "What's with the code-red stuff?"

"It's 'code-red stuff' until we get that damn bomb out of our laps," Crease said hotly to Mother. He said to Liz, more quietly, "I'll chill when I'm not hanging out there naked trying to unload this thing, worrying if somebody accidentally mentioned it on the phone last night to her mother or her girlfriends. Till then, you stay."

"I resent that," Liz said. "You don't know a thing about my life now! How can you assume—"

"Exactly," Crease interrupted, staring her down. "Thank you."

Crease glared at Bishop and the other Sneakers. Bishop glared back. Finally Bishop said, "Alright. She stays."

"Oh, terrific," Liz said, throwing her purse down on the couch. "Thanks for the trust, fellas." She walked over to the window, ran up the shade and stood defiantly looking out.

"There isn't a government on the planet that wouldn't kill us all for that thing," Crease said levelly.

Liz stood exposed in the window for a long moment. Then she pulled the shade down sharply and stood staring at the bunch of them, hugging her arms across her chest.

Crease put his gun in his belt and took charge. "Carl," he said. "Get some circuit wire and put a loop on every window and rig it up to the stove alarm."

"Oh, man," Carl said, "there are a hundred windows."

A look from Crease and Carl got to work. Crease went into the kitchen area and brought out armloads of pots and pans. "Mother, help me with the hi-tech stuff," he said.

"I can't imagine a worse place to try to lock up," Mother said, grabbing up a trash can. "This is like trying to secure a beehive."

Mother filled the trash can with noisy utensils, and he and Crease rigged the area around the elevator with booby traps. Directly across from the sliding doors, they focused the laser machine and flipped the switch. The blue-uniformed holograph guard bearing the shotgun sprang to life, looking menacing.

Mother played a thug coming out of the elevator, confronting the guard, firing on it: "Blam! Blam! That'll sure as hell wake us up."

Bishop did some creative security work while Liz watched disbelieving. He rigged a hammock up under the skylight using bungee cords and a sheet, and he filled it with wine-glasses. Any tampering with the skylight would send the whole thing cascading.

Liz grumpily accepted Bishop's bed to sleep in, and Bishop judiciously foreswore any efforts to share it with her. He found a couch at a discreet distance. Liz lay back and stared at the ceiling, wrestling with a swirl of emotions. How had she once again got herself embroiled in Bishop's outlandish life?

The Sneakers all began settling down for a long cozy night's sleep.

Twenty-two

In vain, it turned out.

Everyone was asleep, on the one bed, the two cots, the couches, the floor. Crease himself finally fell asleep after about an hour, on the floor by the door, gun in hand.

A knock at the stairwell door sent Crease bolt upright. He raised his gun, waited . . . Another knock, and a young woman's voice: "Please. We need help."

"What is it?" Crease growled low.

"Please," came the voice. "I'm sorry to bother you. My baby's got an attack. I have to get him to the emergency room. Please help me."

Crease stood to one side of the door and spoke through the crack. "I can't help you. Go away," he said.

Everyone else in the Lair was awake and watching him.

"Have a heart, mister," the woman intoned piteously. "I got no gas money. My baby. Fifteen dollars is all I need. It's his asthma. I'll pay you back, I swear. I live right down in the basement. We're neighbors. Just gas money. I get my check Thursday."

Crease fumed. He was ninety-percent sure this was a con, if not something far worse. But at the very least, just another con. Then he heard a baby cry outside the door. The baby coughed. Crease cursed.

"Come on, mister," the woman said. "Open the door."

"No! Damn it! Here," he hissed. He got out his wallet and slid a twenty-dollar bill under the door, grumbling to himself. He was convinced he was being scammed, but he wasn't about to open the door to find out.

"Oh, Jesus bless you, sir," the woman said. "Your reward will be in heaven."

"I thought you said it would be on Thursday," Crease said caustically.

"Oh, yeah, mister," the woman said. "I'll be up Thursday, soon's I get my check. I swear. God bless you, sir. God bless your children too."

Crease listened to her footsteps recede. He turned and scanned the room. Everyone turned over and went back to sleep. Crease slid to the floor, eyes wide and staring.

If anyone among the Sneakers was cut from a different mold from Bishop it was Crease. He was no leftie. He started out as an army brat, son of a military father who moved his family every couple of years to a new base somewhere in the U.S. or Europe. Crease was the outsider in every school he attended. As he was about to be accepted as a regular member of a sports team or had just made a real friend, the family would up stakes and move. With every move, Crease became a little more inward turning, a little more determined to be totally self-reliant.

His father had been in army intelligence during the war and was a charter member of the OSS. When Crease was growing up, Crease, Senior was a secretive man who left the impression he was really working for the CIA. He implied there was much more to his life than he could let on. He always carried a double-locked briefcase that he claimed contained, among other important things, a secure phone he could plug in anywhere and send and receive coded messages. Crease never saw this mysterious phone, nor did he ever witness the fruition of any of the grand money-making projects his father claimed to be putting together on the side.

The elder Crease had some involvement with the development of early computers and their use in military intelligence. That much Crease believed. But as the years passed, many of the hints his father dropped to explain his frequent absences from home—the top-secret missions he couldn't divulge—Crease ceased to believe.

When the boy was twelve and the family living in South Carolina, his father left on one of his missions and didn't come back. Just disappeared, leaving his wife and four children with almost no money and no means of support. The army denied knowledge of his whereabouts and refused to pay any further benefits.

Crease lied about his age and got a job in a cable-spinning factory. He helped his frazzled mother support and raise his three younger siblings.

His mother cried often and wondered what had happened. Crease just nursed a monumental rage toward his father. And stayed angry.

He joined the CIA in part to get to the bottom of things, although he did not completely acknowledge his motives at the time. He eventually did find an agency file on his father, but most of it was expunged. The file led him to Key West where he found out that his father had died an alcoholic several years earlier. He never found anyone at the CIA who admitted knowing his father, nor did he get anything from army intelligence records but the barest statistics.

His father took his mysteries to the grave with him. And he left behind a son who hated secrets and secrecy and wanted to live his life in the clear, like an arrow in the blue. He wanted to obey every law, fulfill every obligation and be an upright member of a rock-solid law-abiding society. He wanted his daughter to grow up knowing exactly who her father was and where he was and where he always would be.

When dawn broke, Crease sat in a chair by the door, cup of cold coffee in his hand, eyes still wide and staring. He was compulsively searching the room, the windows, the roofs of nearby buildings. His revolver sat on a small table beside him.

Janek's box sat on Whistler's desk, safe in plain sight.

Twenty-three

The city glistened in the Saturday morning sun as the Sneakers—and the captive Liz—emerged from the back door of their building, putting their coats on. Bishop pulled an aluminum camera case from the back of the van and slipped Janek's black box in it.

Crease walked ahead, his eyes peeled for signs of danger, as the team and Liz proceeded out the alley to the street.

Liz spotted a cab and flagged it. "Well, I really enjoyed sleeping with all you guys," she said. "Don't call me, okay?" She stepped out in the street toward the cab.

"Liz," Bishop called after her, "I'm sorry, I—"

"I hope your little handoff goes well," she said, opening the cab door. "I'd hate for you to have something new to run from." She got in the cab and was gone.

Bishop watched her. There goes a lost cause, he thought. He and Crease got in Bishop's car and drove away.

In a less-than-chic part of town. Bishop pulled his battered, orange Karmann-Ghia over and parked across from a sprawling public grade school. It was comprised of a series of barracks-like single-story wooden buildings and a huge deserted all-blacktop schoolyard with swings and a backstop, but not a blade of grass. As though this central city school district lacked the means and will to tend both grass and children.

Bishop and Crease scanned the plaza that faced the schoolyard and the half-dozen rickety tables near the small food-and-coffee stand on the far side. A few people sat eating and a stream of worshippers passed by, coming from a beautiful old Catholic church down the block. Two joggers ran once around the plaza and out. A scattering of pigeons and sparrows appeared, but not Wallace and Gordon.

A homeless person rolled his shopping cart up to Crease, who was leaning on the Karmann-Ghia, waiting. The man started his spiel. But Crease had been hit on once too often in the last twenty-four hours. When the homeless guy saw his maniac glare, he quickly rolled on by and onto the school playground through a gaping hole in the fence. He lay down on a wooden lunch table and went to sleep.

Bishop searched the plaza with his eyes, then went back to reading the tabloid newspaper headlines displayed in the street boxes opposite the car. HAS QUINTS, EATS FOUR read one headline. QUAYLE COMMITS HANKY-PANKY ON BACK SIDE, CADDY REVEALS read another.

Crease watched a late-model Plymouth circle the plaza. It pulled over and parked on the far side, past the food stand. Crease nudged Bishop. They watched Gordon and Wallace emerge and walk toward the food shack.

Bishop opened the car door and took the aluminum case from the floor.

"Take the gun," Crease said quietly.

"What for?" Bishop said. "The guys are right there. It's over."

Gordon spotted Bishop crossing the plaza with his case. Gordon looked hopeful; Wallace his usual churlish self.

"Good morning," Gordon said.

"Hi," Bishop said. He stopped in front of them, the case hanging noncommittally by his side. The man in the food stand behind Gordon and Wallace was serving espressos to a couple of wise-guy-looking types, right out of *Godfather III*.

"Want a cappuccino?" Gordon said.

"No," Bishop said.

"Any problems?" Wallace said a little suspiciously, eyeing the aluminum case.

"Nope," Bishop said.

"Any luck is a better question," Gordon said.

Bishop handed him the case. Gordon's face relaxed in relief. He opened the case and inspected the box. He turned and looked at Wallace, who just stood there dumbly.

"His money," Gordon said pleasantly.

"Oh," Wallace said, turning and striding back toward the Plymouth.

Gordon rolled his eyes—what a dimbo. He turned the box over in his hand and gave a low appreciative whistle. "You're good, Brice—Bishop," he said. "You've earned your government pay."

Crease, standing by the Karmann-Ghia and too far away to listen to their conversation, glanced idly down at the row of newspaper boxes in front of him. Most were sex rags and tabloids. Crease's eye was drawn to the one *San Francisco Chronicle* box. A headline above the fold on the displayed paper caught Crease's eye. MATHEMATICIAN KILLED—MURDER, ARSON SUSPECTED. With the article was a headshot that looked like Dr. Gunter Janek, but the lower half of the photo and the accompanying story were on the bottom side of the fold. Crease, instantly alarmed, rifled his pockets for change to get the paper out of the box. No change. He yanked on the box, it rattled but wouldn't budge.

Crease looked up toward Bishop and the two NSA agents in sudden fear. Bishop was waiting with Gordon, Wallace was at the trunk of the Plymouth, pulling out a briefcase.

"Hey, Martin! Phone," Crease called, waving.

Bishop turned to see Crease holding up the car phone. "Yeah, in a minute," he called.

"It's . . . your . . . *mother!*" Crease said insistently.

Bishop looked at him puzzled. Crease seemed very serious, agitated. Something's wrong here, Bishop thought, but what? He looked around and noticed that most of the people who had been in the plaza when he entered were no longer there. Only the espresso drinkers remained, leaning at the stand, sipping, their backs to the plaza.

Bishop looked over at Wallace. The bulky man was walking toward him with his hand inside the briefcase.

"She's . . . very old," Bishop said to Gordon. "Excuse me." As Gordon nodded, Bishop walked deliberately toward his own car, his back to the two agents. Bishop's face showed growing uneasiness and confusion. At the car, he leaned half into the driver's side and took the phone that Crease, now in the passenger seat, was holding out with a phony apologetic smile.

"Give me the keys," Crease said through his teeth.

"What?" Bishop said.

"Do it," Crease said without moving his lips.

Bishop glanced at Gordon and Wallace who were now moving toward them. He lifted the phone to his ear while slipping Crease the ignition key. "Hello?" he said into the phone. He heard nothing in the phone. He still didn't understand.

"On my signal," Crease said, low.

"I didn't get the money," Bishop said.

Wallace said something to Gordon, and the two men started to move apart, but kept coming.

Crease slipped the key into the ignition and moved his left foot onto the gas pedal. Gordon and Wallace weren't ten yards away.

"Now," said Crease.

Bishop dropped the phone, grabbed the wheel and pulled his legs inside the car at the exact moment Crease flipped on the ignition and floored the gas.

The Karmann-Ghia screeched off and Bishop slammed his door shut. Gordon and Wallace started to run after them. The two men drinking espresso suddenly dropped their act and ran toward the street, trying to head them off. The derelict supposedly snoozing in the schoolyard did the same.

Bishop took over the gas as the car got up to speed. He took a hard left through an alley to avoid the pursuers. The Karmann-Ghia shot out onto another cross street. "What the hell are we doing?" he said. "I didn't get the money!"

"Just keep going," Crease said, looking back. "Turn when you get there at the big street and look for a newspaper stand."

"Will you give me a damn clue?!" Bishop said. "We just left $175,000 back there!"

Bishop turned onto the wide commercial street.

"There," Crease said. "Halfway down the block. We're in deep shit, I think. I hope I'm wrong."

"What?" Bishop said in frustration. He pulled over in front of a newsstand.

Crease piled out, stuffed a five-dollar bill in the stooped, myopic attendant's hand and grabbed a *Chronicle*. The near-blind attendant peered closely at the bill. It was going to take too long. Crease looked back down the street in dread, and jumped in the car. "Go, go," he said.

Bishop pulled away. "You didn't get your change," Bishop said. "That's the first time I—"

Crease held up the newspaper so Bishop could see the headline and the picture. "Janek's dead," he shouted.

"Jesus. They killed him?" Bishop said, horrified. He looked in the rearview mirror and speeded up.

Crease pounded the paper. "The NSA doesn't kill people, Martin," he said. "Who are they?"

"You said it last night," Bishop said. "There isn't a government on earth that wouldn't kill for that thing."

"Come on, not ours!" Crease said. Bishop's brows went up skeptically. Crease just didn't buy it. "Who were those guys?" he asked.

"There's one way to find out," Bishop said, jamming the car into a tight turn and speeding off to the west.

Bishop raced across the Oakland-Bay Bridge into San Francisco and down 101. He got off and crossed over to Market Street, took a jog past the new Federal office building and into the Western Addition. He sped into the rundown neighborhood he had visited three days before.

He came up on the old Federal building from the same direction as last time and screeched to a stop in front of the abandoned news kiosk out front.

He and Crease piled out of the car—and Bishop looked around in confusion. Where was the Federal building?

"It was on this corner," Bishop said. "I'm sure of it. Am I turned around?" He looked at the surrounding buildings, checked the street signs at the intersection. "No, I'm not," he said. he was at the right place.

"You got the right street?" Crease said.

"It's right," Bishop said, the realization hitting him: The Federal building was no longer there. Instead there was a pile of rubble, and in the middle of it, a parked bulldozer. He looked at the rubble and felt sick.

"Oh, Martin," Crease said. "You didn't fall for that one?"

"They took away my home," a voice said behind them. Bishop and Crease turned. It was the derelict, crouched against the news kiosk. "Help me out, peoples," the wiry old man said. "I got no place to sleep. Got no shelter from the storm."

"How long has this been scheduled?" Bishop said, grabbing the old guy and pointing to the demolished building. The old man stood up straight, and squared his thin shoulders. "The scripture say all God's children deserves shelter from the storm." He smiled crookedly at Crease and Bishop. "Now, seein' mankind can raise up mighty towers," he said, his voice rising, "mightn't he just leave a one or two of 'em stand? For such as me to have a roof? What's the harm? I'm hurtless, gentlemens," he pleaded.

Bishop realized how pointless his question was. He let go of the man's coat.

"Why, if you fellas ever need help," the old boy said, "you come to me, Amos Larue. A name you can trust."

"My God," Bishop said. He looked at Crease. Crease's face had I-told-you-so written all over it.

"You gentlemens are welcome to join me for some pickin's," the derelect said, gesturing generously toward the ruins. A flock of people were making their way onto the site, eyes to the ground, looking for riches.

Bishop realized with a sinking heart that he now had about as much chance as they did of going home with treasure. He thought of the other Sneakers, waiting.

Twenty-four

In the hills above Berkeley, in the scorched earth where the firestorm had reduced hundreds of beautiful houses to charred rubble and a whole forest of redwoods to blackened totems, the rain was making inroads. Small rivulets of mud began to grow into little creeks, as water from higher elevations gathered force and volume and cleared channels down the hillsides.

The moderate rain increased steadily into a torrent, and mud streams began carrying what were once verdant backyards down toward the bay. The streams joined together on the curving driveways and roadways to form mud tributaries, which flowed together at intersections into broad headlong rivers that now carried small uprooted trees and lawn furniture, and lower down, small cars into the neighborhoods unlucky enough to be at the bottom of the Berkeley Hills.

Natural disasters were something Bay Area residents had grown accustomed to expect, but they took an emotional toll, nonetheless, even on the well-off.

The people down in the beat-up southwest section of town around the old Oakland theater, however, didn't honestly give much of a damn about the weather or the mud slides or even the next earthquake. They were worried about the next rent, the next meal.

And though the rain beat on the windows and thunder

rattled the tightly drawn shades, the crew on the third floor of the old Oakland theater paid about as little attention to the weather and its depredations. They were worried whether they would be around to see the next meal.

It was code red again at the Lair, and this time everybody took it seriously. Carl, working feverishly at his computer, suddenly slammed back against his chair in frustration.

Bishop was tearing through dozens of phone books from years past, not finding what he was looking for.

Crease was on the phone—on hold—and looking homicidal.

Only Whistler was composed, as though fate had already dealt him the worst surprise it could have in store, and everything else was just life. He sat off by himself under the skylight, his face turned up toward the pelting rain.

"Damnit, Bobby, don't tell me you can't do it because I know you can!" Crease shouted into the phone. "And don't tell me you won't do it because I've got to have it. Right *now*! No . . . No . . . Christ! Would I ask you if it wasn't goddamn life and death?! It's *real* important to me! . . . of course! . . . Yeah, I'll hold *again*."

Mother was on another phone. He listened, nodding. "Yeah, thanks," he said into the phone. He hung up and turned to the others with a resigned look: "The building's been scheduled for demolition since August," he said. "It's been vacant for a month."

"Shit," Bishop said, slamming his phone books shut. "And the NSA never had an office in San Francisco or Oakland."

Crease was now talking softly into his phone. "Oh, God. You're sure? General knowledge at the Institute? Jesus. . . . Yeah, thanks. Listen, Bobby, I'll remember this." Crease hung up the phone. They were all looking at him. He got to his feet, balled up his fists in exasperation. "Janek's grant was from the NSA. He was already working for the NSA. That $380,000 didn't come from any mysterious Zurich bank account, it came from the U.S. Government."

"Oh no . . . oh no," Mother moaned.

"We've been *had*!" Crease said, picking up the phone and smashing it to the floor. "How could you be so goddamn stupid?!" he shouted at Bishop. "Two guys show up, say they're government, and you just buy it?"

Whistler stood and moved into the middle of them, holding out his hands pacifyingly. "Maybe they *were* government," he said. "Maybe they were somebody else's and maybe they were neither. Bish's mistake, and it's ours too, was thinking we were stepping into a simple arithmetic problem: them plus us equals $175,000. Too easy. We're most likely one part of a hell of a lot more complex bit of algebra."

There was silence as everyone digested that and tried to figure out what it meant.

Whistler listened for a response, but heard nothing. "Think chess," he said.

"And we're pawns," Mother said, holding his head.

Bishop had already been thinking about the limited choice of moves available to them now. He pulled something from his pocket and passed them over to Mother. The tickets Greg had given him three days before.

"Of course," Mother said. "The Bolshoi. Who else steals from the NSA? Whose main mission in life has been feasting off U.S. Intelligence?" He handed the tickets unthinkingly to Whistler.

"Who has a greater need these days for U.S. economic data?" Whistler said, feeling the tickets.

"It was a standard misdirection ploy," Crease said. "Whistler's right; we fell for it."

"KGB rules," Whistler said, holding the tickets out until Bishop reached over and took them.

Bishop headed for Crease's locker and opened it. "Everybody, pack up whatever you can," he ordered. "You're getting out of here."

Mother and Carl began furiously to unplug and stack up various pieces of equipment.

Crease watched as Bishop rummaged in his locker. Bishop found Crease's gun and stuck it in his belt.

"What do you think you're doing?" Crease asked.

Bishop headed for the door. "Greg . . ."

Twenty-five

On stage, a beautiful slender Juliet in diaphanous white tulle was trying to run from her fate. She did a series of poignantly futile *jetés,* a final *petite entrechat* and, despairing, lifted a vial to her lips and drank. The music quavered tragically, Juliet swooned and fell onto a marble slab. The audience sighed.

Up above, on the mezzanine level of the stately old San Francisco Opera House, Bishop proceeded along the burgundy-carpeted hallway, comparing numbers on the private boxes to his ticket stub. At a box near the end of the row, he stopped, quietly opened the door and slipped in.

Greg, silhouetted against the scene of dying Juliet on stage, sat at the front of the darkened box. He leaned back utterly relaxed, absorbed and transported in the aesthetic of the moment. An expensive-looking blonde with unfairly long legs sat coiled at his side.

In flanking boxes and all across the hall sat San Francisco's elite and assorted members of the diplomatic community. The Bolshoi were still an international event in San Francisco, where even the made-in-America Joffrey Ballet drew SRO crowds.

Bishop moved forward silently, pulled out Crease's gun and pressed its cold nose against Greg's neck. "Get rid of the girl," he whispered, lowering the gun and pressing it into the Russian envoy's side.

Greg turned slowly in his seat and looked at Bishop. "Martin. Have you lost your mind?" he said. "Put that—"

Bishop cocked the gun. Greg could hear it. He turned to the girl and said brightly, "Darling, would you excuse us for a moment?"

"But not now!" she said. "It's almost over." She looked at Bishop in annoyance.

"I'll tell you how it ends," Greg said with unflagging courtliness.

The girl looked petulant but gathered her long legs under her, tossed her flaxen mane and exited the box.

Bishop kept the gun in Greg's side. "You will give me back Janek's box," he hissed. Below, Romeo was lamenting what might have been.

"Give it *back*?" Greg said in a low voice, sounding genuinely surprised. "Martin, we don't have it. You must believe me." He turned and faced Bishop squarely.

"The hell with you," Bishop growled. "You used me, now you're setting me up to take the fall for Janek's killing. No, I *don't* believe you."

Patrons in the boxes on both sides shushed them irritably.

Greg shook his head ruefully. "But you should," he said. "You see, if I meant you any harm, you'd be dead by now." He nodded in the direction behind Bishop.

Bishop caught movement from the corner of his eye. He spun around. A tall bald man with cold eyes and a big ugly automatic stood there, ready. He reached forward slowly and took Bishop's gun. He stepped back.

Bishop shook his head at his own continuing stupidity.

"Vsyo normalna," Greg said to the bodyguard. *"Mozhna yekhats."*

The bodyguard hesitated a moment, then shrugged. He handed Greg Bishop's gun, turned around and left.

People in the two neighboring boxes were leaning forward and glaring. Greg stood and bowed quickly to each neighbor. He grasped Bishop's arm and moved with him to the back of the box. He gave Bishop back his gun. "Now do I have more credibility?" he said.

Bishop warily pocketed his gun.

"My friend, we had nothing to do with this Janek business," Greg whispered. "Not for lack of trying, mind you. It is a piece of electronics we'd like to have—we are led to understand it breaks your codes open like a melon."

"Not to mention your codes," Bishop said with a cynical snort.

"Not our codes," Greg said. "Our codes are entirely different from yours. Your top codes, we have never had any luck at breaking. So, Lord knows, we wanted that box. It would certainly even the playing field a bit in this new economic game we are trying to play. But we did not take it. Someone else got there first. The whole episode has been a disaster for us—for me personally."

"Why you?" Bishop said suspiciously.

Greg laughed self-deprecatingly. "So far as tradecraft goes, I have to admit, Martin," he said, "the last half-dozen years have been dismal for me. I can barely remember the last bit of useful information I passed along. I think . . ." He lowered his voice even further, ". . . it had to do with how poorly the Patriot missile was actually doing against the Scuds in the Iraq war. A modest little morsel, I'm afraid. Heh, heh, I got that from the mistress of a company exec I met at the Telluride film festival—to some people it's all just a movie. . . ." He smiled indulgently.

"I suppose you passed that on to the Iraqis," Bishop said.

"Not at all. Saddam was a lost cause from our point of view," Greg said. "Why you gave him a new lease on life, I cannot figure out. Americans are so charmingly quirky in their foreign policy."

"I wouldn't know," Bishop said, noticing over Greg's shoulder that the final act was coming to a close. The audience began to stand and applaud warmly. Bishop had to decide what to do.

Greg joined in the applause. "In fact," he confided to Bishop over the noise, "that awkward little bit of Patriot information came in handy as leverage. We agreed not to divulge it during the war lest it harm your president's public support at home, and in turn he coughed up certain trade credits that proved useful during the last tough winter. It's all just horse trading, Martin. I've been trying to tell you that for years."

"Then who murdered Janek for his box?" Bishop said, hardly in a mood to be lectured at.

"*I* would like to know," Greg said. "I personally would love to have that box, should it come your way and you'd like to help an old friend. I need a real triumph. Even these days, one can be sent home, you know. My God, I would die. I have become too accustomed to the splendors of your mature free-market economy."

Bishop wasn't buying. All that sounded like Greg-style smoke and mirrors to throw him off the scent. No more glib storyteller existed than Greg. "Who set me up?" he said coldly.

"I don't know," Greg said simply. He leaned in close and spoke low, "What I will tell you now, I cannot tell you in this box. Do you understand? Come." He reached for the door.

Bishop hesitated, leery of the tall bald man outside the door with the big pistol.

"Martin," Greg said, "you *must* trust me. Now I am being absolutely level with you. The FBI is convinced my people did this. As long as they believe that, I'm paralyzed. Even my closest sources won't talk to me. I can't even call a girl for a date without turning up on some wiretap."

He held Bishop's eyes, then opened the door and walked out.

Bishop debated for a minute, put his hand on the gun in his pocket and followed.

Greg was waiting for him. The worldly envoy put an arm through his and said, "Tell me what happened."

Twenty-six

Greg's black limousine cruised through the rain-swept streets of the affluent San Francisco neighborhood where many of the nineteenth-century robber barons' mansions now housed foreign consulates and trade missions. From a small bar in the back of the limo, Greg poured Bishop a Stolichnaya and himself a Jack Daniel's. He raised a silent toast, which Bishop half-heartedly reciprocated.

"Whoever set you up is very clever," Greg said. "They have everyone assuming my government—or at least the KGB on its own—is behind it. What other intelligence agency in the world has the motive *and* the spy craft to pull it off? The phony government offices. That was good. And the backgrounding on you—really, pulling Martin Bishop's name from the dustbin of history, an obscure ex-radical from far down on the FBI's wanted list. And finding you, and setting you up. That is all first-rate. No one will believe our denials. Of course, we deny everything."

"Including this—especially if it's your operation," Bishop said cynically. "I'm not convinced."

The limo pulled up to an iron gate in an alley behind an enormous Victorian mansion. Greg zoomed his rear window down. Waiting inside the gate was a young man in an expensive European-cut suit holding two large leather photo albums. The young man stepped through the gate and handed Greg the albums.

"*Spasiba,*" Greg said. Then, he said to the chauffeur: "*Prayekhai neemnozhka.*"

Greg closed the window and the limo drove off. Greg settled back to peruse the books. They were full of men's photographs and bios, Bishop saw, as he nursed his drink.

Greg covered all but one photograph on a page and showed the picture to Bishop. It was a telephoto shot of a middle-aged man leaving a building. "Him?" Greg asked. Bishop shook his head no. Greg kept leafing through the book. "Your government would pay a fortune to look at these books," he said. "Although I'm afraid they are not as current as they used to be."

"You keep tabs on all our agents?" Bishop said, trying to fathom who was in the books.

"Just the ones we think we can turn," Greg said, picking up the other album and opening it. "You know, sexual problems, financial troubles. Now *we* have financial problems." He found another photo, covered all but it, and showed it to Bishop.

"That's the older guy," Bishop said, surprised.

Greg took the book back and read the legend. "A loathsome man named Buddy DeVries, aka Buddy Weber, Buddy Wallace—"

"Wallace," Bishop said. "That's him. How the hell—"

"We considered recruiting him in '83," Greg said. He read further. "Drinking problem, married three times. This fellow was ripe for the picking, I think your phrase is." He shook his head. "We caught him with a fourteen-year-old boy. He was a 'chickenhawk'—the younger the better, for him. He belonged to a child-pornography club. He was so far over the edge, we decided not to touch him; he'd just blow himself out of the water. And here it is, predictable as the tides: left the NSA four years ago. Terminated." He kept reading silently. "Oh my."

"What?" Bishop asked.

As the limo entered a long, brightly lit tunnel under some hills, Greg closed the book and sighed. He looked at Bishop. "You disappeared once before, my friend," he said. "I suggest you do it again."

"Why?" Bishop said. "Who's he working for now?"

Before Greg could answer, a shrill siren interrupted, reverberating loudly in the tunnel. An unmarked car pulled behind them, portable red light flashing from the top.

Greg swiftly slammed his album shut, took the two volumes and shoved them into a small combination safe under the seat. "Your FBI is such a pain in the ass," he said as he twirled the combination and straightened up.

"Who is Wallace working for?" Bishop asked insistently, looking back at the unmarked car.

"Astanoveetyes neemledyena," Greg said to the chauffeur. The chauffeur obeyed by pulling over to the side of the tunnel and stopping. Few cars passed in either direction.

"Martin," Greg said matter-of-factly, "I can offer you asylum inside this car. Technically, it's part of the consulate. Do you wish to defect?"

Bishop looked at him astonished, a wave of cold fear washing through him. "What?!" he asked. "Who is Wallace working for?"

A man knocked on the window beside Greg. Greg buzzed the window down.

The man didn't even look at Greg, he was interested only in Bishop. "Mr. Bishop," he said, "I am Special Agent Michaud, FBI. Please step out of the vehicle."

"Do you wish to defect?" Greg asked Bishop evenly.

Bishop looked across at the bland-faced Michaud staring at him and desperately tried to figure the angles.

"Mr. Bishop, get out of the vehicle now," the agent said, pulling the door open.

Bishop got out of the car. Greg looked sad. "You don't know who to trust," he said, as much to himself as Bishop.

The two agents spun Bishop around against Greg's open door and frisked him. The second agent found the pistol on Bishop and handed it to Agent Michaud.

"Is this loaded?" Michaud asked. Bishop nodded. The second agent abruptly grabbed Bishop from behind and immobilized him with an arm hold. Agent Michaud leaned into the limo and, holding the gun in his gloved right hand, calmly placed it against Greg's head and pulled the trigger. It was like a bomb going off in a tunnel. Before Greg's body even had a chance to slump over, Michaud had moved the gun smoothly into the chauffeur's face and detonated another bomb, and he was dead also.

Bishop's eyes were full of terror as Michaud turned facing him. But the wooden-faced agent didn't raise the gun. Instead he bent over and carefully placed the weapon on the pavement by the car. Then he straightened up and smiled coldly. "Too many secrets," he said.

"Jesus, I don't get it," Bishop muttered in shock.

"You're about to," a voice behind him said. Bishop turned in time to see Wallace, aka Buddy DeVries, swinging a heavy gun butt at him. He went out.

Twenty-seven

Bishop reached consciousness slowly, aware at first of a steady vibration and some painful jouncing of his head. He heard sounds he could not identify, and he saw nothing. He drifted in and out of consciousness for a minute or two, then came awake and tried to sit up. His face and shoulder immediately hit something solid and he fell back down awkwardly. He fumbled in his coat pocket, pulled out a tiny map light attached to his keys and looked around. He was in the trunk of a car.

He rolled over and steadied himself as the car made a series of turns. The tires hit a different road surface and started to whine. Shortly, another severe, high-speed turn slid him headfirst into the side of the trunk and knocked out his map light.

He rode in the dark, tenderly palpating the back of his aching head. Soon the car slowed and made a complete 360-degree turn in an intersection—or so it seemed—and sped off.

After a straight ride of many minutes, the car slowed, made a series of short turns, climbed a hill and Bishop could hear a high-pitched chattering outside, like the sounds of a cocktail party. The sound faded.

The car slowed, and Bishop heard a whirr, a sound like a motorized door opening, as at a loading dock. The car went over a bump and squealed to a stop.

Car doors opened and closed. Footsteps echoed. It was clear to Bishop the car was indoors. He heard muffled

voices. Somebody shouted something. Somebody came
running. There was a silence. The trunk opened.

A glaring light blinded Bishop. He shielded his eyes with
his hands.

"What're you doing up?" Wallace said, and slammed the
butt of his gun against Bishop's head again, knocking him
out.

Twenty-eight

Bishop was propped up, unconscious, in a leather chair
in the middle of a dimly lit room with one bright extensor
light focused on him.

Behind him, in its own glass-enclosed area, was a handsome technological icon—a Cray computer, the world's most
powerful super-computer. It was a tall, imposing piece of
machinery girdled with a curved bench of black leather.
Striations of blinking laser lights ran up and down the green-
and-gold mainframe body—a six-foot-high, four-foot-wide
upraised hand with ruby eyes. It seemed to watch over the
insensate man.

The Cray was only the centerpiece of a large L-shaped
office/computer room lined with other computer worksta-
tions, television monitors displaying stock quotes as in a
brokerage house and no windows.

Opposite the Cray, built into the inside corner of the L,
was a stunning twenty-foot-long saltwater aquarium illuminated from within, tenanted by leopard sharks ceaselessly
patrolling its length.

Two large Mark Stock paintings—spooky dirigibles
looming Hindenburg-esque over gray and black buildings—
dominated one leg of the L. On the walls of the other leg,
a series of Jonathan Borofsky silhouette paintings—life-sized
faceless men with hats, briefcases, bearing macabre witness.

Bishop groaned—throbbing pain stitched his head as he
opened his eyes to the bright pin spot. A man's voice grated
on his aggravated brain.

"Think of it as the key to the biggest vaults in the world," the voice said. "The world runs on information—it's the one true international currency. This is pure power, the main vein to the universal juice, all of it."

Bishop eased himself up on his elbows, his mind slowly coming into focus. He realized the voice was coming from the shadowed far end of the room, a man sitting in a deep swivel chair with his back to Bishop, talking on the phone. The man was wearing a gray suit, but had a samurai knot in the back of his hair. The man's hand was resting on Janek's little black box.

"For instance," the man said, "would you like to cut the loans out from under your favorite developer so you can pick up his properties cheap? How about a TRW financial-information-profile service of your very own?" The man listened for a moment, then laughed. "Just think of me as your Thousand Points of Light. Ciao."

The man hung up and swiveled around just as a wave of nausea swept over Bishop and he passed out again.

The man, fortyish, with thinning hair on his round head and big, vivid dark eyes, stepped over to Bishop. With surprising tenderness, he ran a damp handkerchief across Bishop's brow.

Bishop blinked to, and tried to focus.

"Pain?" the man said.

Bishop groaned. He peered groggily at the man's face, but his features were too distorted to distinguish.

The man held a bottle of aspirin in his left hand. He tapped two out onto his palm. "Try aspirin," he said. Then he held out two closed fists for Bishop to choose from.

Bishop's hazy brain was producing a disturbing hallucination. He pushed it away. "No," he said.

The man leaned into the light and smiled. "Power to the people, Marty," the man said. He opened his fists: They both held aspirin.

"Cosmo," Bishop said, stunned.

"My God," Cosmo said. "Will you look at you? Is that a gray hair, or what?" He beamed down at Bishop.

The two old comrades in arms stared at each other, a reflective beat trying to fit the new images with the old memories.

"I'm sorry if he hurt you," Cosmo said. "I'm afraid Wallace doesn't like you very much. Maybe it's your politics."

Bishop studied the man in a kind of appalled awe. He had no idea what bizarre flow of circumstance had brought them here together. But in front of his eyes was the martyr-ghost who'd haunted him for two decades. The hero of the high holy cause, the inescapable reproach to Bishop's own failed courage and commitment, no matter how he cut it. Here was Cosmo alive, back from the dead and dressed in very different raiment.

Cosmo read Bishop's thoughts. He smiled, and picked up the conversation as if twenty years had not intervened. "Anyway, I couldn't have you talking to the Russians," he said. "Five years ago, who cares? It wouldn't have mattered: We could trust them not to go running to the FBI. And if they did, we could trust the FBI not to believe them. Today, we can't trust anybody."

"Cosmo, what the hell is this?" Bishop said. "What happened?"

"The world changed on us, Marty," Cosmo said. "And *without* our help."

Bishop didn't get it at all. Greg and his chauffeur had just been murdered before his eyes. His own skull felt as though it had been half crushed in. And here was the ghost of Cosmo acting like twenty years ago was yesterday. "What happened?" he said again.

Cosmo held out the aspirin and a glass of water. Bishop took them and just held them, waiting.

"There I was in prison," Cosmo said, talking easily, a meeting of old pals over drinks at a corner bar. "And one day I assist a couple of nice older gentlemen to make some free telephone calls. They turn out to be—let us say—good family men."

"Organized crime," Bishop said, trying to focus.

"Don't kid yourself, it's not that organized." Cosmo chuckled. "Anyway, I arrange for one of the gentlemen, Mr. Battiani, to have a direct line to his bookie and other associates. They arrange for me to get an 'early release' from my unfortunate incarceration."

"How did they do that?" Bishop said, knowing he shouldn't ask.

"You can do anything with money, buy a parole for example," Cosmo said with a half smile.

Bishop rubbed his hands over his eyes, trying to make it all go away. "Why did I ask," he said.

"Once outside," Cosmo said, "his colleagues embrace me. They value me. I learn the meaning of friendship. And"—he sat back down in his chair and touched the computer keyboard—"these are forward-looking men; they value innovation and enterprise. I begin to perform a variety of services."

Cosmo leaned over and typed a few instructions into his computer. A giant brokerage-style display board stretching across the wall above him lit up—a moving ticker for running stock quotes across in lights.

"For starters," he said as he typed, "I reorganize their entire financial operation: budgets, payroll, money laundering, you name it. Then I set up a worldwide network so we can monitor such things as"—he punched a final key—"the street price of brown heroin in Singapore." Letters and numbers blinked across the big board—prices per kilo, refined, unrefined; prices per glassine envelope; and price ranges in different cities: Hong Kong, Bangkok, Hanoi City, Madrid, Rome, Tucson, Miami.

"Oops, looks like we can do better in Sicily today," Cosmo said, punching in some buy/sell commands. "Let's see what Uzis cost in Cairo . . . and Havana." He typed. Uzi prices appeared on the board. "How about a nice Exocet missile?" He typed again. Exocet quotes appeared from Dublin, Brussels, San Diego.

Bishop watched in deepening dismay. Cosmo was pleased. "I'm sure you still keep up on world events," Cosmo said. "You've probably read about the bonanza of Soviet munitions hitting the market. A MIG-25? We can provide the training crew and spare parts. Free enterprise, Marty. It's just sweeping Eastern Europe. Ain't it grand? Tactical nukes are not out of the question."

"You wouldn't do that, Cosmo," Bishop said

"I do need a little something down," Cosmo said with a new coldness. "Marty, join the real world. These are exciting times. The entire Soviet nuclear weapons industry is for sale—nine hundred thousand military and civilian nuke weapons workers, out of work, running around loose, desperate to make a buck? I'm having to fight them off. They're coming to me in droves. My problem is sorting them out. But thanks to you"—he patted Janek's box—"I can now access the CIA's list of those three or four thousand key technicians with hands-on knowledge of advanced atomic weapons design." Cosmo laughed. "So you see, I'm an international headhunter placement agency, too."

"This is one of your perverse fantasies, Cosmo," Bishop said, hoping.

"Our Arab brothers are stinking rich, Marty," Cosmo said. "They want it *now.* They want to kick some condescending Western ass. Here, look at this." He punched some keys. Some cryptic abbreviations and figures ran across the big screen. "Oh, maybe you don't read Russian," he said. "What that is, is the line on an off-the-rack nuclear device I can deliver. It's about the size of a soccer ball, has twice the kick of Hiroshima. Think of the chaos. Oh, Marty, the New World Order isn't going to be designed in Harvard Square, I'm afraid."

Bishop looked sick. He pressed his hands against his skull, trying to make his pain and Cosmo's nightmare vision go away. He stared in disbelief as the man played happily away with his toys.

"My, my, those wacky Afghanis are undercutting those high-priced Argentinian generals again," Cosmo said, turning toward Bishop. "Cool, huh?" His eyes glittered. "And of course the whole network is protected by a very powerful encryption system designed by yours truly, so the Feds can't read it. Nobody can."

"But if the Feds got Janek's box?" Bishop said.

"Disaster," Cosmo said. "Hey, can you believe that Janek? Absolutely brilliant. A first-rate mind."

"And you had him killed," Bishop said.

"He'd have just made another one," Cosmo said. He could see Bishop was horrified. "Marty, I did the guy a favor, alright?" he said. "He was twenty-nine years old. There isn't a mathematician in history who did anything worthwhile after he turned thirty. He went out at the top of his rocket flight. I like to guess I saved him a lifetime of pain and frustration."

"Guess you did Greg a favor too," Bishop said.

"Oh, man," Cosmo said. "I couldn't let the Russians get involved in this. I mean, the FBI is bad enough. But those zany ex-Soviets? Jesus Christ, they're bigger assholes than we are. I had to discourage them in a way they understand."

"That's one way to put it," Bishop said, closing his eyes to relieve his throbbing head.

"Believe me, Marty," Cosmo said, walking to the other end of the room and reaching into a small refrigerator, "we had to have this instrument. And I know that whoever takes such a thing is going to bring down upon their heads a very serious shitstorm." He was speaking loudly from across the room, unwrapping a package of red meat. "Now I cannot expose my employers to this kind of risk, so I think: Who can I get to perform this service for me?" He smiled at Bishop as he stepped to the aquarium and started feeding the leopard sharks with chunks of beef. "Who will be smart enough, skilled in the required arts? And hungry enough for a decent paycheck after all these years?" The feeding frenzy in the tank was churning the water into a murky cloud. "And, if the money wasn't motivation enough, who did I have some leverage on? Really it was a question of who will be sacrificed."

"All to protect the organization," Bishop said.

"Yes," Cosmo said, smiling philosophically.

"No. I don't buy it," Bishop said. "I know you."

Cosmo was deeply pleased. His eyes lit up. He walked over and put a hand on Bishop's shoulder. He started to smile. "God, it's good to see you," he whispered. He put a silencing finger to his lips and pointed to the ceiling. Then he beckoned Bishop to follow him into the glassed-in area where the Cray sat.

Bishop complied. Cosmo closed the glass door and turned to him, speaking with intensity. "Come on, do you really think I give a rat's ass about hookers, or gambling, or the cement business?" he said. "These guys don't know it yet, Marty, but that's not what this is all about. Not for a minute!"

"That's a relief, I think," Bishop said.

"With Janek's baby," Cosmo said, "I can do more than just access data, I can also *change* it. I can manipulate reality. We were going to change the world, Marty. Remember?" he said. "Did you ever get around to actually doing it? No? Well, now I can."

"Really," Bishop said, growing more disheartened than ever. He sat down on the Cray's bench.

"Yes," Cosmo said with conviction. "What's wrong with this country, hmm? Money. You taught me that. Evil defense contractors had it, noble causes did not. Politicians are bought and sold like so much chattel. Our problems multiply: pollution, crime, drugs, poverty, disease, hunger, despair. We throw gobs of money at them, but the problems always get worse. Why is that? Because—and I quote you— money's most powerful ability is to allow bad people to continue doing bad things at the expense of those who don't have it.''

"I still believe that," Bishop said. "Look who you're working for."

"As I said, that's just my day job," Cosmo said gleefully. "Listen, when I was in prison I learned that people don't act on what's real, they act on what they *perceive* to be real. You see where I'm going? Major premise: People keep their money in banks they *perceive to be* financially sound.''

"Minor premise:,'' Bishop said. "If people perceive their bank as shaky, they start to withdraw their money."

Cosmo said, "Conclusion: Pretty soon it *is* financially shaky."

Bishop said, "Consequence: You can make banks fail."

Cosmo hit an imaginary "wrong answer" button. "Bzzz. I've already done that," he said. "Maybe you've read about a few. Think bigger.''

"The stock market," Bishop said.

"Yes," Cosmo said, "and the commodities market, and currency markets.''

"Small countries?" Bishop said sarcastically, goading him.

Cosmo didn't notice the sarcasm. He smiled knowingly. "Why not?" he said. "St. Lucia in the Caribbean. Whole country depends on its coffee crop.'' He pantomimed keying an entry into his computer. "Oops! Coffee futures just took a nosedive," he said. "If I play it right, in about a week or two, that country's in the toilet." He walked around the Cray, spinning out his dream. "Marty, it may take me six months to finesse, but I can make a run on *everything*! Coffee today, the whole Caribbean tomorrow. Pretty soon I can have entire countries defaulting on loans; the pound collapses, the mark, the franc, *gold*! Eventually the dollar.''

He sat down opposite Bishop and spoke carefully and calmly. "I might even be able to crash the whole damn system—the whole world economy. Destroy all records of ownership. Think of it, Marty. No more rich people, no more poor people. Everybody's the same."

Bishop looked at Cosmo, deeply alarmed, trying to square

this talk with his gloating over his worldwide arms and drug trade. It didn't compute. "You haven't gone crazy on me, Cosmo, have you?" he said.

"Who else is going to change the world, Marty?" Cosmo said with genuine belief. "Greenpeace?"

They shared a good laugh. They connected! Cosmo thought.

"I'm finally going to do it, Marty," he said.

Bishop looked at his old friend and voiced a conviction he'd have been wiser to keep to himself. "You *are* crazy," he said.

Cosmo's eyes darkened. He turned away sharply, opened the glass door and stepped back into the main room. He went to his keyboard and typed in something. He dialed a number on his modem and waited.

Bishop called from the glass room. "How did you find me, Cosmo?" he said. "I never leave a trail. I've been out of touch with the underground for years."

"Information—the elixir of life," Cosmo said, speaking loud enough for any eavesdroppers to hear plainly. "I drink it all day long. All kinds and flavors." He typed in more commands. His voice took on an edge. He spoke without turning. "I've never not known where you were, Marty— Canada, Turkey, Orlando, Albany, Oakland. Just in case. What d'ya know, the case arrives."

The phone rang through the modem and answered. "The screen in front of Cosmo filled with garbled characters.

"And I think of you," Cosmo said, "my old and good friend who promised me we wouldn't get in trouble . . . and who, oh so cleverly, I might add, did not."

He plugged a cable from the computer into Janek's box and watched the screen steadily degarble.

"Tomorrow," he said, "they will retrieve your fingerprints from the gun that killed a Russian consular officer. The following day, those prints will be run through an FBI computer, and they will come up with a name: Martin Brice. Then, they will check this same data base in Washington, D.C. that we are in now."

Names and criminal records began appearing on Cosmo's screen. "The FBI's little black book," Cosmo said. "Which, thanks again to you, I am now able to access. Come and look at this."

Bishop walked over behind Cosmo and looked. As if by

magic, the name "MARTIN BRICE" appeared on the terminal, followed by a log line: "WANTED, 12/69, OUTSTANDING FEDERAL AND STATE WARRANTS: SEC AND ICC VIOLATIONS, CONSPIRACY, WIRE FRAUD, COMPUTER BREAKING AND ENTERING, OBSTRUCTION OF FEDERAL PROCESS, MISAPPROPRIATION OF FUNDS, FLIGHT TO AVOID PROSECUTION, DRAFT EVASION . . ."

"Jesus," Bishop said under his breath. He had never seen his rap sheet in black and white. It seemed to go on forever, crimes he hadn't even formulated in his mind.

"Of course, this will not do them much good," Cosmo said, "as no one knows where Martin Brice is, do they? But what if this index entry included an alias?" He typed in AKA MARTIN BISHOP." His finger poised over the "SEND" button.

"Don't do it, Cosmo," Bishop said.

"Pain?" Cosmo said.

Bishop looked at him despairingly.

"Try prison," Cosmo said.

Cosmo looked at him with cold lifeless eyes and hit the "SEND" button. "We both know who our friends are, don't we, Marty?" he said. "No more secrets. Ciao." He nodded to someone behind him. Bishop turned in time to see Gordon step up and expertly slip a forearm chokehold on him.

"Just relax," Gordon said, as Bishop struggled momentarily against the pressure, then collapsed to the floor unconscious.

Twenty-nine

It was nighttime in the Tenderloin. Gordon's Plymouth pulled up to a deserted skid row corner. It sat idling for a few moments. Then Wallace opened the back door and shoved. A body thudded to the ground and rolled.

A sleeping derelict behind a stoop woke briefly and lifted his wispy head to peer at it. The body didn't move. It didn't appear to breathe. The derelict cursed, bundled up his bedding and scuttled farther down the block, looking for a new place to nest. No way he was going to hang around and get rousted by the cops when they came to scrape that poor sucker out of the gutter.

A more fearless and enterprising neighbor sleeping across the street roused himself from his cardboard box, hobbled over and investigated. His industry was rewarded. He bent down and carefully relieved the blindfolded, unconscious Bishop of his wallet and watch. Two other individuals closing on the prize saw they were too late and stood over the body in disgust.

Bishop drifted in and out of consciousness. He was on a concrete floor that smelled of urine. He was cold. Somebody kicked him in the side and shoved him toward the edge of the tier, but he clung desperately to the railing. He looked over—it was five floors down to the prison courtyard. "How's it feel, Mr. Stand-up Guy?" he heard a voice say. "Are they comin' for you? Are they gonna save your ugly chicken neck?" Another kick. "What's so hard about a little prison time?" the voice said. "You'll learn to fit in. You have to fit in where ever you go." Bishop stumbled to his feet and ran along the tier as fast as he could, trying to escape. But every cell he passed had faces full of hate. Exhausted, he fell again. A godfather type, a kindly old Italian gentleman with a compassionate face, came out of his cell. "You need a friend, Marty," he said. And he put a foot on Bishop's back and gave him a sharp shove, off the deck into the abyss. . . .

The two derelicts standing over Bishop jumped in fright at his sudden fit of screaming. As Bishop tried to heave himself up, the bums scurried off. Bishop fell back on his face, unconscious.

In the morning, a transient wearing work gloves and two overcoats approached. He circled the body, carefully took off his bulky gloves and went to work. He searched Bishop's pockets and, finding no spoils for his exertions, straightened up and spat on the still man's bloodied head. Then he noticed Bishop's jacket and attempted to pry it off.

That was enough finally to waken the still-blindfolded Bishop—who sat up on the curb dazedly. He clawed off the blindfold, and looked at the marauder. The bum smiled. "How are ya keepin' today, bud?" he said ingratiatingly.

"You'd be smart not to sleep right in the street. Them bus drivers, you know, have no regard." He strolled off.

Bishop felt his head for blood, felt his limbs for broken bones—surprised actually to be alive. He vaguely remembered a horrible dream. He pulled himself up and shuffled painfully to a nearby pay phone. He searched his pockets but found no change—found nothing. A bag lady bundled up in a spittle-encrusted angora scarf approached him with a surly look. She was just sticking out her hand to panhandle him when Bishop put the bite on her.

"You got a quarter?" he rasped, lifting the phone off its cradle.

The bag lady pulled her hand back with a snarl. "What kind of Christians are they?" she said. "The Navy sent pickaninny babies to Ireland for twenty years. Twenty years!" She gave Bishop the evil eye and walked away.

Bishop noticed the wire on the phone receiver he was holding had long since been severed from the box. He carefully hung it up and shuffled off after the bag lady.

Thirty

The disheveled man limping along the sidewalk in the affluent Nob Hill district occasioned little interest. Several women hurrying to work and a couple of blue-haired Ladies-Who-Lunch coming out of their condos took an especially wide berth. Bishop did look like a psycho who'd failed to return to the home after a weekend furlough: gutter-filthy clothes, blood on his shirt, bruised, swollen face. But that didn't make him an unusual figure in an American city in the nineties.

He stopped before a handsome brownstone building at the top of a steep, tree-lined street. He buttoned his jacket and pushed through the front door, when he was stopped by a portly doorman with a choleric Irish face.

The doorman just shook his head and pushed Bishop firmly toward the street. "No go, buster," the doorman said.

"Cut it out!" Bishop said angrily, pushing back. "You

know me. I used to . . . go out with Liz . . . Elizabeth Barker.'' Two residents passing on their way out, looked at Bishop nervously but didn't stop.

"Buddy, no doubt you had your day," the doorman said, trying to get Bishop through the door. "Sure you're a good-looking guy, I'll bet the ladies were all over you. Now how's about not giving me a hard time.''

Bishop had one arm out bracing himself against the door frame, about to flip out of control, when Liz stepped out of the elevator. She was immediately aware of the raised voices and struggle. She rushed forward.

"It's okay," she said to the doorman. "I know him." The doorman looked skeptical. "I'll take responsibility, Ben. Let him go.''

The doorman reluctantly stepped aside. His blood was up. He wanted to kick Bishop's ass. Bishop shrugged his jacket straight, fury in his eyes.

Liz saw he was in a very emotional state. Without a word, she helped him gently back inside and got him a glass of water at the lobby fountain. She let him sit silently for a minute, getting hold of himself.

"The paper said Greg was killed," she said. "I was worried about you. I called your number, and someone answered. I didn't recognize the voice.''

Bishop grimaced anew when he heard that. "That son of a bitch," he said, looking around like a trapped animal.

"I guess I didn't take all this seriously enough," she said. "Would it help if I called the police?''

Bishop looked at her in alarm. "Lord, no," he said. He just sat there in silence, staring at the wall, emotionally exhausted.

"Um, what are you doing here, Bishop?" she said at last.

Bishop looked at her vacantly, then pulled himself together, took a breath and forced a smile. "This guy comes home from work early," he said. "Unexpectedly. He goes upstairs and finds his wife in bed. He opens his closet and sees his partner just standing in there, hiding, wearing *his* bathrobe. The guy looks at his wife . . . looks at his partner hiding in there. He says, 'Shmuel! What are you doing here?' And Shmuel says, 'Everybody's got to be somewhere.' "

Liz wasn't sure if she should laugh or cry. She laughed.

"I can't do it alone, Liz," Bishop said.

Liz wrestled with herself for a moment, then nodded. She helped him to his feet and into the elevator.

Thirty-one

Liz let him into her apartment and locked and bolted the door behind them.

Bishop looked around. He hadn't forgotten the uncomplicated elegance of her place, the lack of clutter, the few carefully chosen furnishings: Alessi bowl on a polished marble coffee table, David Hockney acrylic over the couch, cut flowers, Wassily chairs, a nineteen-inch Proton TV. Her affluent upbringing plus fancy education could have equaled stuffy upper-crust tastes. But not Liz. She had a knack for surprising. Facing the kitchen was a series of strange Duane Michaels' narrative photographs, erotic and surreal. By the bedroom was a genuinely unsettling painting of an obese little boy peering through a heavy iron door. On the bathroom door was a bleak American-Gothic Lyle Lovett concert poster on one side, a Jimi Hendrix poster on the other. Eclectic and a little off the rails. Bishop felt at home.

First, he grumpily scouted the place looking for signs of some other regular man. Liz watched him, knowing exactly what he was doing. He found none.

"Maybe a shower?" Liz asked delicately. She pointed him toward the bathroom, opening the towel closet.

"I have to use your phone," he said. She retreated into the kitchen. Bishop sat in a chair and dialed. Then, into the phone: "It's bad. We need to meet. Not at the Lair."

Thirty-two

Crease didn't feel safe keeping his family at their apartment in the Noe Valley section of San Francisco. He had taken them to his wife's sister's house in a gated community near Stinson Beach, up the Marin coast from the city. Marta, Caroline's sister, was married to John, a prosperous commercial real-estate broker in his late thirties who had gotten rich in the bottom times of the eighties. Law enforcement was John's first love, even though the closest he came was volunteering in the sheriff's auxilliary. He worshipped the ground Crease walked on. He listened as Crease talked on the phone.

"I been holding my breath, man," Crease said. "Yes. I'll pick them up on the way." He hung up, and called another number. "Carl Arbogast, please. It's a what? . . . Yes, I'm sure he's staying there. Diane somebody . . ." He waited, shaking his head. "Carl? What the hell are you doing staying in a girls' dorm? Oh. Diane is your cousin. Fine. No. Nobody would ever think to look for you in a girls' dorm. Here's what you do: Get over to the houseboat, tell them I'll pick you all up in half an hour. No, I'll tell you then. And everybody bring a change of clothes."

He got off the phone. John, a thin, intense man with glasses, started in. "You're on a case, aren't you? Once CIA, always CIA, am I right? I mean, do they ever really let you go? The best cover for a double agent or an undercover is a guy who's supposedly retired from the business, isn't that true?"

"Not in my case, John," Crease said, getting up and heading for the bedroom. "Listen, thanks for taking us in on short notice like this. If Caroline and Christine could stay here a couple days . . ."

"Absolutely," John said. "As long as they need to. And I haven't seen *you* since I don't know when. I barely know your name." He followed Crease into the bedroom and watched as his brother-in-law threw some clothes into a bag and checked his gun and ammunition.

"You expecting any visitors?" Crease said.

"None," John said.

"Let the guard at the gate know that," Crease said. "And tell him to call you if anybody wants in."

"Affirmative," John said, "Oh hey, talk about burying the lead. I officially applied to the Agency. I found out I'm not too old."

"You're kidding?" Crease said, appalled.

"I'm gonna see some action yet," John said.

"The Agency is a headless horseman, John," Crease said.

"Nowadays it's a place for economists and women photo analysts. You'll get more action working on that ice-pick murder in Stinson Beach." He picked up his bag and headed for the door.

"Agh, kitchen murders don't interest me," John said. "The Russian diplomat who was murdered in San Francisco last night, though, I got a theory about that."

"I'd like to hear all about it when I get back," Crease said, shaking his brother-in-law's hand. "I'll stop by the pool and say goodbye to the girls." He walked out the door.

Thirty-three

Carl loped along one of the rickety gangways that linked the houseboats into one big ragtag community. An ad hoc housing development, this network of barge-based dwellings on the Sausalito shore within sight of the Golden Gate Bridge was Outlaw City. The ramshackle floating abodes were home to bikers, refugees from the sixties, Libertarians, survivalists and others who found it impossible to live according to code.

Seven years before, Mother had come across a blind guy wandering in a daze at a Dead concert where his seeing-eye dog had been trampled to death. Mother put the lad up for a few days on his houseboat and saw him through his grief. They never got around to getting Whistler a new dog or another place to stay.

Instead, they put together their electronic and auditory talents and started an underground recording studio. They found the perfect locale: the third subbasement of a nondescript cinderblock building that during World War II had been a secret U.S. Air Force propaganda film studio. Mother and Whistler came to be revered among new young Bay Area artists as the cheapest place in the known universe to make professional quality demo tapes.

Bishop heard about them through a computer bulletin board called HAIRNET, specializing in "specialty" (read "almost legal") services for barter. He sought them out and traded some studio tapes he had of a little-known Dylan-

Lennon jam, in return for their help in one of his early sneaks—breaking into the system that controlled the timing of traffic lights in the city. Together they created the greatest rush-hour traffic jam in the history of San Francisco, attributed at the time to a massive power surge originating at the Grand Coulee Dam in Washington state. Thus began the Sneakers.

Back then, Mother had tried to be married for a while. He moved Whistler out and moved Barbara in. Barbara was a flamboyant, red-haired fashion editor at the *San Francisco Examiner*. Mother fell in love with her bright Irish eyes and the astounding way she had of reciting Yeats to him during lovemaking. She saw right through Mother the Slob and fell in love with the pilgrim soul in the maverick barque.

Then she realized she really couldn't stand the smell of dead fish every morning and every night. And he realized he never wanted to go completely ashore. So they divorced.

Mother went and retrieved Whistler from where he was living in the third subbasement of the air force film studio. It was disconcerting for other people—finding him down there moving around perfectly happy in the pitch dark.

Now Mother was lying in a chaise out on the houseboat deck, listening to Whistler's new girlfriend, Dustin, singing for him in the bedroom. Today it was "Pie Jesu" from Andrew Lloyd Weber's *Requiem*, in a voice whose heartbreaking purity sent the aural-erotic Whistler to a place no man had gone before.

Then, after the briefest sex, the slender, perfect Dustin came out on the deck for some moments of nude obeisance to the glorious noonday sun. She brushed her long pale blond hair a few dozen times on each side. She smiled at Mother, pulled on her T-shirt and cutoffs, went inside and kissed Whistler and split.

Whistler wandered out. "Can you believe that voice?" he said. "God's gift to man."

Mother's sanity nearly cracked. "Whistler," he croaked weakly. "You have to give her to me. Please. You have no *idea* what she looks like. You don't care! You just crave her voice. Let me crave the rest of her."

"Yeah, who needs a body when you've got pipes like that?" Whistler said. He went back inside whistling the "Pie Jesu."

Mother was literally tearing at his hair when a new arrival

announced him or herself seismically, sending shock waves along the shaky gangway well before they came into sight around the neighboring barges. Mother retreated inside just in case and locked the door.

Then Carl bounded into view.

Chapter Thirty-four

Crease parked the red van around the corner from Liz's place. The Sneakers got out separately and entered Liz's building at discreet intervals.

When Bishop emerged from the shower looking and feeling almost half human, Liz was feeding coffee and fruit to the men, who were riveted to a TV news broadcast. A file photo of Greg was on the screen, chroma-keyed next to the anchorman.

". . . The FBI spokesman," said the anchorman, "reported that fingerprints found on the embassy car matched those taken from the office of a Bay Area think-tank researcher found mysteriously murdered two days ago. The connection was made after a local radio station received an anonymous tip linking the two sets of killings."

"Yeah, I bet it was anonymous," Bishop said. "That bastard." Crease and Mother glanced at Bishop and back at the story.

"The FBI refused to speculate on motive, saying it is much too early in the investigation. One source close to the probe, however, told our reporter that the double limousine murder had the look of an espionage-for-cash deal gone sour. And that the killer in both this and the think-tank case had all the earmarks of a trained assassin. The source indicated the FBI was very optimistic about establishing the identity of the killer, given the excellent quality of the two sets of prints. There is speculation that the FBI's computerized fingerprint databank has already matched up the prints with a suspect, but the FBI spokesman refused to confirm or deny that rumor."

Bishop shut off the TV with the remote. He looked ashen. He stared at the blank TV in silence.

"Sit down, Marty," Liz said quietly. She pushed up a chair for him among the Sneakers. He sat, and she leaned on the wall nearby, frightened for him.

"Alright," Crease said, quietly and firmly. "Martin is in deep. We're all in deep. We have to go to the NSA. We've got to come clean and tell them everything we know."

"So we can help them get back the ultimate Big Brother Machine?" Mother said. "No way!"

"We can't just leave that thing with the mob!" Crease said, heating up. "And we have no way in hell of getting it back ourselves. It's time we called the authorities."

Mother threw up his hands. "Oh, brilliant," he said. "Crease, we are accessories to espionage and murder."

"Worse," Whistler said from his chair by the window. "If they can make a case that Bishop killed Janek in the course of robbing him, we'd all be charged right along with him. It's called felony murder. We could all get death."

Everyone in the room looked at Whistler in shock. A chorus of angry exclamations bubbled up.

"All the more reason to turn ourselves in now," Crease said, trying to keep himself calm, "while we can still cut a deal."

"With what?! We got bupkus!" Mother said, jumping to his feet. "We walk into the cops and give 'em back the box?! Which we ain't got a clue in hell where it is! Or maybe we just turn over the money?! That glorious $175,000 fee we got paid! I'm gonna die laughing. We are chump city." He walked out of the circle. "You heard Whistler: We turn ourselves in, we fry."

"The electric chair. Jeez," Carl said, his voice quavering. "And I've never even gotten laid."

They all looked at him. He realized what he'd said. "With somebody I'm in love with, I mean!" he said hastily. "You know, real sex, love—shit, I've gotten laid."

Liz couldn't help smiling. The Sneakers chuckled—all except Crease.

"You think I like this?" he growled. "I've got a family, goddamn it. We've—got—no—other—choice!"

"Yes, we do," Bishop said.

All eyes turned to him.

"Crease is right, we'll call the authorities," Bishop said. "But we make the call our way. At our choosing. Unload the van. Bring it all up."

"What do you mean? Here?" Liz said, alarmed.

"Here," Bishop said, shrugging.

Liz looked at him hard for a beat, pondering. She made up her mind and turned to the other Sneakers. "You guys are in trouble," she said sweetly. "Would you like to move your stuff in and use my apartment for a while?"

They got the point. Suddenly they were falling all over each other jabbering simultaneously, asking Liz very politely if it would be okay with her if they used her place. Thank you a thousand times. Incredibly sorry for the terrible inconvenience. We'll be eternally grateful, et cetera. Bishop looked at her sheepishly.

"Of course you're welcome here, you louts," she said with a wry look. "Now I guess I'll take my last undisturbed shower." She reached over, picked up her Alessi bowl and disappeared into the bedroom.

The Sneakers gave each other guilty looks, then bolted for the outside door.

Thirty-five

When Liz reemerged, changed from her going-to-work clothes into jeans, she stopped in the doorway and held her head. It was more than she'd bargained for, and she had thought she had known what to expect. Her apartment had undergone radical surgery.

What was once elegantly sparse now looked like a Circuit City going-out-of-business sale, crammed to the rafters with much of the gear from the Lair and the van. Electronic equipment was piled on bridge tables, electrical cords ran everywhere, and Mother was nailing some kind of very-low-frequency, long-array antenna all the way across the living-room wall, causing great chunks of plaster to crumble to the floor.

Liz moaned and raised her hand to protest. But most of the damage was already done. She held her tongue, while vowing to herself: never again.

She went over to the entrance foyer to help Crease roll in a machine of some kind.

In the living room, Whistler sat in a makeshift cockpit surrounded by computer monitors, scopes, tone generators and his Braille readers, all hooked up to a telephone.

Crease hooked up his machine—a graph-making device resembling a lie detector—to the same phone. "A voice stress analyzer," he said to Liz. "Not as accurate as a polygraph, but it'll do."

Bishop surveyed the setup uneasily. "Are we being brilliant, or are we throwing ourselves to the lions?"

"Lions!" shouted Mother.

"Brilliant!" Carl shouted back.

As long as they were actively doing something, this pack of unhousebroken hyenas bristled with upbeat conviction. Bishop smiled.

"I'm going to bounce the call through six different relay stations, and off four satellites," Whistler said with relish. "It'll be the hardest trace they've ever seen."

"Let's do it," Bishop said.

Carl handed Bishop his little phone book, pointing to a number. Bishop dialed. Liz watched, engrossed. She had no idea what they were up to.

After two rings, a woman's voice answered over the speaker phone. "Fort Meade, Maryland. Good afternoon," she said.

"Try Director Ops," Crease said to Bishop.

"Uh, Director of Operations, please," Bishop said into the phone. There was a pause.

"What extension, please?" said the woman.

"I'm sorry, I forget the number," Bishop said. "But I need the director of operations. It's very important."

"What extension, please," the woman repeated.

Bishop looked to Crease for help.

"Try their computer section . . . No, technical research," Liz piped up. The team looked at her appreciatively.

"Give me the Research section. It's an emergency," Bishop said and held his breath.

"I need an extension or a name," the woman said, her tone unchanging.

Bishop looked at Crease and Mother in desperation. A long moment passed as they racked their brains.

"Setec Astronomy," Bishop blurted to the operator.

Another pause. Then the woman said: "One moment please."

The team members heard her ring an extension and put Bishop on hold. They looked at each other hopefully.

Whistler, headphones on and wired into his array of machines, quickly doused their spirits. "They've started the trace," he said.

On the computer screen at Whistler's side, a blue line on a color graphics map of the U.S. and Europe displayed the circuitous route Whistler had devised to place this phone call from San Francisco to Fort Meade, Maryland. The first link went to Denver, then Comstar satellite to New York, Transcom satellite relay to London, satellite to Geneva, land line to Bonn, satellite back across to Toronto, land line down to Buffalo, Comstar to Washington, D.C., cellular across D.C. land line to Baltimore, then to Fort Meade.

Now a blinking red line—signifying the trace—began to extend back along the final leg of the call, from Fort Meade to Baltimore, as the superior NSA equipment went to work to backtrack the call.

"Who is this, please?" a man's basso voice came over the speaker phone.

"It's my dime, I'll ask the questions," Bishop said. "Who are you?"

"Let's say my name is Mr. Abbott," the man said in his sonorous tones.

Crease, reading the graph line on the voice-stress analyzer, nodded to Bishop. "It's true," he said.

"Shit," Whistler said. "They're into the D.C. cellular matrix already. They are fast." On the computer screen, the NSA trace had made the first two connections and was looking for the third.

"Mr. Abbott, are you interested in Setec Astronomy?" Bishop asked.

"I'm interested in all kinds of astronomy," Abbott said.

"That's cute," Bishop said. "Maybe I need to talk to somebody who isn't so cute. Are you interested?"

"If I knew more I could be interested," Abbott came back.

Crease nodded. The stress-analyzer graph tracking was steady. More truth.

"They've got through St. Louis and they're across Comstar to Buffalo and Toronto," Whistler said. "These guys

are something else.'' The red blinking trace line now snaked
north from Washington and up into Canada.

"I need to know if you're someone who can make a
deal?'' Bishop said into the phone.

"Go on,'' Abbott said.

"Can—you—deal?!'' Bishop said, exasperated.

"Yes,'' Abbott's distinctive deep voice came back.

The stress line continued steady. Crease nodded.

"Shit, they got the transatlantic satellite and the Bonn
land line all in the same jump,'' Whistler said to Bishop.
"How the hell'd they do that?! You got less than half a
minute.''

"If I come in with what I know, will you guarantee my
safety?'' Bishop asked Abbott urgently.

"Do you have the time,'' Abbott said calmly.

"No,'' Bishop said.

There was dead air. Whistler's screen showed the red trace
closing in through Geneva and London and finding New
York. "Fifteen seconds,'' he said.

"Can you guarantee my safety?'' Bishop said with greater
urgency.

"Where is the item?'' Abbott asked.

"Can—you—guarantee—my—safety?!'' Bishop said.

"Yes. I guarantee your safety,'' Abbott said.

"Eight seconds,'' Whistler said. "They're through New
York.''

Crease's graph was spiking. "He's lying!'' Crease said.

Whistler's screen showed the red line hitting Denver and
casting about for the last link to the Bay Area. Liz watched,
terrified.

"Hang up! They've almost got us,'' Whistler said.

"He's lying!'' Crease hissed.

"Hang up!'' Whistler spouted.

Bishop hung up. His heart was racing, and sweat was
pouring off his forehead. Liz stood against the wall gripping
her coffee cup with white knuckles. The team took a long
time to calm down.

"We're screwed,'' Crease said quietly.

Thirty-six

Liz and Bishop served the others, then sat down for a last supper of canned hash, cottage cheese and bagels—all the food to be found in the house.

"There's got to be another way to cut a deal with these freaks," Mother said, mixing his cottage cheese and hash together with ketchup and Worcestershire sauce, and taking in big forkfuls.

"If we had the box, yes," Crease said, picking at his food. "Without it, no."

"So let's get it," Carl said in a barely audible voice.

"What?" Whistler said. He knew very well what Carl had said.

"He said, 'So let's get the freaking thing'!" Mother said.

Bishop looked at them. "I don't know where it is, remember?" he said.

They ate in silence for a while, lost in their sordid thoughts.

"You have *no* idea where they took you?" Crease said. "Even a hint, something they said? You were with this guy Cosmo for at least half an hour, you said."

Bishop was exasperated. "They threw me in a trunk and drove around in circles," he said. "It could be next door, it could be a hundred miles away." He chewed and tormented himself. "It could be underground, it could be a high rise. Forget it."

But Whistler, a fish who plied other waters and swam in a different ether, saw an opening here, not a closing. "Bish, what did it sound like?" he said.

"What?" Bishop said, in no mood.

"When you were in the trunk," Whistler said. "What did the road sound like?"

Bishop looked at him. "I don't know," he said. "A highway. Regular highway."

Whistler felt his way to a synthesizer, turned it on and

started it making white noise, a tires-on-highway noise.
"Did you go over gravel?" he asked. "Speed bumps? A
bridge?"

"A bridge. Yeah," Bishop said. "Big bridge."

Mother grabbed a map and snapped it open. "Four
bridges in the Bay Area," he said.

"Toll booth?" Carl piped up. "Oh. Never mind. They
all have tolls."

"Was the Golden Gate fogged in last night?" Whistler
asked.

"Yes," Crease said.

"Did you hear a foghorn?" Whistler said to Bishop.

Bishop thought back. "No," he said.

"Scratch the Golden Gate," Crease said.

"That leaves three," Mother said.

"What did it sound like?" Whistler said. "Did you go
through a tunnel in the middle?"

"I'm not . . . no," Bishop said. "No tunnel."

"Scratch the Bay Bridge," Crease said.

"That leaves two," Mother said. "San Mateo or Dumbarton."

"What did it sound like?" Whistler said yet again. "Did
it change in the middle, like metal grating? Whining?"

"No. No whining," Bishop said.

Whistler was synthesizing the tire sounds on different road
surfaces.

"Lower," Bishop said.

Whistler altered the sound.

Bishop listened carefully. "Lower," he said.

Whistler lowered the pitch.

"There was a recurring sound," Bishop remembered.

"Like seams—concrete or metal expansion joints?"
Whistler said. He synthesized the sound. "Like this," he
said.

"Yeah," Bishop said. "That sounds familiar."

Thirty-seven

They listened now to the same sound produced not by the synthesizer, but by the tires of the Sneakers' van speeding over the expansion joints of the Dumbarton Bridge.

Mother was driving. Crease, Whistler, Carl and Bishop were in the back with the maps.

As for Liz, Bishop had politely thanked her for her offer of field assistance and requested that she man the home front while they made this foray. Liz had politely refused. Bishop had insisted. Liz had told him in Technicolor to bugger off. She'd come this far, invested this much, and she was going all the way. Bishop had been at a loss for words.

Liz was now in the van, in the shotgun seat next to Mother, as the team crossed the Dumbarton Bridge.

The van came down off the bridge. "Now what?" Mother asked.

Bishop, lying back by the rear doors with his eyes closed, was trying to relive the ride. "Smooth for a while, pretty straight, ten or fifteen minutes," he said. "Then a series of turns. Then bumps, rough ones—a whole bunch."

Crease scanned the maps. "Railroad tracks," he said. He called to Mother, "Right on Antrim, left on 84."

Mother followed the instructions. They sped down into the Silicon Valley for some minutes, then turned right on Antrim and rolled through East Palo Alto into Santa Clara County. They were in techno-electronics heartland.

"What do you remember next?" Whistler said.

"A . . . cocktail party," Bishop said, still lying with his eyes closed.

"What?" Crease said.

"It sounded like we drove through . . . a cocktail party," Bishop said. "Like chattering. It was right at the end."

They all looked at each other. "Great," Crease said. "We'll look for a cocktail party on the other side of the railroad tracks. I need a drink."

"What's the exit where the tracks are?" Whistler said.

"There are . . . one, two . . . three," Mother said, checking his map. "Ogilvie, Florinda and Crescent."

"There's a body of water, a man-made lake out here somewhere," Whistler said.

The Sneakers exchanged puzzled looks.

"Out Crescent a little ways—a reservoir," Carl said, looking up from his country topographical map.

"Stay on Crescent," Whistler said. "Get off at the reservoir."

"There's a cocktail party at the reservoir?" Crease said, highly dubious.

"Yes," Whistler said with a broad smile.

Thirty-eight

In the gathering dusk, the Sneakers and Liz stood by the van, parked on a curving road above a brush-covered hillside. A sound very much like a high-decibel cocktail party washed over them. They looked at each other and laughed.

"Very good, Bish," Whistler said. "Remind me to make you an honorary blind person."

Bishop smiled. "Remind me to send your ears and brain to the Smithsonian when you finally check out," he said, putting an arm around the blind man.

Below them, thousands of cackling geese were feeding, strutting and chattering on the verge of the Crestvale Reservoir. They sounded at a distance like a country-club crowd who'd just heard phenomenal news from their brokers—excitedly gabbing and celebrating over the white wine and brie.

"Great," Bishop said. "Where does this road go?"

Carl had his maps out. "Nowhere," he said. "It ends right around that hill."

"What's around the hill?" Crease said, scanning the landscape with field glasses.

"Nothing but private property," Carl said.

They all looked at each other in discouragement. Then it dawned on them that this might not be bad news at all, but exactly the answer they were looking for. They looked at each other and piled back in the van.

Crease drove on around the hillside, climbing steeply to the crest. As they came over the top, off to the right and slightly below them was a long, sprawling building with a gold facade. It was a company of some kind, set off on the outer edge of the suburban landscape.

Carl checked it out with binoculars. "Forget it," he said. "It's a toy company." He read out the sign on the well-tended front lawn between the flower beds: PLAYTRONICS—EDUCATIONAL SOFTWARE AND COMPUTER GAMES.

Bishop took the binoculars and looked: a modernistic structure with reflective gold windows presenting an opaque face to the world. Ten-foot-high wire fencing topped by barbed wire enclosed the grounds. "Toy company, my ass," he said. "That's laser fencing. There's high voltage on the perimeter, and the whole building says 'Go away.' That's Cosmo, I know it."

"Whistler, you Vulcan," Mother said. "You did the impossible again." One by one the other Sneakers gave Whistler a congratulatory squeeze or punch.

"That part was easy," Whistler said. "Now we gotta get close enough to smell the spoor."

Since he went blind as a kid from a degenerative pigmentary disorder that came with his genes, Whistler had never taken the easy route. Growing up in a tiny artists' colony on Puget Sound in Washington state, he'd wanted to be a painter like his father, who more than made a living at it. For months every summer and during Christmas vacations, father and son trekked along the rugged British Columbia coast. Young Whistler did the practical camping chores while his father translated the rocky seaside escarpments and high pines into surreal cathedrallike images. He helped create a Northwest Waterways school that took something from the Hudson River school of the last century.

Whistler's artistic dream dissolved with his sight. So too, paradoxically, did his tolerance for the overwhelmingly gray and blustery climate of his northwest birthplace. Now he craved the *feel* of the sun on his skin. He insisted that the pineal gland deep in his brain needed it. He went to college in Southern California, at Cal Tech.

Though he started in Engineering Physics, he veered into

Astrophysics, finding that his sightlessness uniquely suited him to the Einsteinian method of theoretical physics' mind experiments. He proved to be first-rate at "wild ideas," the kind of free invention that led Einstein to his Special Theory of Relativity and latter astronomers to discoveries like black holes and galactic string theory.

Whistler was contentedly working on his Ph.D. thesis—an inflationary theory positing a gigantic expansion of the universe in the first infinitesimal fraction of the first nanosecond to account for the universe's odd homogeneity—when he ran into a snag. It was an earthbound snag, in the form of a woman. His thesis adviser's young wife took to dropping in at Whistler's apartment to straighten up the place for him. Soon she was doing much more, and soon enough they got caught. His thesis adviser was also the chairman of his department. Goodbye Ph.D.

Whistler got an okay job doing radio astronomy analysis at JPL. But after a few years of listening to umpteen-billion-year-old background radiation left over from the Big Bang, he ceased to care so passionately about the spaces between stars where no human race is. He decided he needed to work where there were more warm bodies. First he got a job at IBM—it felt more like Mars. So he went the other direction—a job at a Los Angeles record company as a sound engineer. He was checking out the competition at a Dead concert in San Francisco when he lost his dog and Mother found him.

On the hillside above the Playtronics Computer Game Company, Bishop turned back to the other Sneakers, grim-faced. "This is it," he said to the others. "Any second thoughts?"

They looked at each other. Nobody said anything. They shook their heads no, their tense faces reflecting at least some understanding of the possible dangers ahead.

Liz, however, was wide-eyed with anticipation. She had heard much about Bishop's sneaks, his black-hat jobs, but had never seen it happen firsthand.

"Mother, set up the directional," Bishop said. "Carl, video. Let's go."

Liz moved out of the way as the team jumped into action. They dragged equipment from the van and set it up as unobtrusively as possible, using bushes as a blind.

Mother looked through the telescopic eyepiece of a long-range shotgun microphone. He centered the scope on a smoked-glass window on the second floor of Playtronics and adjusted the image—as the picture came into focus so did the sounds.

"Second floor, northwest, number two," Mother said.

Whistler, listening intently on a headset, translated the vague sounds. "That's a bathroom," he said. "The ladies' room, in fact. Wait . . . Jesus! They're talking about a black box!" He listened as the Sneakers held their breath. "Never mind," Whistler said. "Black fox, they said—fur coat. False alarm."

Mother moved the mike to the next window. "Second floor, northwest, number three."

Crease made notes on a hurriedly sketched, approximate floor plan of the building.

Whistler listened to that window for a moment and said, "Emergency exit."

"How do you know that?" Mother said, amazed, staring into the eyepiece and trying to imagine what would identify the space.

"I can hear the emergency floodlights' battery recharging," Whistler said.

Mother shook his head in awe. Crease dutifully noted the information on his diagram.

"Give me the six hundred," Bishop said. Carl handed him a long lens that he screwed onto a tripod-mounted video camera aimed down the hill. Carl then ranged along the road, gathering branches and uprooting small shrubs.

Liz, eager for a role, carried Carl's findings back to Bishop and returned for more.

A pickup truck hove into view on a turn in the road and came toward them. The other Sneakers melted into the bushes and into the van. Liz grabbed Carl, pushed him against a tree and was giving him a smoky kiss as the pickup rolled by. The driver honked and hooted and kept going. Liz released Carl, gave him a sweet smile and got back to work. Carl followed with rubbery knees.

Whistler, listening at another window, said, "Crease, what's this mean? 'My voice is my passport. Verify me.' "

"May be some sort of voiceprint ID,' Crease said, writing it down. "I'll check it out when we get back."

"What's my location now?" Whistler asked.

Mother sighted through the scope of the shotgun mike. "Third floor, southwest corner," he said.

"That room is bursting with ultrasonic," Whistler said. "I've never heard sensors that powerful." He took off the earphones. "Someone's very serious about keeping people out of that room."

"Ground zero?" Mother said.

"That could very well be the navel we want to contemplate," Whistler said.

Bishop finished sighting the lens of the video camera. He bent down and programed the VCR, which Carl had rigged in the bushes. Carl completed the job by camouflaging the camera and VCR with more bushes and branches. The camera started clicking faintly every few seconds.

Bishop hovered a few moments to make sure it was working correctly. He climbed in the van and signaled Mother to take off. They drove away.

"You see, it's pretty uneventful," Bishop said to Liz. "You'll never want to go again."

"Oh, I learned something," Liz said.

"Oh, what?" Bishop said, waiting to hear something complimentary about their professionalism.

"I found out that Carl's a great kisser," she said, smiling at the boy. Carl blushed scarlet and sank down in his seat. The other Sneakers chuckled benevolently.

Carl, originally from West Virginia, got to San Francisco by way of the Gulf Coast and Galveston. His father, Becean Arbogast, was a guitar-playing swain who formed the first rock-and-roll band ever in his West Virginia mountain hometown of Cypress Piddlin. Becean's sporting with Dotty, the best-looking girl in the next town who was one of his band's three groupies, led to the birth of Carl when both parents were only seventeen.

Within two years the little family moved to Pascagoula, on the Alabama Gulf, where Becean got offshore oil work. As the oil-rig company expanded west to Gulf Port, Mississippi, and then Morgan City, Louisiana, Becean and Dotty moved with them, raising little Carl in sweltering week-to-week motels, about which he remembered only the tiny courtyard swimming pools with the Astroturf decks and floating cigarette butts.

The Arbogasts' big break came twofold when Becean got

a job as a field foreman for an oil exploration company out of Houston, and Dotty got a shot on *The Price Is Right*. Becean was making enough for the family to take out a mortgage on a modest house in Galveston. And after Dotty won prizes four days running on the quiz show, they had a thing or two to put in the house.

Carl, who was eleven at the time, marks *The Price Is Right* as the beginning of the end for the Arbogast family. Then, they felt anointed, touched by luck. They were on a run and life was coming up roses. However, with a house furnished with table service for twelve, a marbelized roll-top bar, a curly-maple chiffonier, Reynolds aluminum siding and a wall clock framed in lightning bolts, the Arbogasts had appearances to keep up. They began to battle over what further essentials had to be bought and to drink to allay the stress of the bills that piled up.

Within a year they had sold off most of the game-show winnings to pay debts and taxes, and had split up. Dotty kept just one thing from her four days of glory—the white mink stole. She moved to San Francisco to try her hand at exotic dancing.

Carl opted to stay with his father who, however, spent up to ninety days at a time out on oil rigs in the gulf. It was after Carl got into trouble fooling with his school's computer that school authorities discovered he was living virtually on his own as a minor. He was sent to live with his mother.

Dotty was now a topless bartender in San Francisco. She begrudgingly took her son into her little second-floor flat near the Haight. She was after all still a young woman and liked to bring men home now and then. She kept the identity of her place of employ a deep secret from Carl, who in turn had no desire to visit Mom at work. When Dotty brought home a guy—some of them not much older than Carl—he would run out and sleep in an all-night movie theater.

Dotty conscientiously enrolled Carl in high school. But Carl soon stopped going and found a job at an electronics repair shop, acting as the mouthpiece for a Thailander who spoke almost no English but knew his electronics and was willing to share it.

On one of his days off, Carl ran into Marty Bishop at a pick-your-parts auto junkyard. The boy was salvaging old car radios and Bishop was foraging for an undamaged rocker

panel for his aged Karmann-Ghia. Bishop hired the eager
kid to do some outside wiring for him at the Lair. Soon Carl
was doing other odd jobs, and within two years was a
Sneaker-in-training.

Thirty-nine

A day and a half after their discovery of Playtronics,
the Sneakers had decorated the walls of Liz's apartment with
surveillance stills of Playtronics from all angles. And they
had for the watching a cartoonlike motion picture of their
target. Through a time-lapse video, a compressed vision of
a Playtronics corporate day came to life.

While a digital readout at the bottom of the screen showed
the date and time, the first segment of tape showed Playtronics employees at the end of their work day switching off
their office lights, zipping out to their cars and emptying the
parking lot. The night passed quickly. Daybreak saw the
place gradually come to life again. Cars arrived, zinged
around searching for parking places, people entered the
building.

"Okay, jack it up," Bishop said.

Mother switched to fast motion. In twenty seconds an
entire day unfolded. Clouds scudded past overhead. People
raced in and out of the building. The sky darkened, a small
storm front passed, the sun came back out. People gathered
on the lawn for what seemed only a nanosecond, plopping
down, gobbling their lunches, jumping up, streaking back
inside. Deliveries were made in a flash. It grew dark. Lights
in the building turned on momentarily, then most went off
as the workday ended. People streamed out to their cars and
raced away into the night.

"Slow it down," Bishop said. He huddled with Carl and
Mother in front of the video console.

"This is the room with the ultrasonic motion detectors
Whistler heard," Mother said. "They never turn the lights
off, so we can't tell when whoever works in there leaves."

"But the parking lot empties out completely," Carl offered. "Everyone does leave."

"That's gotta be the computer room I was in," Bishop said. "Run it back. Let's figure out who works next door."

Mother put the tape in reverse. Bishop got up and crossed to the kitchen, passing Liz on the phone.

"No, Mom," she was saying, "tonight's *not* a good night to drop by. Just because. Do I have to spell it out? Alright, I have five guys here all looking at me hungrily." "Four," Whistler called from somewhere in the apartment; the guy heard everything.

"Okay, four," Liz said to her mother. "The fifth guy is blind and he's *listening* to me hungrily."

She rolled her eyes at Bishop, who smiled and walked on toward the kitchen.

"Mom, the point is, I'm entertaining someone," Liz continued, exasperated.

Entering the kitchen, Bishop passed Whistler standing at a counter, expertly dicing vegetables. It was Whistler's turn to make dinner. Bishop heard a sexy woman's voice say, "My voice is my passport. Verify me." Crease was at work erecting a large metal enclosure the size and shape of a telephone booth. The cartons from which he had assembled it—labelled PROTEK: SECURITY FOR A MODERN AGE—were piled in a corner.

"It's called the Mantrap," Crease said. "Imagine there's a hallway past this booth. The only way to get to it is to go through the booth first." He handed Bishop a black plastic ID card and gestured for him to try it out.

Bishop entered the booth. In front of him was an exit door, tightly closed. On the left wall of the booth was a microphone/speaker and a computer terminal displaying the messages:

"1. INSERT IDENTIFICATION CARD

2. READ FOLLOWING MESSAGE"

Bishop inserted the black plastic ID card. The steel entrance door accordioned shut behind him with a loud metallic snap. He was now locked in the box. The terminal display changed to read:

"HI. MY NAME IS [YOUR NAME HERE]. MY VOICE IS MY PASSPORT. VERIFY ME."

"You can't get out," Crease said, "unless your voice-print matches the one encoded on the card."

Bishop nodded and recited aloud: "Hi. My name is Martin Bishop. My voice is my passport. Verify me.'' Nothing happened. ''Great,'' he said. ''Now get me out of here.''

Crease inserted a card into a slot by the sliding door. It opened. Bishop stepped out.

''Can we beat it with tape?'' he said to Crease. ''Faking it on DAT?''

''Even with DAT,'' Crease said, ''I don't know. It's got to be within an almost impossibly narrow range of individual markers—timbre, rhythm, inflection. Faking it'd be real tough.''

''So we'll have to go Plan B—up close and personal,'' Bishop said sourly. ''What'd you find out about the motion detectors?''

''I'm picking one up later today,'' Crease said. ''Makes beating this look easy.''

Liz had been standing in the kitchen doorway, watching quietly. Whistler somehow knew she was there. He probably smelled her shampoo. ''Point me to a high-sided skillet, Liz,'' he said. ''I am making Piccoli's secret primavera sauce.''

''How're you doing that?'' Liz said, leading him to the pans. ''Piccoli never tells his recipes.''

''I figured out the recipe the first time I tasted it,'' Whistler said. ''I have a precocious palate too. It comes with the ears.''

''Bish, I think we found our man,'' Mother called from the living room.

Bishop walked out and looked at Mother's video screen. The time code said 7:22 P.M. Mother pointed to the always-lit computer room and the adjacent room, also still lit.

''Watch the room next to the target,'' Mother said. Suddenly the lights went out in the adjacent room. ''Now watch who comes out,'' he said.

At 7:23 P.M., a young oriental woman dressed in sneakers and a tennis dress and carrying a sports bag exited the building. She got in a white Miata and zoomed out of the parking lot.

''Keep watching,'' Mother said.

At 7:25 P.M., a tall, geeky-looking sandy-haired man in corduroy and Hush Puppies exited. He carried a notebook stuffed with loose papers under his arm. He zipped away in a Mazda sports car.

Mother upped the tape speed. No one else left the building until after 8 P.M.

"So it's one of those two," Bishop said.

"Right," Mother said. He went to warp speed on the tape. An entire day blinked by. "Now here's the next evening." He slowed it. 7:03 P.M., the same adjacent office went dark. 7:06 P.M., the sandy-haired fellow appeared out front, and no one else for a long stretch of time. Mother backed up to the man and froze the tape.

"Good," Bishop said. "We'll use his office to get to the computer room. Can we get plates?"

Mother fast forwarded until the man got to his car, then he zoomed the image closer. The car's back license plate read "IQ 180."

"Cute," Bishop said. "Alright, let's do this guy. Carl, find out what's in the data bases about him, everything—not just present-day stuff. Crease, you play architect. Mother, get out the Batmobile."

Mother got his nickname when he was driving a cab in Washington, D.C., after his prison gig. He was living with two guys he had gone to Harvard with, in a sprawling fifth-floor apartment near Dupont Circle. They were now lawyers with the government and got a kick out of sharing quarters with a convicted felon.

Mother had a habit of bringing home strays—people and animals—from his cab or from the street. He would let the cab dispatcher know, as a precaution, when he was taking a hard-luck passenger home with him. Soon his radio call-number was just "Mother." Everybody at the decrepit cab company garage down in the Southeast section predicted a short life for him.

He would bring home an angry Vietnam vet and feed him for a couple of days. Or a Bangladeshi immigrant who hadn't yet figured out the system. Or a Midwestern runaway or hooker or junkie—anybody whose story, however thin, touched Mother's imagination. He got robbed often but took it philosophically, figuring that only the desperately needy would do that to him.

Mother's personal cross to bear was being the son of a famous father. A celebrated child psychiatrist and writer, his father assumed that given his own insights into child rearing, his son could hardly be anything but squared away.

Mother acted squared away as long as he could—until he couldn't any longer.

Just out of Harvard, he was working as a *Washington Post* cub reporter, trying to live up to his father's standards and in his own mind, failing. A guy representing himself as an underground Timothy Leary drug acolyte lured him, on the promise of a Pulitzer prize story, into breaking into a National Institute of Mental Health lab. They were after proof of U.S. Army LSD experiments on prisoners.

Before he was two steps inside the door, Mother was arrested, and his coconspirator got away. Years later, the unnamed coconspirator admitted he was an FBI stooge out to embarrass *The Washington Post* and the army admitted the LSD experiments.

Eighteen months in federal prison pretty much freed Mother of any pressure to emulate his father. He went in the other direction: drove the cab, befriended lowlifes, did every natural and synthetic drug he could get his hands on, and tried every form of sexual expression available this side of Rangoon.

By the time his father suddenly died six years later, Mother had gone deep within on his quest for understanding and had fried many brain cells on the journey. He took his inheritance, went to New York and established a small magazine of the paranormal and freaky called *Nnexion*. He commissioned and published articles aimed at discovering the hidden connections between people—a force or particle, like the hard-to-detect gravity waves or gravitons, holding humankind together. Mother called that particle the "humitron," and he used up his inheritance trying to prove its existence.

In San Francisco, he was pursuing his researches through drug-free contemplation, meditation and poetry writing—while writing a screenplay on the side—when he met Whistler and eventually Bishop. Of the six animals living on the houseboat when Mother adopted Whistler, only the one-winged seagull didn't take to him at first. He ran at him and pecked his ankles until Whistler quickly learned seagull. Then they worked it out.

Forty

It used to be called the Santa Clara Valley. In those former days, the twenty-mile-long, two-mile-wide alluvial plain curving around the Bay at the bottom of the San Francisco peninsula was known mostly for its rich black soil. Ranchers and farmers coveted this fertile land like none other in California. Mild climate, reasonably plentiful rainfall and, tempered by the heat-compensating influences of the Bay's large body of water, a dearth of crop-killing freezes, it was made for fruits and vegetables.

A new crop grew up in the late 1960s and early 1970s—silicon microchips—and they changed the nature and name of the place. The bucolic valley became Silicon Valley, the London, Paris and Florence of the Electronics Revolution. Scientists, engineers and entrepreneurs poured into these few loamy square miles to sow their technological brilliance and get rich. Manicured industrial parks took over the farmlands and orchards as a couple thousand energetic firms began perfecting the harvesting the miraculous chips. Apartment and condo complexes went up. Big homes rose up in the Coast Hills. Land values rocketed. Population swelled and traffic snarls signaled that the valley was forever changed.

And the moral values changed too. There was so much money to be made so fast that ambition and greed became the ruling ethos. Firms boomed overnight and some went bust just as quickly. Smart men who were unlucky gnashed their teeth as they watched other smart lucky men get unprecedentedly wealthy. Some looked for shortcuts. There were many Cosmos out there, looking to get their hands, by means fair or foul, on the next magic box to come out of the high-tech temples.

Bishop and his men owed their livelihood, at least in part, to the proliferation of one of the foul means—industrial espionage. Ideas were as good as gold—better, because one innovative idea could be spun into a pharaoh's treasure. Somebody had to safeguard the ideas, protect the makers from the marauders. The Sneakers knew their way around Silicon Valley. It was where their business had been born.

Crease trudged into the Santa Clara County building, an L-shaped brick-and-glass structure that had replaced the quaint stone county building when the Silicon Valley's population multiplied tenfold in the 1970s.

Crease had a story ready and some fake ID. He was an OSHA inspector following up on an unsafe-practices allegation at a computer toy company, Playtronics. Employees were complaining of fumes and headaches. He needed the building's original blueprints to determine if the paints-and-solvents areas could be venting into office areas.

Not a terribly original story, he thought. And an iffy ID. He had made it himself. But it had worked before.

When he walked into the County Recorder's Office, however, and caught a glimpse of the woman clerk looking at herself in a hand mirror back at her desk, he instantly changed his tack. The woman was examining her face closely, peering behind her ears, stretching her jaw, turning her head this way and that, looking pleased.

Crease walked up to the counter and rang the bell. As the woman approached the desk, Crease saw a thirty-seven or thirty-eight-year-old with a crisp, fashionable haircut, bright lipstick and a brand new facelift. She smiled.

"Wow! You look great," Crease said. "You been doing something since the last time I was in here, Lynn." He read her nametag. "You been working out?"

Lynn blushed, pleased. "Oh, no," she said. "Just got a haircut."

"Come on," Crease said. "You're into yoga or something. Doin' something right. I never noticed what a doll you are, hiding behind that counter." He flashed a great smile. "They changed the light in here, is that it?"

"No, same lights," Lynn said. She couldn't stop herself from grinning. "Gee, I've forgotten your name."

"Donald," Crease said. The hell with the story, he thought, go right for it. "I'm here for the usual—blueprint file. This time Playtronics, up there on the east slope."

"Sure, Donald," Lynn said. "No problem." She gave him another warm smile and retreated into the stacks.

* * *

Bishop was on the hillside high above Playtronics. He set up a still camera on a tripod, affixed a very long lens with its own support. He positioned himself and drew a bead on the different groups of office workers lunching on the grass.

He waited patiently as the employees leaned and shifted, looking for the right shot. Through the viewfinder he was homing in on their security badges. But he couldn't get a full-on, unmoving view of one. Then he had good luck. A new arrival sat down and laid aside her things. There was a fully exposed security badge on the woman's coat lying on the grass. He clicked away.

The gray Mazda RX-7 with the "IQ-180" license plates left the Playtronics parking lot at dusk. Mother's version of the Batmobile: his belching, polluting VW Rabbit convertible with a fake-wood car phone on the dash, picked up the Mazda at the first intersection and followed it down the street.

The Mazda accelerated to a fast speed. Mother wound the VW out trying to keep up. The guy turned onto a broader boulevard, pulled into the right lane and slowed so suddenly that Mother had to go sailing right by. He was sure the guy had made him. But, in fact, the sandy-haired man was dawdling along in the righthand lane to light his pipe. Then he sped up, passed Mother and the tail was on again.

Mother managed to follow the guy to The Oasis Bar and Grill in Palo Alto. By the time Mother parked down the street and sidled in, Mr. IQ-180 was seated at a table by himself toward the rear of the crowded restaurant.

Mother took a position at the bar and went to work. He ordered a draft, and when the aging surfer-boy bartender with the prematurely sun-wrinkled face and fading blond ponytail put it down in front of him, Mother laid out two twenties on the bar. "This one's my drinking, this one's for you," Mother said to the man, laying a finger on each of the bills.

The barkeep nodded and knocked the bar with his knuckle. "Sit tight," he said, and went off to serve some customers. He came back and leaned on the bar opposite Mother.

"The tall guy sitting at a table by himself back there," Mother said. "He a regular?"

"Yep," the bartender said. Then said no more, just looked at Mother.

Mother put another twenty on the top of the first twenty in the tip pile. It was the right thing to do.

"Three nights a week, at least. And he's always alone," the bartender said. "I assume he's one of you."

Mother looked at him surprised.

"A wire for hire," the bartender said. "An operative."

Mother still played dumb.

"You see the booth behind him? With the five people in it?" the bartender asked.

Mother nodded.

"Well, watch your guy for a minute," the bartender said. "And by the way, also watch the secretary type on the other side of the booth by the salad bar, with the pink hair."

Mother watched Mr. IQ-180, who was sitting with the menu in his hands but wasn't reading it. He was staring straight ahead, plainly listening to what was being said in the booth behind him. The same with the pink-haired lady. She was just loitering near the salad bar, plate in hand but putting nothing on it.

"What's so interesting?" Mother asked. The five figures in the booth were all very serious. A nervous middle-aged accountant type was scribbling figures on his place mat as he talked. A large bald man listened intently. Two junior executives took notes in identical black notebooks. And a young man in his twenties, dressed in blue jeans and a dashiki, absently listened while his eyes wandered to the TV set above the bar.

"From what I hear," the bartender said, "Harry—he's the marketing VP—is telling the president his projections can't be met."

Underneath the bleached ponytail, Mother thought, this barman knows his stuff. "The president's the bald one?" Mother said.

"No, the kid's the president," the bartender said. "Now, I'm pretty sure your guy there, the loner, is an amateur—a wannabe. I've talked to him a bunch of times. Don't know his name. He'll sit up here until a promising table develops, then sit down near it. Another one of these?" he said, picking up Mother's empty.

"No thanks," Mother said. He was barely sipping his beer.

"But the woman at the salad bar is a pro," the barkeep

said. "Harriet Parker, one of the top undercover operatives in the valley."

"Her?" Mother said in disbelief.

"She's got total recall," the surfer-man said. "People hire her just to ride the elevators in competitors' buildings. The CIA uses her from time to time, I'm told."

"Impressive," Mother said. "They ever use you?"

"I don't work for the goverment," the bartender said.

"Why's that?" Mother said.

"It's a long story," he said. "Going way back to the Democratic convention in Chicago in '68. The government made an impression on my head with a riot stick and it changed my outlook." He nodded toward the salad bar. "Check that out."

Mother followed his look. A big Hell's Angels type was stepping between Harriet Parker and the booth.

"That's Curtis," the bartender said. "He's the kid's bodyguard."

Harriet looked at the walking wall, gave up and actually started putting some salad on her plate.

The business meal in the booth was breaking up. Mr. IQ-180 hunched forward and got very busy eating bread sticks and butter.

Harry, the marketing VP, gathered some papers and followed the others out, leaving his scribbled-on place mat.

"The place mat," the bartender said. "Watch what happens."

As if on cue, Mr. IQ-180 turned toward the empty booth, Harriet took a step toward it and Harry, the VP, stopped, realizing what he'd done and hurried back to the table. He snatched up the place mat, folded it neatly, stuck it in his breast pocket and walked out.

"It's not over yet," the bartender said.

A busboy cleared the table, carefully removed the tablecloth and folded it. He looked around, walked over to the booth where Harriet was now sitting and dropped the tablecloth surreptitiously on the banquette. Harriet slipped him a twenty.

"She'll try to read it off the cloth," Mother said. "My God, it's a jungle in here."

"The stakes are high, man," the bartender said. "So what's your interest?"

"Agh, forget about me," Mother said, laying another

twenty down on top of the first two. "Tell me more about our guy."

Forty-one

Liz knocked impatiently at her own bathroom door. "One minute," Bishop called from inside.

"I hate to intrude on your 'guy things,' " Liz said, "but are you men really going to the bathroom together?"

"Almost done," Mother called. "Be right out."

Inside, under a red light, Bishop and Mother watched an image appear on a sheet of photographic paper in a tray of chemical developer. One of Mother's surveillance photos: Mr. IQ-180 getting into his car. Bishop quickly dunked others and Mother pulled out finished ones as they developed, and hung them along the shower curtain rod to dry. Pictures of the subject driving in traffic, parking at an apartment complex, walking up to his ground-floor apartment, opening his door, entering.

Liz paced outside. "Should I go to my neighbor's?" She said petulantly. "I have to go."

"Lord, no," Bishop called. "Another few seconds."

He pulled out the last two prints. The first was the geeky guy coming out of his apartment in his baggy pj's to pick up the morning paper. "This guy lives alone," Bishop said, noting the pj's

"Right," Mother said. "No pets. No alarm system. And regular hours. Mr. Clockwork. Leaves for work at eight-thirty. Quits work at night at seven-thirty." He shook off the last print. "And this is what gets him into the parking lot," he said, showing a shot of a parking sticker on the front side of the car's rearview mirror.

"Good work, Mother," Bishop said. "We'll make one of those for the van."

Mother leaned against the sink, forgetting about Liz. "Three nights a week this guy eats at The Oasis Bar and Grill," he said. "Industry hangout—techies, businessmen, secretaries, hustlers. He eats alone, never talks to anybody, but always sits near whoever's talking shop. Eavesdropping, looking for that edge. Bartender says the guy's obsessed about making his killing, pissed off that he's not already rich. Says guys like him are a dime a dozen out there.''

Liz banged again on the door, one hard whack. "That's it, I'm going," she said, irate.

"Hey, no," Bishop said, as he and Mother came breezing out of the bathroom, carrying still-wet prints of blowups of the Playtronics' security badges. He gave Liz a smile. She gave him a punch.

Oh-oh, thought Bishop. Privacy threshold busted. Serious stroking and adjustments were required.

Liz slammed the bathroom door shut. They could hear an exclamation of disgust from her as she waded through the mess in there.

Bishop and Mother continued toward the living room, past walls tacked up with Crease's blueprints of Playtronics building plans, marked in yellow highlighter to indicate the location of the sensors. On the third-floor blueprint, one corridor was conspicuously marked in red.

"According to our friendly bartender," Mother went on, "Mr. IQ-180's father got off to a big start in the early Silicon Valley gold rush. He lived high, built a big house up in the Coast Hills, vacations in Cabo, five cars.''

"This guy wants to live up to Daddy?" Bishop said.

"Worse than that," Mother said. "The old man went down in flames. The son's desperate to prove he's smarter and better. He's scared shitless he's gonna end up just like him.''

"What happened to the father?" Bishop said.

"First the wife left him, went back to Boston," Mother said. "She didn't take to the life—seven-day work weeks, boozing, girlfriends—take your pick. The old boy continues living like a winner—Porsche, fancy clothes. The salary doesn't cover it; he drinks more, debts pile up. So he gets together with a couple MBAs, creates his own company to market one of the early voice-recognition chips that he steals from the company he's working for. They set up a dummy company overseas. They raise some money, spend too much of it, raise some more, spend it, et cetera. The whole thing blows up. Now he's in jail on tax fraud, industrial theft, SEC violations.''

"Not a pretty picture," Bishop said. "That's some baggage for our boy to carry around.''

"He's not a happy camper," Mother said. "He's ready to kill for the big fortuna. I got some more stuff in the car," he said, heading for the door.

"Check this out," Carl called to Bishop. Laboring at his computer, Carl had managed to hack his way into California State Department of Motor Vehicles computer files.

Bishop leaned over to see the entry on Carl's CRT. "What'd you get?" he said.

"His name is Werner Brandes," Carl said, reading from the DMV file: "Single, six-feet-one, one hundred seventy-four pounds, must wear glasses to drive, no outstanding tickets or warrants. And . . ." He picked up some sheets of scratch paper. "According to his TRW credit file, police file, and trade association file, he has a $750 limit on his Visa card. No other cards. No delinquencies or other bad marks in his TRW credit sheet—no bad debts, no bounced checks. No mortgage. Has rented in the same place for the last eight years, owns his car outright. Very clean dude."

"Going the opposite route from his father," Bishop said. "*Anything* interesting?"

"No police record, no firearms registered in his name," Carl said. "Member, International Microchip Designer Association, and chairman of their social committee."

"Great," Bishop said. "The world's most boring human."

"I accessed his bank account at Highland National," Carl said.

"Great. That's not easy," Bishop said.

"Actually, it was," Carl said. "I got a teller to tell me his PIN number because I had his mother's maiden name and stuff from the other files. He's got a savings account with about $7,000, few hundred in his checking, no record of a brokerage account. Figured out his annual salary from his pay deposits—$38,000 a year."

"That's pretty low," Bishop said. "He's got a nice top-floor office in the restricted area at Playtronics. He must be doing important work for Cosmo, but doing it cheap. Why?"

"Well, he's worked at six different companies in the valley in the last eight years," Carl said, checking his notes. "Always left on okay terms, never got fired. And judging by the salary, most of his moves were lateral."

"Looking for the fast track," Bishop said. He shook his head. "An unhappy man. Cosmo picked him up at a discount."

"Here's a wrinkle," Carl said. "He once took ballet lessons and he cheats at golf."

"How'd you find that out?" Bishop said. "Not that it helps us."

"Pretext call," Carl said, "to his college faculty dorm advisor. I said I was going a bio piece for the Microchip Designers Bulletin. The guy remembered Werner: A brilliant student in physics. Never dated. Always seemed a little pissed off that the world hadn't recognized his brilliance. Never in any trouble. He also said he thought the guy's father was once a biggie in the valley but lost his shirt."

"Ambitious, hardworking engineer, looking for the brass ring," Bishop said. "There oughta be some chink there. Maybe golf is the way in."

"He gave up golf a couple years ago," Carl said. "Greens' fees got too expensive. He gets his exercise from a stationary bike. Rents six videos every weekend."

"Worse and worse," Bishop groaned. "How the hell we gonna get close enough to record him?"

Liz, glowering, came in from the bathroom, just as the front door opened and Mother clambered in dragging two full garbage bags, one of them leaking a brown liquid.

"Oh, Mother," Liz said, going for a towel.

"Sorry, Liz," Mother said. "This is from the guy's house."

"And thank you for bringing it into mine," Liz moaned, throwing down the towel. She glared at Bishop, stalked into the bedroom and swung the door shut.

Bishop raised a cautionary hand and went over to the bedroom door. He knocked quietly and went in, closing the door behind him.

Liz, gazing out the window toward Golden Gate Park didn't turn.

"We'll be out of here as soon as we can," Bishop said. "We'll leave now, just say it. You've been great."

"No," Liz said flatly. "It's not that."

"We're playing too much of Mother's heavy metal and not enough Jimi Hendrix," Bishop said.

"Bishop!" Liz said, riled. "You're not taking me seriously."

Bishop looked at her, confused. He had no idea what *was* bothering her.

"You're not taking me seriously," she repeated. "I'm a cum laude graduate of a top-rated university. I was a National Merit Scholar. I have a mathematics Ph.D. and an MBA, and six years experience in international banking and monetary strategy! I worked for the World Bank in India where I redesigned the banking policy of a whole state. I've been around the block a few times!"

Bishop looked at her blankly.

"Is it because I'm now doing something I love better—teaching music to gifted children—that you treat me like a schoolgirl, like I don't know the difference between megabyte and a dog bite?" she said.

"Oh," Bishop said, taken aback.

"Oh!" Liz said.

"I'm sorry, I had no idea," Bishop said. "I just assumed . . . I was just trying to . . . my intention's always been to . . ."

"Well, cut it out!" Liz said

"Sure," Bishop said, looking stunned.

She put her chin in the air and swept by him, banging open the bedroom door and joining the other Sneakers outside. Bishop followed her out, unsure of what had just happened.

The three years Bishop had had with Liz were the nearest to normality he'd experienced. They had crossed paths at an ineffably romantic spot: the supermarket vegetable section, where Bishop had been at a loss to distinguish watercress from several other leafy greens. He turned to her for help. He was a pushover for her cool certainty—about vegetables and about him. It was all they could do to finish that first salad together before finding themselves whisked together in a fine emulsion.

As a child of privilege and a daughter of an International Harvester executive posted abroad, Liz had spent her formative teenage years in Paris. She took piano lessons from Nadia Boulanger and gave her first piano recital at the hallowed Salle Pleyel. Defying her aspiring parents, she then eschewed the concert piano and dug her fingers into the far more gritty pursuit of applied mathematics.

When she met Bishop, she had just come home from a

tour in India and Thailand for the World Bank and was in
the throes of a career change. She was tired of ocean hop-
ping and wanted a home. She was tired of numbers crunch-
ing and wanted to regain the harmonies of music. She was
at that age. She'd never put it that way herself, but she was
getting ready to nest.

It was what ultimately blew her and Bishop out of the
water. He wanted to desperately. But he couldn't.

Mother had the trash spread out on the dining room table.
He and Crease were picking at it distastefully. Liz marched
right over and dug in, getting her hands dirty, helping sort
through it. She found something.

"Phone bill," she announced. "Let's see: phone bill, no
long distance."

"Club Med brochure," Bishop noted. "Ticket stub to a
Barry Manilow concert. Here we go!" He read from a let-
ter, " 'Dear Compudater: Welcome to the world of automated compatibility.' He's a computer dater!"

"I love it," Crease said. "Let's get him a date."

"Damn straight," Mother said. *"Cherchez la femme."*

"Or let *la femme cherchez* Werner," Crease said.
"What's the name of the girl we used for the cereal company sneak last year?"

"Sandi Krieger?" Bishop said. "Forget it, she married a
cop. How about Barbara? She's cute."

"Forget her," Mother said. "She regards this work as
juvenile. That's why she divorced me." He returned the
Sneakers' jaundiced looks with defiance. "What about
Flo?" he said.

"Yeah, *she*'s buff," Carl said.

"Fellas, fellas, look at this guy's trash," Liz said. "He's
not looking for buff." Liz held up a box of Lean Cuisine
with the empty food tray carefully rinsed out and returned
to the box and closed up neatly. She presented as evidence
an empty toothpaste tube perfectly rolled up with every last
smidgen squeezed out.

"It's the nicest trash I've ever seen," Mother said.

"The man who rolled this tube of Crest," Liz said, "is
looking for someone meticulous, refined . . . anal."

Bishop and the rest of the Sneakers just stared at her. And
smiled. Liz blinked.

"What?" she said.

Forty-two

"I can't do this!" Liz said, standing before her closet. "It's pretending to be someone else. I'd be too embarrassed. It's not me."

All five Sneakers were in her bedroom—wardrobe consultants for her first solo sneak job.

"Which 'me' are you talking about?" Bishop said. "The international finance expert who's been around the block a few times, or the Ph.D. mathematician who—?"

Liz looked at him balefully. He shut up.

"Just be yourself, that'll be perfect," Carl said enthusiastically.

"Here, bold colors," Crease said, pulling out a yellow-and-red sundress.

"That's for the beach," Liz said, taking it and putting it back.

"This is it," Mother said. He had a short black sheath in his hand, a very low-cut number. "A little cleavage."

"Mother, what are you thinking?!" Liz said. "Never mind. I genuinely don't want to know what's going on in your mind."

"This might be trickier than you think," Mother said. "You gotta keep him interested."

"Hey, cool it, you guys," Bishop said, taking the dress from Mother, putting it back. "Slacks and a sweater."

Well, that may be going too far the other way, Liz's look said.

Whistler had his hands on the knobs of the second drawer of Liz's bureau. "Lace lingerie and nylon stockings are essential. May I?" he said.

"Whistler!" Liz said, outraged, "How'd you know that's my underwear drawer?!"

Whistler slid open the drawer, dipped his hand in the right corner and pulled out a patchouli sachet. "Could smell this from across the room," he said.

"Amazing," Liz said matter-of-factly. "Put it back. And

this guy isn't going to be seeing any lacy underwear, I can promise you.''

"Just a peek?" Carl said.

"Carl!" everybody said at once. Carl looked sheepish.

"Here, this will be perfect," Whistler said, picking out one of Liz's perfumes by smell. "And every time he gets bored, cross your legs. The 'shssssss' sound of stockings rubbing against each other"—he shook his head—"sets a man free."

"That's it!" Liz said. "Get out of here, all of you. If I don't know how to dress for a date by now, we're in big trouble."

Forty-three

In a horseshoe-shaped Naugahyde booth, at a table decorated with a red-netted candle-in-a-cup, way in the back of the Steak 'N' Stein Restaurant, Werner Brandes waited nervously. He wore his favorite hound's-tooth, check jacket over a new burgundy turtleneck. He was facing the back wall of the restaurant, busily peeling the red plastic netting from the candle. Periodically he jiggled his side pocket to make sure his keys were there and patted his breast pocket for his wallet. He poured some salt in the ashtray, then wiped it out with a napkin.

"Werner?" came a feminine voice, finally.

He looked up to see Liz smiling weakly.

"Hi. I'm . . . Doris," she said.

Werner half stood and shook her hand. He almost made eye contact. "Hi," he said. "Ready for the salad bar?" He furtively checked her out as she slid in the booth: nice, tidy pulled-back hair, clean face—very little makeup; simple, elegant dark suit and blouse with choker collar, tiny earrings, small clutch handbag with a built-in executive organizer. He noticed that and he *liked* it. Couldn't take his eyes off the combo handbag-organizer.

"You go ahead," Liz said. "I'm . . . trying to quit."

"All right, I'll be right back," Werner said. He took his plate and left. Liz adjusted the right sleeve of her jacket, making sure the small microphone up there was concealed. She looked around, opened her purse/organizer to the middle page, which read: Hi. My name is Werner Brandes. My voice is my passport. Verify me.

She crossed out the word "Hi" and closed the organizer just as Werner returned, his plate overflowing with garbanzo beans and green onions.

Liz smiled and moved over to sit next to him. She put her hand on his shoulder, the mike just inches from his mouth. He barely concealed his alarm. He blushed and dug into his food.

"So . . . You have such an interesting name," Liz said. "How exactly do you pronounce it?"

"Mmmnnner Mmmmmdess," he said with his mouth full.

Liz looked at the back of his head as he dove for more salad. It was going to be a long evening. She started to unbutton the high-necked collar of her blouse, but thought better of it. As soon as the waiter came within forty feet she got his attention and ordered drinks. She settled back.

Forty-four

A green light blinked insidiously on a small laminated box in Liz's apartment. Bishop and Crease stood behind the box and nodded to Mother across the room. Mother dropped a large feather, and an alarm wailed.

"It can sense a fly passing gas at fifty yards," Crease said. "It's infrared/ultrasonic. Best combination motion and heat sensor on the market." He reset it. He breathed on it. The alarm wailed. "It responds to thermal differentials too," he explained.

"Does this have a happy ending?" Bishop said, looking discouraged.

"Watch," Mother said. He held a Ping-Pong ball above the sensor and dropped it. Nothing happened. Mother beamed.

"Perfect," Bishop said. "I'll just climb inside a Ping-Pong ball and you guys can roll me into that room."

"Hold on," Crease said, "Okay: size is one way to defeat the sensor. but so is speed." He wrapped a swatch of rubbery material around his arm.

Crease moved his arm *very* slowly in front of the sensor. Nothing happened.

"If we wrap you in this stuff," Mother said, "—think of it as a stealth suit—and bring the temperature in the computer room up to 98.6, I figure you've got a top speed of about two inches a second."

Bishop looked at Mother as though he was out of his mind. "You're the one who knows tai chi," he said. "You're trained for this." He smiled. "Thank God."

"Forget it!" Mother said.

"Come on, it'll be fun for you," Bishop said.

"You want me to dress up in a rubber suit," he said, "smuggle me past guards with loaded shotguns, and put me into a room where if I move any faster than one inch a second, I'm live bait for the Mafia? You call that fun?"

"You're so negative," Bishop said.

"I can't do it," Mother said.

"Why not?" Bishop said.

"If anything happens to me, who'll take care of Whistler?" he blurted.

There was an embarrassed silence. Whistler stopped what he was doing and tilted his head. Mother looked plaintively at Bishop. Bishop smiled wanly.

"Hey, Mother?" Whistler said.

"Yeah?" Mother said.

"If anything happens to Bishop, who'll take care of you?"

The Sneakers all hooted and chortled. It took Mother a few seconds to find it funny, but he did.

"On second thought, this is my gig," Bishop said. "Mother's too big a target."

Mother gratefully handed him a familiar-looking answering machine. "This is the same model answering machine Janek used for the shell of the box," he said. "I thought you'd like to practice with it. Get used to the weight of it."

Crease smiled. "Some guys get all the fun stuff," he said, heading for the door.

Mother followed him out. Bishop looked at the answering machine as if it were a dead otter. He put it under his arm and started trying to cross the room at two inches a second.

He moved like an arthritic praying mantis. The alarm
wailed.

Forty-five

Liz sat alone in the Naugahyde booth. The table was
swept clean except for her and Werner's drinks and the
plastic-wrapped candle. The restaurant was empty, chairs
were upturned on nearby tables and a busboy was emptying
the salad bar. Liz looked frazzled, but her jaw was still set
as firm as the Dutch boy's with his finger in the dike.

She opened her purse/organizer and checked the all-
important phrase: Hi. My name is Werner Brandes. My
voice is my passport. Verify me. All the words had been
crossed out except one: Passport. Liz quickly shut the book
and snapped it as Werner, checking to see his fly was
zipped, came into view. He sat down across from her.

"Now, what about travel?" Liz said, summoning up
perky interest from somewhere. "Where do you like to go?
Europe? Mexico?"

"I don't know. I've never been out of the country," Werner said. He looked around at the waiter and bartender eyeing them tiredly. "I think they want us to leave." He slid
out of the booth and stood awkwardly, waiting.

Liz reached out, grabbed his sleeve and pulled him down
next to her. "I know real men like you don't let themselves
get pushed around by waiters and busboys," she said, smiling at him playfully. "You know, I really love the sound of
your voice," she said, tilting her head and eyeing him.

"Really," he said. "I always thought it was nasal and
pinched."

"No, it's lovely," Liz said. "And there's this one word . . .
I'd . . . I've always loved this word. Oh, you wouldn't.
Never mind. You'd think it was silly."

"No, what?" Werner said.

"I'd really like to hear you say 'passport,' " Liz said.

He looked at her strangely. "You're ribbing me," he
said. "I don't have too big a sense of humor, maybe you

noticed. I got ribbed enough as a kid to last me a lifetime. Let's leave now.'' He started to get up again.

"Werner! Dear Werner," she said, pulling him back down, sliding close. "I'm *not* ribbing you. It's just, when two people really hit it off—as we have—and one of them asks the other to do a little favor for no reason, don't you think the other person should just *do* the first person that silly little favor?" She looked deeply into his eyes.

"You want me to do something?" Werner said.

"I really want to see your passport," Liz replied.

Werner shrugged. "You want to see my . . . ?"

Liz nodded.

Werner shrugged again. "I don't have one. Why do you want to see my passport?"

Liz beamed and kissed him on the cheek. He was thrilled.

"Passport, passport, passport!" Werner said, thrilled.

"Please," Liz exclaimed, closing her eyes in relief. "Not too much on the first date." She pushed him ahead of her out of the booth and started toward the door.

Werner followed, entranced. He didn't have a clue where Liz was coming from, but he was delighted with his apparent prowess. He caught up with her. "Would you like to have breakfast with me sometime," he said.

"Sure. Fine," Liz said.

"Shall I phone you . . . or nudge you?" Werner said.

Liz barreled through the door, eyes straight ahead.

Werner hurried out the door after her, patting his jacket's pockets to make sure he had his keys and his wallet.

Forty-six

It was dead quiet in Liz's condo. Low light filtered out from the bathroom into the living room, revealing Sneakers asleep on couches and the floor. One Sneaker was awake, however, and a green eye was watching him. Bishop, poised with one leg up, both arms outstretched, was practicing his two-inch-per-second walk towards the infrared sensor.

The front door opened and Liz swept in, holding up her

microtape. Seeing Bishop up and awake, she announced triumphantly, "I got it."

Bishop jumped. The alarm wailed. Sleeping Sneakers lurched to their feet in terror. Crease, fumbling for his gun, shouted, "Freeze!"

Liz screamed. Mother roared. Bishop leapt for the sensor and switched it off. "Okay okay okay," he said loudly, holding out his hands pacifyingly. All parties took a moment to calm down—the anxiety quotient was pretty high in this crowd.

"I got it," Liz repeated weakly, holding up the microtape.

Assorted halfhearted cheers rose from the members, as much as they could muster in their frayed states. They flopped down in their sleeping niches and tried to zone out.

Liz gave Bishop the microtape. He took it and walked her toward the bedroom door, stepping over bodies. "Good work," he said. "Thanks."

"I'll say," Liz said. "He asked me out for tomorrow night." As Bishop chuckled, Liz added, "I told him I'd see him."

"Really?" Bishop said, trying not to show his surprise—or was it a tinge of jealousy?

"Uh huh," Liz said, enjoying this. "Well, he's cute. And really smart. And, you know, he seemed to sort of . . . like me . . . a lot." She said that with a faraway gaze. Bishop looked genuinely alarmed.

Liz came back down to earth. "It *is* tomorrow night, isn't it?" she said with a faint smile.

Bishop visibly loosened up. He looked at her impressed.

"I figured you wouldn't want him showing up at the office at a bad time, so . . ." she said.

"Well, since you're so popular," Bishop said, "maybe I better put in a bid for the night after."

"The night after?" Liz repeated quizzically, as if she had been unconsciously regarding tomorrow night as the end, one way or another. Now the conscious thought occurred to her there actually might not be a night after for Bishop. They were at her bedroom door. "I'd like that," she said in answer to his question.

"Yeah," Bishop said, trying for a smile.

"You okay?" Liz said. "You seem pretty tense."

"Yeah, you know," Bishop said.

"Bishop, what makes you think you can pull this off?" Liz said, touching his arm.

"What choice do I have?" he said.

"And afterwards," she said. "What are you going to do then?"

"I'd really like . . . to have a life," he said. "I've seen the pictures. It looks like fun." He smiled. "I'd like to get my name back. And I'd like to maybe do some of the things I didn't let myself do right the first time."

There was a long pause during which each wondered if one or two people would go through the door. Two voices argued within Liz, and finally one of them convinced her she had courted enough heartache with this man for a lifetime. "Well, good night," she said.

"Good night," Bishop said.

Liz kissed him on the cheek, innocently. He stopped her and kissed her on the lips. They held a look. Then they pulled apart. Liz turned slowly, went inside and closed the door behind her. Better safe than sunk, the voice said. But the other voice nagged at her too: no risk, no rapture.

Bishop made his way toward an open spot of carpet in the hall. He took a throw pillow and lay down, using his baseball jacket as a blanket.

Liz took off her suit and silk shirt and threw it all in the corner of the closet for the cleaners. She went into the bathroom in bra and panties and looked in the mirror. She turned around and walked back to the door to the living room.

Bishop got up and walked in his bare feet back down the hallway to Liz's bedroom door. He stood there. He leaned his forehead against the door.

On the other side of the door, Liz put her hand on the doorknob. The voices spoke again. She pulled her hand away and turned back toward the bed.

Bishop turned, padded back down the hallway to his bed on the floor.

Forty-seven

The bulky, stooped Mexican gardener, moved by the conviction that the border of pink azaleas around the entrance needed enlivening, had brought a wheelbarrow full of red flowers to plant at the corners and the ends of rows.

Garbed in khaki coveralls and protected from the hot sun by an ancient canvas hat, he knelt in the dirt and worked hard, troweling, planting, clipping and trimming. Soon sweat was dripping from his handsome Zapata mustache. Then he heard nature's call. He pocketed his clippers, laid his trowel carefully in the wheelbarrow and timidly went up the front steps of Playtronics.

He passed through the colorful lobby with its large graphics of toys in cheery primary colors. He diffidently approached the entrance guard, who looked up from his copy of *The Star.*

"*Muy caliente,*" the gardener said in his Mexican accent. "*Hay bano en este piso? Es urgente.*"

The jowly thick-necked guard looked at him narrowly.

"Bathroom?" the gardener tried in English.

The guard pointed to a nearby bathroom. The gardener hurried toward it, smiling gratefully.

In the bathroom, the gardener took off the annoying hat and mustaches and pocketed them. It was Mother. He went straight into the last stall, stood on the john and removed the corner ceiling tiles.

He hoisted himself into the opening, no small job given his girth. The push-ups paid off. After much grunting, he disappeared from view.

The guard at the security desk out front looked up from his *Star.* He looked over at the bathroom and checked his watch. It had been awhile and that gardener still hadn't come out. He got up and sauntered over to the bathroom, checking to make sure he had his firearm. He stuck his head inside and saw no one. He bent down and looked under the three stalls. Nothing. He started back to his desk, puzzled.

Should he worry about it? Should he call the guard commander?

Then he noticed the gardener, back outside, trimming azaleas. The guard stared at him in wonder, thinking deep. He shrugged, shook his head and got back up on his guard chair. He picked up the *Star* and read on.

Outside, Carl, dressed exactly as Mother had been, wearing the same bushy mustache, worked away in the garden.

Mother crouched in the elevator chase, the vertical cut that ran up and down the back of the noisy elevator shaft in which a car was descending. The car passed him and stopped at the ground floor. Mother knew he had to jump, and he was scared to death, almost ready to cry. He was not built right for this sport. He crossed himself. And leaped.

He grabbed at the main cables which supported the elevator. One hand slipped off one cable, but he managed to hang on with the other one. He hugged his fat body to the cables and rode down with the car into the basement.

Whistler, in the Sneakers' van, was putting the final touches on the doctored microtape. He stopped it in his editing machine and made a diagonal cut across the tape. He spliced in another piece. Listening intently, he ran the tape over a sound reader. "Hi. . . . My name . . . is . . . Werner Brandes. . . . My . . . voice . . . is my . . . passport. . . . Verify . . . me," it said. Whistler nodded, satisfied.

Mother shinnied down the side of the elevator car, tiptoed across some steel support beams and flattened himself in the vertical chase as much as a round, fat person could. The elevator lurched upward. Once it was clear, he lowered himself gingerly to the ground and made his way out of the elevator shaft. He quickly crossed the basement and pulled open the door to the dimly lit boiler room.

He went straight to an unmarked metal cabinet on the wall opposite the door. He opened it and played his mini-flashlight along rows of electromechanical thermostats. The second row down he came to one marked 315–COMPUTERS. Into this he patched a digital temperature-control box, custom-designed to override Playtronics' automated thermostat. On this piggyback override were two digital readouts. The top one was labeled "TARGET TEMPERATURE: 98.6," the bottom one read "CURRENT TEMPERATURE: 68.0."

Mother activated the override box. Nearby the furnace fired up with a roar. The "CURRENT TEMPERATURE" reading began to blink: 68.1 . . . 68.2 . . . 68.3.

Heavy footsteps on the stairs were coming down fast. Mother swung the cabinet door shut and crawled behind the furnace. A security guard came lunging into the room, swearing.

"You'd think I was a goddamn janitor," the guard groused. He searched around in a utility alcove, ranting. "I am a highly trained paramilitary! I am not a towel boy! I am trained in automatic weapons fire, in high explosives and in state-of-the-art terrorist inter*diction*!" He stomped out of the utility alcove with an armload of toilet paper. He banged open the door to the boiler room, crossed the basement and went up the stairs.

Mother came out from behind the furnace, dripping with sweat.

Forty-eight

"It's getting hot in here," Liz said to her date, the swashbuckling Werner. Tonight Werner was wearing his at-home outfit: a too-large T-shirt with USER FRIENDLY on the front and RAM (RANDOM ACCESS MALE) on the back. The T-shirt was tucked into loose-fitting lederhosen with suspenders, an outfit Liz kept looking away from, then looking back at in awe. Werner was cooking "Doris" his special "microbiotic" dinner in his apartment near the Stanford campus.

"You don't mind, do you?" Liz said, crossing and opening the kitchen window, and leaning against it attractively. Tonight Liz was in sleek black slacks and heels, and casual cashmere sweater with long sleeves and high roll-neck that climbed almost to her chin.

"No, not at all," Werner said as he chopped his carrots, jicama, fennel, turnip and raw catfish into tiny, perfectly cubical chunks. "Treat it as your own house." He proudly glanced over, admiring his date, not believing his good luck. Liz *was* ravishing, in a silky buttoned-up way.

"Do you cook a lot?" Liz said interestedly.

"From time to time," Werner said. "I enjoy handling raw food. It's kind of, you know, sensual." He was wearing big yellow rubber gloves.

As Werner ducked his head into a low cabinet looking for a pan cover, Liz quickly dipped into the pocket of his jacket draped over the chair near her.

"I know that's a funny thing to say," he said, "but I think food is a pretty gut-level experience. Ha ha, sorry for the pun."

"Ha ha. A pretty good one," Liz said with a congenial smile.

Werner turned his back to steam his vegetables. Liz kept talking and backhanded his wallet out the window. "Why do you call it microbiotic food?" she said, wiggling the wallet frantically behind her.

A hand reached up from the shrubbery and took the wallet. It was Carl. He hunkered in the dirt and rifled the billfold.

"You'll see," Werner said. "It has just micro-calorie content, and zero animal fat, zero cholesterol, and primo fiber. And it's like poached in champale. And I make it without the secret killer."

"What's that?" Liz said.

"Salt," Werner said. "You're going to flip, I can tell you now. This is one of the three things I make really well. In this one, it's the presentation. Kinda my signature thing. You'll see. Want another drink while I pound these breasts?"

"I'm fine," Liz said, watching as Werner laid out chicken breasts and proceeded to hammer them with a toothed mallet.

"Pounding sort of predigests the meat," Werner said. "It really does more than tenderize it. I start with free-range chicken, too. Though there actually aren't any government standards on what free-range means. I mean, how big is the range? What grows there? So you never really know."

"You pay a lot of attention to what you eat, huh?" Liz said.

Outside, Carl searched through Werner's wallet.

"Funny you should say that," Werner said. "I've been researching the ideal diet. You know what it is? Don't laugh."

"What?" Liz said, full of bright-eyed curiosity.

"The bottom of a monkey cage. There, I knew you'd laugh," he said, as Liz tried not to look sick.

"What are you talking about?" she said.

"It's true," he said. "You've got your grains, your fruit, seeds. It's low in calories, it's high fiber. We could learn from monkeys."

"Fascinating," Liz said, trying to look thoughtful.

In the bushes, Carl found what he was looking for—the Playtronics' electronic key card. He stood and made a lame-sounding bird call that anybody listening would have taken for a secret signal.

"You wouldn't know it," Werner said, "but on a no-fat monkey diet I've lost thirty pounds. These things used to fit me." He pulled out the slack waist of his lederhosen.

"No. Thirty pounds?" Liz said, backing up to the window again.

"Really," Werner said. "You know how big a ten-pound bag of sugar is? Well, picture—"

"Oh my God, is that a cockroach?" Liz said pointing.

Startled and concerned, Werner searched intently around the bottom cupboards where Liz had pointed.

Liz was starting to reach her hand out the window behind her when Werner popped back up and shrugged.

"Nada," he said.

"I guess you scared it away," she said. "Thanks for caring. I like a clean man."

Werner smiled happily and went back to his pounding. "Anyway," he said, "I've figured out that chicken is the key to the world's cuisine. It's pretty much the universal food." He flipped the breasts and pounded some more. "This is French, this recipe. I call it *'Poulet au Bleu'* because I poach it rare in the champale. The only drawback, and this happens every time—"

"I think someone's at the door," Liz said, looking toward the vestibule.

Werner stripped off his rubber gloves and walked to the front door. Liz quickly reached behind her, and Carl slapped the wallet into her hand. She pulled it back inside and slipped it into the pocket of Werner's jacket just as he turned around.

"Nope," he said, walking back, putting on his gloves. "Nobody here but us mice."

Carl sprinted across the condo lawn, jumped a low hedge and ran to his car.

"Getting hungry?" Werner said pleasantly.

"Am I," Liz said, letting out a sigh of relief.

Forty-nine

Werner's electronic key card passed under the laser sensor.

In the Playtronics' security headquarters behind the elevators on the first floor, two guards turned at the sound of the jingling alert bell. They scanned a bank of closed-circuit TV screens. A computer automatically typed out onto silver paper: "06/23/92—7:28 P.M.—Werner Brandes—Front Entrance."

At the front desk, Bishop, carrying a briefcase and wearing eyeglasses and a Playtronics ID badge bearing his own likeness, was automatically admitted into the facility past the guard. The guard, immersed in *Soldier of Fortune* magazine, barely glanced up.

Bishop walked past the elevators trying not to betray his nervousness, and continued down the corridor to the stairwell. He turned into the stairwell and climbed briskly to the first-floor landing where two closed-circuit TV cameras were mounted side by side on the wall, one looking up, one looking down.

Moving beneath them, out of their range, Bishop plucked a small transmitter from his briefcase and, almost in one motion, clamped its two leads to a cable and pushed the tiny transmitter up behind one of the cameras. He resumed his climb up the stairs.

Parked a block and a half away down the tree-lined street, with clear sight lines to Playtronics, was the Sneakers' van.

Inside the van, Crease and Whistler sat waiting at the video console, both wearing headsets. Abruptly, the console's eight video monitors blinked on, giving Crease a "guard's-eye view" from within Playtronics.

The first three monitors showed the front entrance, the Mantrap on the third floor and a service area at the rear of the building. The other five showed a rotating series of corridors, stairwells and doorways throughout the building, the view changing every twenty seconds.

"You're clear right up to the Mantrap," Crease said into his headset. On one of the monitors he was watching Bishop climb the stairs to the third floor. When Bishop turned the corner, he went off that monitor and appeared on another one covering the third-floor hallway.

Bishop, listening to the Sneaker van through a tiny clear plastic tube that curled from his glasses into his ear, paused in front of the Mantrap. SECURE AREA: AUTHORIZED ACCESS ONLY a sign read. Bishop fought the nervous urge to glance back down the corridor, and stepped confidently into the metal booth. He pulled out Werner's access card for the second time. He inserted it into the waiting slot. The doors slid shut behind him.

Bishop pulled a mini-tape recorder from his sports jacket pocket, held it a foot from the Mantrap's microphone and turned it on: "Hi—my name—is—Werner Brandes—my—voice—is my—passport—verify—me."

Bishop waited anxiously while the voice was analyzed. Silence.

In the van, Crease and Whistler sweated.

Someone came out of an office down the hall and walked up to the Mantrap. Bishop didn't dare turn to look. At that moment the screen in the Mantrap lit up. It read: "THANK YOU, WERNER." The door leading into the high-security area slid noiselessly open. Bishop mouthed, "Thank *you*."

In the van, Crease saw Bishop exit the Mantrap. "Yes!" he breathed.

Bishop took long strides to ensure he had turned the corner by the time the following employee cleared the Mantrap. He noticed the cheery Playtronics colors were gone, replaced by flat gray on the walls, industrial carpeting on the floors. Every door was metal and shut tight, with a keycard access slot next to it. The hall windows had heavy security screens. No art on the walls. Wiring leading from the ceiling to every doorframe.

Bishop turned down another corridor and passed the

Computer Room where he had been held and ranted at
by Cosmo on both the evils and the opportunities of the
Post-Communist world. As he passed close by the door,
with its big sign, RESTRICTED ENTRY, an incredibly sensitive
motion sensor triggered an automated voice that said,
"PLEASE STEP BACK. YOU HAVE ACTIVATED MY
PROXIMITY CONTROL WARNING. INSERT YOUR
ACCESS CARD AND STEP BACK UNTIL CLEARED."
Bishop's heart almost stopped when the voice began.

As did the hearts in the Sneakers' van. "Sorry," Crease
said into the headset. "That's a new bit of security not on
the plans I have here. Hope there aren't any more new
ones."

Bishop tried to calm his beating heart as he moved along
to Werner's office next door and inserted his key card. The
door clicked open.

At the guard station on the first floor, the computer printer
spat out another entry on silver paper: "06/23/92—7:35
P.M.—Werner Brandes—Entry—Rm 317."

Bishop walked in, closed the door behind him, made sure
it was locked and let out a whoosh of semirelief. "So far
so good," he whispered into the mike up his sleeve. "Now
for the hard part."

Fifty

Momentarily secure behind the locked door of Werner's office, Bishop moved over to the desk, opened his
briefcase and removed some tools. He stripped off his jacket
and the rest of his clothes. Underneath, he wore a black
neoprene wet suit.

"The Beast from the Black Lagoon," Whistler said from
his seat in the van, as though he could see Bishop's every
move.

"I'm already boiling in this thing," Bishop groused in a
whisper. "The next sneak, *I* stay in the van, Whistler goes."

"I'm ready to go in, Coach," Whistler said.

Mother, downstairs in the boiler room, was sweating
heavily. He checked the readout on his piggyback thermo-

stat: 88.1 degrees and rising. He fanned himself with a newspaper and moved as far from the direct heat of the boiler as the room would allow. He collapsed in a heap in the corner and panted like a dog.

Acoustical tiles now lay on the floor below a hole in Werner's office ceiling. A chair on top of a table stood beneath the hole. Bishop's neoprene-clad feet were disappearing from view in the direction of the computer room next door.

Bishop inched along a makeshift catwalk above the third floor to a position just over the near corner of the computer room. He waited there listening, making doubly sure their intelligence was correct—the instrument-filled room was empty.

"I'm about to peel it," he whispered into his mike.

"No change here," Crease said in his ear. "Take it down strong."

Bishop carefully removed an acoustic tile from the corner of the ceiling and peered in. All quiet. He removed three more, leaned into the hole and scanned the room.

In the glassed-off section stood the giant green-and-gold Cray computer, and attached to it by a silver umbilical, was Janek's black box. It sat on a desk right out in the open, unprotected except by the locked outside door and the killer ultrasonic sensor with the green eye.

Bishop craned around the room, searching. The green eye was nowhere to be seen. He leaned out further. "I don't see the one-eyed monster," he said.

The men in the van looked puzzled. "Whistler, are you absolutely sure you heard right?" Bishop said through their headsets. "I don't see any Smart-Eyes TDS-1000 with that blinking green—Aaagghh!"

"You found it," Whistler said. "Probably right under your nose."

"Ahhhh . . . Whoa, that was dumb," Bishop breathed, pulling himself ever so slowly back into the hole. "It's just below me, to my left. I'm behind it now." Below him to the left was the hypersensitive ultrasonic sensor, emerald eye blinking with silent vigilance.

He unzipped his wet suit a few inches and pulled an ultrasonic sniffer from inside. It looked like a TV remote control with a glass nipple on the end. He lowered it very slowly through the opening. There was no sound. He lowered the

sniffer farther out into the room, away from the corner. It
started to tick. He whispered into his mike: "There's a
three-foot area in the corner out of the sensor's range."

"Good, hang on," Crease said in his ear. "Mother,"
Bishop heard Crease say, "what's our reading?"

Miserable, dripping, exhausted from the heat, Mother
heaved his large body up and staggered over to the thermostat box. He checked the digital display. "What we got
here . . . is 98.6 and holding. And one fricasseed goose.
Can I please get out of here?"

"No way, man," Crease said in his ear. "Everybody
maintains. Go ahead, Bish."

Mother slouched back to his corner, stripping off his shirt.
He wrung a stream of sweat out of it, draped it over his
head and sat back down.

Bishop began slowly lowering himself into the "free
zone" in the corner of the computer room, beginning the
dangerous ballet he had rehearsed.

Fifty-one

Werner's condo was getting uncomfortably hot again
for Liz. Werner sat alarmingly close to her on the couch.

"No, really," Liz said, "it was delicious." In front of
her on the coffee table were their dinner plates, three bottles
of wine and several half-filled wineglasses. Werner's two
plates were clean. One of Liz's plates held a half-eaten *poulet au bleu* sticking up out of a melted-butter sauce now
congealed to the consistency of the La Brea tar pits. On
Liz's other plate were concentric circles of different diced
vegetables, each ring punctuated by a pearl onion, boiled
potato or other round vegetable to give the effect of electrons orbiting an atomic nucleus. Liz had nibbled out a
smallish wedge of vegetables, but the designer look was
largely intact.

"I just couldn't bear to, you know. . . ." she said. "It's
so striking."

"I overcooked the carrots," Werner said.

"No, I like them really squishy like that," Liz said, taking a small forkful from the third ring.

Werner faked a yawn, using the gesture to sneak his arm around her. Liz, the hair on the back of her neck standing up, instantly decided it was time to be dazzled by Werner's sophisticated taste in wines. "What was that fabulous wine with the chicken?" she said. "I've never tasted anything quite like it."

Werner beamed. "Oh, a fetching little Alsatian wine," he said with a knowing chortle. "A Lacrimae Sanctae Odiliae. Not so easy to get in the Silicon Valley."

"I would never have guessed you were a wine connoisseur," she said admiringly.

"I am a bit of a corksniffer," he said modestly, swirling his claret in his glass. "This Petrus, for example—better with bourgeois cuisine like this than cuisine classique, don't you know. If you're going to eat haut and want a Bordeaux, I like a Cheval Blanc myself."

"Where did you learn all that?" Liz gushed.

"Actually my family had quite a wine cellar for a while," he said. "Then my father drank it all." He laughed bitterly.

"Really?" Liz said.

"Agh, ancient history," Werner said. "He was an idiot." He picked up another glass. "Now this Grand Echezeaux, I particularly like the undertones of toasty oak, don't you? So right for a Burgundy."

"Uh, let me see," Liz said, raising her glass of Burgundy and sipping. "Gee, I see what you mean." She nodded appreciatively and searched her mind desperately for the next diversion as Werner's arm snaked around her shoulder again. "What's this?" she said. Great luck. Something else to be fascinated with on the coffee table—a toy cocker spaniel. "Don't tell me you're a dog lover too?" She leaned forward and stroked the little animal.

"Watch," Werner said, casually rubbing Liz's back. "Play dead!" The dog flopped over on its side.

Liz thought that *was* clever. But it was becoming painfully clear her general enthusiasm was translating itself in Werner's mind into only one thing. "Hmm, great," she said evenly, trying to back him off.

"I designed the voice recognition chip," Werner said, massaging the back of her neck.

"What a thing to do," Liz said, very uncomfortable with

his hand where it was. Oh God, she thought, what am I going to do now?

"Watch," Werner said again. "Do your business!"

The dog lifted its leg. Liz was grossed out and also inspired. There was an opening.

"That's so cute," she said. "Where's the bathroom?"

Werner pointed. "Just walk straight forward," he said.

And as Liz skittered out of the room, the mechanical doggie did as bid: It goose-stepped straight forward along the coffee table, plowing headfirst into Liz's purse-organizer, knocking it on the floor and spilling its contents. "Oh, pooch, look what you've done to Doris's pocketbook," Werner said.

He scooped up Liz's wallet and started to put it back in the purse when he noticed her driver's license. His face fell, then turned bright red. Her name wasn't Doris.

When Liz walked out of the bathroom, her pocketbook was back on the table, intact. Pooch sat there, innocent. Werner sat there, composed.

Liz sat down across from him, armed and ready with a new topic. "Gee, I noticed," she said, "that you have all your books and albums and CDs alphabetized by artist. I've always organized my things by category. Do you believe that shows men's and women's brains are inherently different?"

"What do you say we go for a drive . . . Doris?" Werner said.

Fifty-two

Bishop had left the "free zone" way behind—about four feet. He was inching his way through the superheated room, surrounded by swirls of menacing ultrasound and infrared rays. The black box was still a tantalizing twenty-five feet away. At this rate, it would take him half the night. He tried to concentrate on nothing but smooth movement, but his mind wandered to Liz in the clutches of that techno-geek. He stopped dead, picturing the possibilities. Keep moving, he told himself. Liz is formidable; she can cope with whatever comes up.

* * *

Werner and Liz drove silently through the exurbs of the Silicon Valley. They had been driving for some minutes when Liz realized with relief that Werner had run out of self-aggrandizing jabber. She looked at his chilly expression, and suddenly his un-Werner-like silence made her nervous.

"Boy, this *was* fun," she said. "Wanna head back? I've got an early day tomorrow. Bet you do too."

"We're almost there," Werner said.

"Almost where?" Liz said.

He said nothing, and kept driving, stonily silent. Liz tried to keep her I-can-handle-anything face on, but she couldn't imagine any way this latest turn augured well for her. Things were veering off a predictable course. If this guy had sex games in mind, she felt she could probably handle it. She hoped that was all it was, but it didn't feel that way.

Werner rounded a corner, drove up a tree-lined street and turned in a drive. A long, gold-facaded industrial building loomed up before them. The headlights illuminated the company sign amid the pink and red-bordered azaleas: PLAYTRONICS—EDUCATIONAL SOFTWARE AND COMPUTER GAMES.

"Wh-what is it?" Liz said, doing her best to quell the sick feeling in the pit of her stomach.

"It's where I work . . . *Elizabeth*," Werner said.

"Oh, God," Liz said with a nervous laugh, "nobody calls me that anymore." She playfully stroked Werner's shoulder. "How did you know that was my—other name, you—funny man?"

"Just do me one little favor, alright?" Werner said.

"Sure," Liz said, nodding hopefully.

"I really want to see your 'passport,' " Werner said.

Liz felt genuinely ill. And scared. She looked puzzled at him as though he was speaking Sanskrit, and kept her mouth shut.

Fifty-three

Bishop was still perambulating with slow-motion grace across the Sahara of space separating him from the box. He was about halfway, arms outstretched for balance, and sweating.

A faint whining intruded on his consciousness. A mosquito landed on his hand. He decided to ignore it.

"Mosquito," the attentive Whistler said in his ear. "Don't let it bother you."

Bishop rolled his eyes. Thanks. Easy for you to say. He pressed on. The mosquito whined again and landed on his forehead. Bishop tried to disregard it, but his concentration was shot. He attempted to dislodge the beast by vigorously working his eyebrows. The mosquito eventually got bored and flew off.

Only to land on Bishop's nose. It looked to have a wing-span of about four feet and an eight-inch needle, which it started to stick in.

"I hear it, Bish," Whistler said. "Let it take a drink and it'll leave."

Bishop was madly scrunching and unscrunching his nose. Which caused the insect to relocate on his upper lip. To hell with Whistler's armchair advice, Bishop thought. This is war. He curled his tongue upward and ate the mosquito. His eyes showed a mixture of disgust and crazed triumph.

Carl, in the driver's seat of the van, sang along quietly with Tom Waits on his headphones.

He casually looked out the window and saw something that startled him. He grabbed up his binoculars and focused at the license plate of the gray sportscar that had just entered the Playtronics parking lot. "IQ 180" he read. He turned and threw open the sliding panel that separated the cab from the van's work area.

"Crease," he said. "It's Werner!"

Crease grabbed the glasses and looked. In the parking lot, the car door on Werner's side swung open and Werner stepped out. He walked around and pulled Liz out by the arm. He pushed her forward toward the building.

"Martin! We've got trouble," Crease said into his head-set.

In the computer room, Bishop was on the verge of success. His hand, only inches away from Janek's box when he heard Crease announce Werner's and Liz's arrival, started to tremble. He picked up the box and began ever so slowly unscrewing the umbilical linking it to the Cray. "One thing I *can't* do is hurry," he said through clenched teeth. "Just head them off before they get in the lobby."

Werner pushed Liz roughly in through the glass front doors. Liz resisted, desperately trying to think her way out of this. "Werner, you're hurting me," she said. He nudged her along toward the guard station.

She stopped, put her hand up and managed an apologetic smile. "It's a joke, a game I play," she said. "It's nothing to get this bent out of shape about. You'd be making a big mistake to take it personally. Now c'mon, let's go home."

"I already made a big mistake," he said. He grasped her roughly by the arm and led her to the guard desk. "I'm Dr. Brandes," he said to the guard. "I work on three, and I believe this *phony* is in some kind of plot to break into my office."

"Lemme see your entry card," the guard said, putting down his tabloid, eyeing them both warily.

Werner pulled out his wallet, reached to slide his key card out of the individual slot where he always kept it. No card. He hastily sorted through the other cards. It was gone. "You took my card!" he growled through his teeth at Liz. He lunged for her. "Where's my card?! How'd you get my wallet?"

The guard jumped over his desk and grabbed Werner, pulling him off Liz. He pushed Werner back and unholstered his revolver. He held it pointed in the air and stepped back carefully behind his desk. "You both stand right there!" he barked, picking up the phone. Into the phone he said gravely, "Sir, we have a problem."

Bishop had the late Gunter Janek's black box cradled in his arms. He was inching for the "safety zone" corner of

the computer room, dripping with sweat. He had less than
ten feet to go. His muscles ached from the excruciating
moonwalk he was doing and from the added tension of
knowing Liz was in danger.

In the lobby, Werner and Liz glowered at each other,
watched over by the security guard. Liz wasn't giving up.
"You're a stubborn man, Werner," she said. "I understand
your work is sensitive. You have to be careful. But I'm really
disappointed you seem willing to trash our new friendship."

"You're quite a Jezebel, 'Doris,' " Werner said. "I'm
not talking to you."

Reinforcements arrived. Wallace and Gordon were
dressed in their usual gray business suits.

Werner, anxious and embarrassed, stepped forward. "I'm
terribly sorry to bother you gentlemen," he said, "but I'm
afraid someone is trying to get into my office."

The men looked at Liz, who was not about to cave. She
rolled her eyes as though Werner was three cards short of a
deck. "This is nonsense," she said. "I'm certainly not trying to get into his office. I was playing a silly game that
backfired. If Werner knew me better, he'd never be making
this fuss." She smiled ruefully at Gordon and Wallace.
"Please, let's just say goodnight. I'll explain it all to
Werner in the car."

Wallace studied Liz, as if trying to see into her brain.

"Let's take a look at his office," said a male figure striding in through the front door.

Liz turned and recognized Cosmo from Bishop's descrip-
tion.

"I'm a little surprised, Werner," Cosmo said. "Being
led around by our dick, are we?"

"Well, maybe it's nothing, sir," Werner said with a lame
half-laugh. "I just didn't want to take the chance."

"It better be nothing," Cosmo said, "or you are."

Wallace grabbed Liz by the arm, shoved her through the
guard post and fairly dragged her down the hall.

On the third floor, Bishop dropped from the crawl space
back into Werner's office. It was strewn with his clothes and
tools.

                         * * *

Cosmo and the rest of the entourage rode up in an elevator and arrived at the third floor. There they were met by three guards who had hustled up the stairwell from other parts of the building.

In Werner's office, Bishop furiously grabbed clothes and tools, throwing them up in the crawl space.

Gordon took a minute to deactivate the Mantrap, and the congregation moved down the hall toward Werner's office.

Bishop hauled himself up into the crawl space. He scrambled, trying to get the ceiling tiles to fall into place.

The door swung open and the armed guards entered, guns drawn . . . just as the last tile settled into its square.

Cosmo's men and Liz looked around expectantly. Liz gritted her teeth in fear. They gazed upon an empty office: no clothes or tools strewn about, no chair on the desk, no ceiling tiles removed. The guards moved across the room, checking behind the desk, checking the windows, the vents. Nothing appeared to have been touched. Liz let out her breath in silent relief.

Cosmo looked at Werner questioningly. "Well?"

Werner walked over and examined his desk irritably. He tested the locked drawers. He looked around at the walls, the ceiling.

Just above the acoustic tiles overhead, Bishop balanced precariously on the narrow catwalk beam, his arms full of his clothes, tools, briefcase and Janek's box. Sweat ran off his head and face and was caught, most of it, in his bundled-up clothes. One stream, however, made it's way down the outside of the arm of Bishop's wet suit and dripped off his elbow. Unbeknownst to him, it started to pool on the upper surface of the tile and seep into it.

Cosmo walked out of Werner's office, followed by a sheepish Werner and a secretly elated Liz. The guards took one last look around—one of them circled the desk—and left, making sure the door was locked behind them.

Had they taken a last look *upward,* they would have seen a dark stain spreading out slowly on one of the ceiling tiles. A drop of sweat hit the desk with a splat.

"You keep suspicious company, Miss—?" Cosmo said as they headed back down the third-floor hallway.

"Barker," Liz said boldly. "Elizabeth Barker."

"I'm very sorry we troubled you," Cosmo said. The

name seemed familiar somewhere deep in his consciousness.

"Not as sorry as I am . . . Werner!" Liz said, turning to
the mortified and furious chip designer. "You just have to
learn to trust people."

Bishop, listening to their muffled conversation before they
turned the corner and moved out of range, whispered into
his mike: "They're letting her go."

"The gods are with us," Crease said in his earpiece. "Is
baby still safe?"

"Never better," Bishop said, carefully shifting his
weight, getting ready to descend back into Werner's office.
"Let me know when they clear the building," he whispered
to Crease.

As they entered the lobby, Wallace walked a few feet to
the side, eyeing Liz. "I'm sorry," he said to no one in
particular. "There's something that smells like fish here."

Cosmo and Liz both looked at him. "You should check
this guy for rabies," Liz said, feeling a little cocky.

"Rabies only occurs in warm-blooded creatures," Cosmo
said dryly.

Wallace, bristling, turned on his heel and headed back
down the hallway. Gordon followed him.

Cosmo gave Liz an apologetic smile. She lifted her chin
and headed for the front entrance. She gave Werner a last
look. "This is my last computer date!" she said.

At that Cosmo stopped. He stared at Liz. Then he called
out: "Wait!" He snapped his fingers loudly. "Guard!" he
shouted.

The guard stepped in front of Liz and held the door
closed. Wallace and Gordon came pounding back toward
the front. All eyes turned to Cosmo.

Cosmo looked at Liz, then at Werner. "A computer
matched her with him?" he said. "I don't think so."

Liz realized that her loose lips had just sunk her ship and
the Sneakers' as well. She mouthed "Shit!" to herself.

"Martin," Cosmo said to Liz, and Liz's name came
flooding back to him from one of the files on Bishop. "You
and Marty." He instantly saw the whole picture. He raced
down the hall toward the stairs.

Gordon and Wallace followed. Two guards grabbed Liz
and muscled her in the same direction. Werner stood there
with his mouth open.

Fifty-four

Cosmo flung open the door to the computer room, triggering a howling alarm. He stopped dead as a wave of heat stunned him. "Why's it so hot in here?" he said, certain something was really wrong. He raced to the Cray. Janek's box was gone. "Shi-it!" he said through his teeth, gripping the edge of the desk to keep control. "Goddamn it to hell."

He turned and grabbed Liz hard. "He'll pay and you'll pay," he snarled. "Make it easy on yourself by telling me where he is."

"I don't know what you're—"

Cosmo threw her halfway across the room. He punched an intercom on his desk and barked into it: "The man Bishop—tall, fair-haired—he's loose in the building and has my merchandise. Use your goddamned weapons, just get him. Whoever does will be very rich. And somebody check what's going on in the bloody boiler room!"

The Sneakers in the van heard the screeching alarms go off and watched floodlights jump up all over the outside of the building. Within seconds, station wagons appeared, each full of armed guards. They spread out around the building.

On his console of monitors, Crease watched guards armed with shotguns racing up stairs inside Playtronics, through corridors, in and out of rooms. "Martin, we've got more guards than ticks on a hound," he rasped. "Six in the front lobby, four in the south corridor, second floor. Five in upstairs north—"

"Guards in the boiler room!" Carl yelped, pointing to a monitor.

"Jesus!" Crease said. "Mother, you got trouble," he said into his headset.

In the basement, Mother crouched behind some wooden pallets and watched a guard, revolver drawn, burst through the door into the outer room and work his way in his direction through a maze of heating pipes. Mother was paralyzed with fear. "I can handle it," he said. It convinced no one. "What—the—fuck—do—I—do?" he choked into his headset.

Carl, frantically consulting the blueprints of the basement, poked a trembling finger at a shaded area. "Heating ducts!" he said to Crease. "Over the furnace."

"You'll be okay," Crease said levelly to Mother. "Just find the heating ducts above the furnace." He checked the blueprint. "They'll get you to the elevator chase."

Mother inched his way on hands and knees toward the heating ducts. The guard was no more than ten feet away through the maze of pipes. No way Mother could get up in the galvanized heating duct without being heard.

The guard put his foot carefully against a stack of wooden pallets and shoved, toppling them, ready with his revolver for whatever might be behind them. Mother used the noise as cover and hauled his large frame up into a blistering hot duct with amazing agility.

He disappeared from view just as the guard made his way past—crouched, sweating, scared himself.

Bishop, immobile in a crawl space somewhere above the third floor, lay in the dark and sweated. "Come on, you guys, my ass is grass up here," he whispered. "I just remembered I had a claustrophobic fit once when I was a kid. I got lost in a cave."

"Now you tell us," Whistler said from the van. "How'd you get out of that?"

"The fire department," Bishop said.

Crease, poring furiously over building plans, said "That's it! Staring me right in the face. Martin, there's a fire escape at the end of the north corridor," he said. "You've got to break through a couple of firewalls. They're just pasteboard. Go directly north about thirty yards. Once you're there, let me know."

Cosmo, standing over a set of monitors in the computer room, scanned the same scenes Crease was watching. Cosmo, too, was reading floor plans, except his were illuminated electronic displays. He barked orders into his intercom microphone. "He'd be in a crawl space. Break through. Get men up in there. Don't leave any of the ground-floor exits uncovered for a millisecond, inside and out.''

Liz decided the best defense was still a feisty offense. She stalked back and forth on the far side of the sweltering computer room, glaring angrily, watched by Gordon. ''This is just crazy insane!'' she said to Cosmo. ''What are you looking for? Little men running around inside your walls?!''

Cosmo picked up a handgun and fired one shot across the room, shattering a computer terminal next to Liz's head. Liz shut up, sat down and hugged herself tight. That had not been a fruitful tack; she searched for one that might allow her to get through this alive.

Next door in Werner's office, a guard noticed the sweat stain on the ceiling. He used the butt of his shotgun to break through into the crawl space. He found Bishop's clothes. ''Affirmative on the crawl space,'' the guard said into his walkie-talkie. ''Third floor, southwest corner. The guy left some stuff up here. I'm going up.''

With Janek's box in his hand, Bishop crawled as fast as he could through wires and cables along a crawl space. He came to the firewall Crease had described. ''I see closed-circuit TV cables,'' he whispered into his mike. ''I think I'm over the corridor.''

''Don't move,'' Crease commanded. He was watching Wallace and three shotgun-wielding guards making their way down the hall, opening offices, looking inside. The three guards, in the lead, were disappearing around a corner when the scene on the monitor switched to a different corridor. ''Damn. Hold on,'' Crease said.

Bishop crouched, frozen in silence, listening for clues about what was going on in the hallway below.

Wallace was still there, looking around and listening.

Crease, watching the monitor which now showed the entrance, covered his mouthpiece with his hand. ''Shit!'' he said. ''I won't get that hallway back for a minute and a half.''

''Can you leave him there that long,'' Whistler said.

''I'd rather not,'' Crease said. He uncovered his mouthpiece and spoke to Bishop: ''I lost the picture, but I think you're probably clear by now.''

Bishop turned his head sharply, thinking he heard footsteps below him. His earpiece fell out just as Crease spoke.

Bishop tried to smother it with his hand, but the tiny voice rang out against the silence.

Wallace heard something. He turned, looked up at the ceiling and realized his prey was just overhead. He raised his pump shotgun and blasted it into the ceiling.

The blast tore through the tiles about twenty feet from Bishop.

Wallace pumped the shotgun and fired again, a couple feet closer. And again, closer. Bishop cowered against the firewall, unable to retreat. Wallace pumped, blasted, pumped, blasted—methodically walking up the corridor. The ducting was blown apart, chunks flying at Bishop, falling around Wallace in the corridor. Another two shots and pieces of Bishop would be flying around the corridor, dripping off the wall.

"Hold it! Cease fire!" came Cosmo's command over the PA system.

Whitened by plaster dust, tasting it and breathing the cordite from the shells, Wallace couldn't stop. He pumped his weapon and fired another explosion into the ceiling.

"Wallace, heel!" Cosmo shouted. "If you shoot up that box, you're dead."

Wallace looked around to see how Cosmo could know what he was doing.

Bishop crouched against the firewall, the last shotgun rupture right next to his feet.

"Marty?" Cosmo's echoing omniscient voice came over the PA. "I know you are in the building, and I know you can hear me."

In the computer room, Cosmo, a gun in one hand, PA mike in the other, watched his bank of monitors and spoke to Bishop. And his strange and sad confessional reverberated throughout the empty labs, offices and hallways of the whole building.

"Oh God, you should not have come back, Marty," Cosmo said. "I won and you lost, and if our friendship had meant anything to you at all, that's how you should have left it. But you always had to be the one on top, didn't you? You were the one who got away with things, while I never did. You always got the girl, while I never did." Cosmo walked around Liz, who was sitting stolidly in a chair. "At least until now," he said. "She's lovely, Marty." He leaned suddenly and shoved the gun's barrel viciously into Liz's breast. She let out a short sharp scream which went out over the mike.

Bishop reacted, his face contorted in anger and fear. "I've got the girl, Marty," Cosmo's voice rang out. "And if you do not give me back my box, I will kill her." Silence. Cosmo watched the monitor. He waited. "And if you're not inclined to take me seriously, I'll remind you how quickly and mercilessly your friend Greg was deleted . . . just for being your friend, I might add."

He waited in silence, watching the monitors. Nothing.

In the crawl space, pinned against the bulkhead by shotgun holes, Bishop listened. There had to be a way out. Below him he heard Wallace cock his shotgun again.

"Marty, for God's sake, bring me the box," Cosmo's voice echoed godlike through the corridors. "I'm losing patience fast. You must know that the people in this building will never let either of you live if you try to get out."

In the computer room, Cosmo pulled up a chair opposite Liz and sat facing her. "I am your way out," he said into the mike. "And I am your only way out. Please. For Liz's sake, bring me the box now. If I wanted you dead, Marty, you would be dead. I cannot kill you."

Bishop was exhausted—out of ideas and out of range of help from his friends.

"You *have* to trust me," Cosmo's voice resounded.

Bishop stuffed Janek's box into his wet suit. He whispered something into his lapel mike. Then he moved down to the blown-open part of the ceiling.

Wallace raised his shotgun just as a ceiling tile was kicked out. Bishop lowered himself into the corridor. By now, half a dozen guards were running toward them from both directions, shotguns ready.

Wallace looked at Bishop as though he wanted to squeeze his head off and spit down his neck.

Fifty-five

Wallace used his shotgun to push Bishop, carrying Janek's box, into the computer room. The temperature had fallen halfway to normal. Cosmo was back in charge of his own building.

"Good evening, Marty," he said to Bishop. He opened his hands with a rueful look. "Why?" he said.

Bishop put the box on the table between him and Cosmo and turned to Liz, taking her hand.

"You picked a hell of a time to finally be there for me," she said, standing and hugging his arm.

"Let her go," Bishop said to Cosmo.

Cosmo picked up Janek's box and smiled expansively. "Marty, there are two kinds of dreamers," he said. "There's the right kind, like me. I dream things that never were and invent ways to get them—some nice ways, some a little rough maybe. That's what it takes to be great." He put the magic box back on the table by the Cray and picked up his gun. "You're the other kind of dreamer, Marty," he said "Like most of those clowns back then—the wrong kind. Not tough enough, not real-world enough. You dream about the way things ought to be and when the world says no-no, you run away to Canada with your tail between your legs."

Cosmo walked over and looked Bishop in the eye. "Did you expend an ounce of mental energy trying to figure a way to get me out of the pen, Marty? An ounce? Did you say, 'Hey, this isn't right, I'm a smart guy, I'll at least try to help the poor sonofabitch?' Of course, you didn't. The Daddies were out to smack your wrists with a ruler; you scurried away and hid. I hated to see it happening. I tried to deny it, but that's the stuff of scumbag cowardice."

Bishop took the onslaught silently, leery of triggering a psychotic explosion.

Cosmo stared at Bishop. "But you're you, after all. You're not me," he said. "I cannot kill my friend." He put his handgun down on his desk.

Bishop breathed easier.

Cosmo turned to Wallace. "Kill my friend," he said. He walked toward the door without looking back.

"Cosmo," Bishop said. Liz looked at Cosmo in terror.

"You see what I mean, Marty?" Cosmo said, facing the door. "You *dreamed* I was really going to let you go free. That's pathetic. You've just never grown up." He half turned and looked at Gordon. "Make them dead," he said, and walked out the door.

While Cosmo talked, Bishop noticed a ceiling fixture behind Gordon and Wallace starting to jiggle.

As the door clicked shut, Wallace grinned and leveled the shotgun at Bishop. "You didn't really think we were going to let you walk, did you?" he said. "I told him the first time was a mistake."

"You didn't really think I was going to let you have the box, did you?" Bishop said.

That confused the doltish Wallace. "What?" he said.

A ceiling fixture close to the two men jiggled.

"Now," Bishop said.

"Damn right, now," Wallace said, raising the shotgun toward Bishop's belly.

"Mother, now!" Bishop blurted into his lapel mike.

With a mighty crash and the splintering of tiles, Mother, screaming in fear, plummeted through the ceiling on top of Gordon.

Wallace spun, his shotgun went off, barely missing Bishop and Liz.

Mother pummeled the stunned Gordon while Bishop jumped Wallace before he could get off another shot. He wrenched at the weapon and it went clattering away across the desk top onto the floor. As the two men wrestled, Liz dove for the shotgun. She grabbed it and fired it into the ceiling.

"Next sonofabitch who moves, I plug," she yelled, and expertly pumped home another shell.

Mother pounded on Gordon's head frantically. Then staggered to his feet like an exhausted Sumo wrestler, heart pounding, leaving Gordon lying there dazed.

Bishop clambered up, helping the winded, scarlet-faced Wallace to his feet—then smashed him in the mug with all his might. Wallace went down across a desk, rolled and thudded to the floor. He dragged himself up and came back at Bishop. Bishop hit him again, and this time Wallace collapsed like a column of water.

"What the hell were you waiting for?" Bishop, puffing, yelled at Mother, who was leaning on the console, trying to get his jello legs to firm up. He was shaking all over.

"Courage," Mother gasped. He was just on the edge of blowing his lunch.

"Uh, can we go now," Liz said, her own hands, holding the big shotgun, beginning to shake visibly.

Bishop grabbed Janek's box and the three of them ran out the door.

Fifty-six

Bishop and Liz rounded the corner down by the Mantrap and saw five guards coming their way from the far end of the corridor. They spun back as the guards leveled their Uzis and fired at them. The wall where they had been standing went up in smoke, falling in shreds. Electric cables inside the wall split apart with a shower of sparks.

Bishop whispered hoarsely into his mike as they ran the opposite way along the west corridor. "Crease, we're going for the north fire escape. Are we clear?"

Crease trained binoculars on the flood-lit building. He saw four guards climbing up the north fire escape. "Negative!" he shouted. "Not clear! You got four goons going up!"

"We're screwed," Bishop said. The Uzi guards were pounding toward the corner. They were trapped.

Bishop read the sign on a trash chute behind Liz: CLASSIFIED TRASH, it said. "That's us," Bishop said, grabbing Liz and pushing her toward the chute. He yanked up the lid, but Mother stepped in front.

"You first, Mother," Liz said. "At least you'll bounce." He was in the chute and had plunged out of sight in a blink. Liz jumped. Bishop followed. The guards rounded the corner to find the hallway deserted.

Mother gathered speed as he tumbled down the slanting aluminum chute and ultimately landed in something soft—a huge pile of waste paper. Liz followed, landing on something softer—Mother. He wrenched her out of the way just as Bishop landed with a thump, barely missing them both. Mother sat up wheezing, holding his gut, trying to get some breath in his lungs.

They were in a sheet metal trough, enclosed on top by narrow steel mesh. A clanking sound started up, and the whole pile started rumbling, moving backward.

"Conveyor belt," Bishop said.

They turned to see where they were headed. Ten feet ahead of them were gaping steel jaws holding six sets of whirling razor-sharp steel blades.

"We're in a big shredder!" Mother said. "Good God! Just like the giant one I read they got at the NSA—the world's biggest—shreds seventy-five thousand pounds a day. It's amazing."

"Did you read how you get out of it if you fall in?" Liz said.

"No way out!" Mother said. "That's the whole idea of these things. It's a sealed system that's activated by the weight of the trash. You have to know that whatever you put in the chute can't be touched until it's shredded."

"Great," Bishop said as all three of them started crawling away from the steel blades. They grabbed onto the bottom of the chute and were just regrouping when a large scooper propelled them backward toward the blades.

"Crease!" Mother yelled into his mike. "I've got something about shredders in one of my tech manuals. I think it's the green one."

Outside in the van, Crease started tearing through piles of technical manuals.

"Uh, or the orange one," Mother said over the mike.

The shredding blades loomed closer. Mother frantically searched through his tool kit. "Maybe if I can induce a current, I might be able to short out the system," he said.

Liz watched Mother's futile pawing in his tool kit as the whirring blades mulched big mouthfuls only a few feet from them. "Oh, fuck that shit!" she said with mortal impatience. She grabbed the tool case and threw it into the blades. The tool case ripped to shreds, the flashing blades rocketing tools in every direction like shrapnel. As human feet were about to get sliced and diced, some of Mother's larger tools got caught in the blades, jamming them. The system shut down.

"Sometimes low tech is the best," Liz said. "You know what I mean?"

With great relief, Mother and Bishop pulled the shattered blades apart and the three of them climbed through the broken shredder. On the other side they ended up in a pile of confetti in another enclosed trough.

"How do we get out of *here*?" Bishop said.

As if responding to his question, the top of the trough opened mechanically.

"Thank you," Bishop said.

Six metal nozzles swung over the top. There was a hissing sound.

"Oh no!" Bishop said.

"Acid shower!" Mother shouted.

They scrambled up the sides of the bin as the burning acid shot out of the nozzles. As he pushed Liz up, acid sprayed Bishop's arm, melting the wet suit. He clambered up. They reached the top of the bin, climbed over and dropped to the floor, everybody in one piece.

Fifty-seven

They emerged into the basement. Mother knew it well. He led them to the rear where there was a ramp up to an enclosed loading dock at the street level. They ran up the ramp and along the loading dock. They peered out the back window into the parking lot. Guards rolled by outside in a station wagon. They ducked down and Bishop looked around. Behind them was a set of interior doors through which guards could come at any moment.

"Up here," Bishop said, leading the way up a narrow utility stairs to a door that opened onto the roof. They exited and crouched down behind the ledge at the edge of the roof.

"Crease," Bishop said into the mike. "We're on the roof of the rear loading dock. There's a fire ladder on the east end. Can you get to us?"

In the van, Crease clambered up into the driver's seat. "I'll get as close as I can," Crease said.

"Where are you?" Bishop said. Off in the distance he saw headlights flash on and off once. "Beautiful," Bishop said. "Come and get us."

In the head security station, Cosmo's wrath was biblical. He was trying to watch all the closed-circuit monitors at once, twitching this way and that like a man in the grip of madness. "Seal the parking lot!" he screamed into the PA. "Double the fence voltage. Nobody gets out of here!"

Crease, with Carl next to him in the front of the van, moved the vehicle forward and scanned the parking lot, looking for the right moment to storm the Playtronics' gate. "Here we come," Crease said into his mike. He took off his headset and was about to accelerate through the gate when two guards appeared out of nowhere and thrust their shotguns through the side windows.

"Keep your hands where I can see them and step out of the van," said the guard with his weapon on Crease.

Crease and Carl exchanged looks of frustration. Carl got out as ordered. Crease delayed, trying to quickly figure out the angles.

"You too, Midnight," the guard said.

Crease's eyes narrowed dangerously. He looked at the man for a beat, then he complied, taking his time.

In the rear compartment of the van, invisible in the darkness behind the closed panel, sat Whistler. He waited until the guards had moved Crease and Carl a few feet away from the door. Then he turned on his headset and whispered, "Bish, they got Crease and Carl."

On the roof, Bishop, Liz and Mother were poised to climb down the fire ladder. "Shit," Bishop said.

"Look!" Mother said, pointing the length of the parking lot. Six utility trucks, dragging large cannisters on wheels, were circling the building and stopping at roughly equal distances. Security guards jumped out, opened the cannisters and started pulling man-sized coils of barbed-wirelike stuff across the blacktop.

"Razor-wire," Mother said. "We're gonna be in a cage." The three of them crouched back down behind the ledge.

The guards stretched out the huge, lethal slinkies in both directions, aiming at closing off the entire building.

"It's now or never, Whistler," Bishop said into his mike. "You've got to do it."

"What?!" Mother said.

"Do what?" Whistler whispered, equally baffled.

"You gotta drive," Bishop said. "I'll talk you through it. Hurry."

Whistler's face lit up. He moved as stealthily as possible toward the front of the van. He silently slid back the front panel and listened. The guards with Crease and Carl were off a few yards to the left and to the rear.

One guard was frisking Carl as the other held a shotgun on Crease. Crease's eyes widened as he saw Whistler noiselessly climbing into the driver's seat of the van.

In the cockpit, Whistler felt the wheel, found the gearshift, got his foot poised on the accelerator of the idling van. "Okay, now what?" he whispered.

"The gate is about thirty yards behind you," Bishop said. "Put it in reverse and floor it."

"What's reverse?" Whistler said.

Bishop stared at the van in the distance, about to have a heart attack. "One down," he said.

Crease, being frisked by a guard, was keeping an eye on Whistler. He saw the blind man bend. Was he reaching for the gearshift? Crease turned to Carl and snarled through gritted teeth: "Did I ever tell you why I had to leave the CIA?"

"Uh, no," Carl said, looking at Crease as though he was crazy.

At that moment the van popped into gear and jerked backward. The two Playtronics guards spun at the sound. Crease made a terrifying animal growl and leapt for one of them, grabbing the shotgun from his hand and slamming the butt into the other guard's stomach, doubling him over. He sideswiped the first guard's head with the heavy barrel of the shotgun, knocking him cold. The other guard started to rise. Crease made another primordial bellow and chopped him on the back of the neck. The man crumpled and lay still. Crease wrenched out the man's .45 automatic. He was in a colossal rage.

Carl had never seen him like this. "Wow," he said.

"Mother-*fuckers*-mess with me," Crease growled. "I bust they fucking head!"

"Alright!" Carl said. He was thrilled to finally hear Crease talk the talk. He put out two hands for Crease to slap. Wrong move. Crease froze him with a glare and, with effort, got very straight again.

Whistler in the van was barreling fast in reverse toward the gate. He was terrified. "Bish? Bish?" he said. "I'm going backwards."

"Doing fine, doing fine," Bishop said, watching from the top of the loading dock. "Hit the brakes. *Now!*"

Whistler stomped on the brakes, held the wheel rigid and prayed. The van fishtailed wildly, bucking and swaying and slid to a stop, miraculously upright, five feet from the gate.

"Now turn the wheel right, push the gearshift forward and floor it," Bishop barked.

Whistler ground the gears, turned hard right and pushed the accelerator. The van jumped forward, made it through the gate and kept veering right.

"Straighten out! Straighten out!" Bishop said.

Whistler straightened the wheel and sped forward—headed right for some parked cars.

"Whoa! Go left!" Bishop said.

Whistler swung the wheel to his left—now heading for some other parked cars.

"Nooo! *My* left," Bishop said. "Go right!"

"What," Whistler said, confused for one of the few times in his life.

"Go right! Go right!" Bishop said.

Whistler wrenched the van hard right, managing just to graze three or four of the cars. He sped through a wide gap where the razor-wire barrier hadn't been linked up.

"Beautiful!" Bishop said. "Keep coming. Five more seconds, then stop."

On the loading dock roof, Bishop motioned for Liz and Mother to scramble down the ladder to the ground. "Okay, now!" Bishop yelled into his mike.

Whistler, headed at the loading dock, didn't react quite in time. He stood on the brakes but skidded straight into the loading dock's truck-tire bumpers and bounced back. "I'll just stop here," he said.

Mother and Liz dashed to the van. They piled in.

"Some driving, Whistler," Mother said.

Whistler made no move to give up the driver's seat. "Where to?" he said.

"Gimme that!" Mother said, climbing past Whistler, pushing him over and taking the wheel.

On the roof, Bishop had one foot on the ladder, about to descend.

"You will give me the box right now," said Cosmo, appearing out of the dark, "or I will kill you as we speak."

Bishop straightened. Cosmo walked across the roof toward him, gun in hand, a tight, paranoid look on his face.

Bishop looked at his old friend and played a hunch.
"No," he said. He put one foot back on the ladder.

In one motion, Cosmo lifted the gun and fired. The bullet
missed Bishop's head by inches. Bishop froze, precariously
balanced on the top rung of the ladder. He looked at Cosmo,
still advancing, gun leveled, now smiling sadistically. The
smile chilled Bishop to the bone. He climbed back on the
roof. Slowly, he reached into his backpack and withdrew
Janek's box. He extended it toward Cosmo.

Keeping the gun trained on Bishop, Cosmo reached for
the box and grasped it. But Bishop didn't let go.

"You could have shared this with me," Cosmo said,
keeping the gun pointed.

"I know," Bishop said, still holding on to the box.

"You could have had the power," Cosmo said.

"I guess I just don't want it," Bishop said.

"I don't believe you," said his old comrade in arms.

For answer, Bishop let the box go. "I've lived in shadows
for twenty years, Cosmo," he said. "I'm tired of it. It's
boxes inside of boxes, doors within doors. It's too complicated. And I don't want it." He turned toward the edge of
the roof.

"Marty, I hear what you're saying and it's oh so sad,"
Cosmo said. "But the moral niceties are fucked, haven't
you noticed? The kinder, gentler ideology won, the evil em-
pire got shitcanned and nothing's changed. Doesn't that tell
you something? Doesn't that give you a clue about how
much of a shit the world gives about our little moral crises—
what we used to call *values*!" Cosmo moved in close,
speaking with great urgency. "The world isn't run by weapons anymore, Marty," he said. "Or oil, or even money. It's
run by little ones and zeroes. Little bits of data. It's all just
electrons."

"You were always better at physics than me, Cosmo,"
Bishop said, putting both feet on the ladder.

Cosmo, more desperate than ever to make his point,
grabbed Bishop's arm. "You think it's still the Free Speech
movement at Berkeley, Marty. It's a war, a world war. And
not about who's got the Sudetenland or the Balkans or Ku-
wait or the bomb. It's about *who controls the information*!
What you see and hear and what you think, what your kids
are gonna think whether you want them to or not. It's already so far out of hand, it's a joke! *It's all about the infor-*

mation. Control or be controlled. There's no Canada in this war, Marty. Will you listen to me?''

''If you're smart, you'll destroy that thing,'' Bishop said, looking Cosmo in the eye. He started down the ladder.

''Don't go,'' Cosmo said.

Bishop looked up to see Cosmo looking ineffably sad. ''Good luck, Cosmo,'' Bishop said. He climbed down to the asphalt parking lot.

Cosmo stood stock-still, completely alone. He looked down at the box. He offhandedly snapped the top off to double-check the innards. He looked—and it took a second to register. What he saw were the guts of an ordinary answering machine, not Janek's decoder.

The white light of a panning searchlight flared onto him and seared him in its beam. A hot flash of mortification and rage swept over him. ''Stop them! In the rear parking lot!'' he screamed. He dashed along the edge of the roof and fired his automatic down at the Sneakers' van as Bishop scrambled aboard. The van reversed away from the loading dock and squealed across the parking lot.

Mother, at the wheel, aimed the van at the rapidly closing gap in the razor-wire barrier. A searchlight picked out the van. Guards in station wagons converged from other parts of the property. Guards on foot rushed to finish closing the razor-wire barrier.

Mother saw the van was going to get there too late. He changed his aim slightly, steering directly at one of the guards hauling the wire. The man jerked around, looked into the onrushing headlights and dove for his life. The van broke through the edge of the barrier and kept going, heading for the parking lot gate only fifty yards straight ahead.

Waiting in the shadows a few dozen yards past the gate, cheering them on, were Crease and Carl.

There was one catch. One end of the coil of razor-wire caught onto the rear bumper. As the coiled wire stretched out, the van started to slow down. Liz looked out the back window at the station wagons closing in. ''You better step on it,'' she called out.

''Good idea,'' Bishop said. He swung open the back door and, leaning out and hanging onto the handle, kicked at the wire snagged in the bumper. A bullet zipped by. Bishop jerked his head and shoulders back in the van. ''Shit!'' he said.

Another round whacked into the door of the van from a station wagon closing fast. Leaning from the passenger window, taking aim with a Luger, was Wallace. Bishop leaned out and gave the bumper another kick, then another. The wire stayed knotted tight around the bumper, growing more and more taut. One more kick from Bishop, and the whole bumper ripped off the old van.

Like a giant lethal slingshot, the razor-wire sprang back toward Wallace's station wagon. The loose bumper clanged around one side of the wagon, ensnaring the whole front of the vehicle with wire, ripping its tires to shreds. The wagon slewed out of control, hit a concrete divider broadside and flipped over. It burst into flames.

Bishop pulled the back door shut as Mother headed like a kamikaze directly at the locked gate. The three guards there scattered. The van crashed through the tall sturdy wire gate and miraculously kept going. Forty yards down the entrance drive, Carl jumped out from behind a eucalyptus tree waving frantically. Mother slowed long enough for him and Crease to pile in. They sped away into the night.

Bishop stared out the rear window, able to pick out Cosmo's outline against a backdrop of searchlights on the Playtronics roof. Just before the van turned and he lost sight of his ex-comrade in arms, Bishop saw several other figures join him on the roof.

Cosmo stood with his useless guards at the edge of the roof, watching Janek's box get away. He turned and strode quickly for the stairs.

In the computer room, he gathered a few items from his desk and stowed them in his briefcase. He crossed to the door and opened it to leave. Standing outside gazing at him were three meaty bodyguard types in cheap suits along with a gray-faced man in an expensive double-breasted blue pinstripe.

"The board of directors would rather you stayed here for a while," the gray-faced man said impassively. His arms hung straight at his sides. His eyes were dead, like a shark's.

Cosmo looked at the man icily, then did the only wise thing. He backed up and slammed the door shut. He looked around, but there was obviously no way out. His eyes went to the console of video monitors. On one of them he saw himself, standing by the door with his briefcase in his hand.

He was being surveilled in his own office. He spun around, looking for the camera. He couldn't spot it. Now he was on a second monitor, and a third. His head jerked around looking. Now a fourth. He was being watched from every angle.

Defeated, he sat down in his chair and sighed. "The nineties suck," he said.

Fifty-eight

In the predawn, with Mother driving, the van screamed north out of the Silicon Valley, flat out. Bishop and Crease watched for pursuers. As soon as they hit the straightaway over the salt marshes, they saw that they were in the clear. They sped on toward the Dumbarton Bridge and the Oakland side of the Bay. The team flaked out in the back, completely spent from their ordeal.

"We're going home, guys," Mother crowed. "Back to the Lair. Feels like we been gone a year."

"We can open the windows and play some sounds," Carl said.

"No more hiding in the shadows, Bish," Whistler said. "I don't know how you held up all these years, but man, it's over."

Bishop took a second Janek-style answering machine out of his backpack and pried off the top. This one was the real one, with the oddly ribbed box inside containing all of Janek's electronics, including the coveted large, black, shiny chip. "You know what I can't believe?" he said. "We just pulled off the greatest sneak in history, and we can't tell a soul about it."

"You know what I can't believe?" Liz said. "We fought World War Three for this incredibly valuable box and now we've got it, it's worth nothing to us unless we give it up. I mean for all its power, there's nothing we could do with it that would be legal or honest."

The Sneakers exchanged glances. "Hey," Mother said, "what could the government do with it that would be legal or honest?"

"Mother, I hate to admit it, but you may be right for

once," Crease said wearily from the floor somewhere in the back.

Mother looked surprised and gratified.

The other Sneakers mulled over the fact that this was a glorious victory that left them in many ways exactly where they had started.

"What I can't believe is, you guys aren't letting me drive home," Whistler said, sitting up front looking out the windshield like an avid nine-year-old.

Everybody laughed and howled about Whistler's incredible driving.

"Man, did we kick some ass back there!" Mother exulted as they crossed the middle of the Dumbarton Bridge and sailed into home territory. Even Bishop was breathing easy at last, winding down.

"Whoa!" Mother said, jamming on the brakes. The van swerved to a halt. A car had stopped short in front of him. "Drive, jerk!" he said, honking his horn loudly.

A second car, a late-model sedan, appeared from nowhere and screeched to a stop on the van's left. Another late-model sedan, a blue one, pulled up behind the van, trapping it.

Quickly, six federal agent types, including a woman, jumped out of their cars and surrounded the van. All six agents bristled with weapons—automatic pistols and shotguns. The two closest agents showed badges to Mother. "National Security Agency," one of the men said.

The female agent, a blonde with no-nonsense short hair and a no-nonsense shotgun in her hands, pulled open the back door and pointed her weapon. "All of you. Step out of the vehicle," she said. "Hands over your head. Move."

The bone-weary Sneakers and Liz clambered out into the cool predawn air. Bishop, before emerging, quickly stuffed Janek's box inside his wet suit. He stepped out into the pool of light. The agents lined them up, pushing them rudely against the side of the van.

"Mr. Bishop," said a deep-voiced black man, stepping out of the trailing blue sedan and coming forward. "I'm Senior Agent-In-Charge Bernard Abbott. We spoke on the phone."

"Abbott," Bishop said, looking at the big man in the dapper Navy overcoat. "How long have you—?"

"Since shortly after your phone call. We've been keeping

an eye on you," Abbott said. "Our toughest trace ever. We'd never have gotten you without a brand-new computer vectoring technology we were trying out. Borrowed from the NASA-JPL radio astronomy program. We can sort through the junk and pick up ghost traces of telephone signals for as long as fifteen seconds after hang up. It's helpful." He chuckled and walked around in front of the Sneakers. "Now, you help me," he said. "I believe you have something that belongs to me."

Bishop considered for a moment, then took a chance. He took a fast step forward, abruptly brushing past the nearest agent, catching him off guard. He stepped up on the curb and walked directly to the bridge railing before anyone could stop him. In the same move, he withdrew Janek's box from his wet suit and placed it on the parapet—inches from watery oblivion. He held up his hand in warning as the agents moved forward. "Stay right there," Bishop said to the advancing agents. They stopped.

Bishop looked at Crease and the other Sneakers. "It's interesting seeing the NSA here, don't you think?" he said. "I mean, the NSA doesn't have black-bag teams. You guys are supposed to be stuck in listening posts all over the world, bent over your computers, not out here with guns. Isn't the FBI supposed to do this kind of thing for you?"

"Absolutely," Abbott said. "This is outside the NSA's usual jurisdiction. But in cases of supreme urgency, we can employ any reasonable means to attain our needs."

"Your needs," Bishop said. "Such as making sure nobody else knows about Janek's little box."

"I wonder why everybody shouldn't know?" Crease said, scowling at Abbott. "Can you answer that?"

"It's NSA's box. We paid Janek well," Abbott said with an evenness that betrayed mounting discomfort. "Let's end the game. Step away from the box."

"I keep thinking of something Greg told me," Bishop said, staying close to the box. "He said our codes were based on an entirely different system from the Russian codes. So this box wouldn't work on their codes. The only thing it's good for is breaking American codes . . . spying on Americans."

Abbott's face hardened perceptibly.

"So you mean with a box like this," Mother said innocently, "they could read the FBI's mail?" He sauntered over to Bishop's side as he spoke.

"Or the CIA's or the White House's or Congress's mail?" Whistler said, following Mother.

"Imagine how mad Congress is going to be when they hear about this?" Mother said.

"On the other hand," Crease said, "if the other children got this toy, they could turn around and read the NSA's mail." Crease took Liz's and Carl's arms and led them across to stand by Bishop.

"The watchers would be watchable," Bishop said. "No more secrets."

The Sneakers and Liz stood together at the parapet, facing the fidgeting, heavily armed NSA agents. They were looking to Abbott for a signal to move in.

"What do you want, Mr. Bishop," Abbott said tightly.

Bishop answered without hesitation. "Clean up my record and get out of my life," he said.

"I don't have much choice, do I," Abbott said with forced affability. He gestured to his agents to lower their weapons.

"Not if you don't want to read about this in *Newsweek*," Bishop said.

Abbott looked at Bishop narrowly for a moment, then nodded. "Deal," he said. He held his hand out for the box.

Mother interrupted. "Not so fast," he said. "I want a Winnebago."

"What?!" Abbott said.

"Fully equipped, with a solar roof and super-wide tires," Mother said.

"This isn't a car dealership, buddy," Abbott said, bristling.

"He wants a Winnebago," Bishop said, nodding understandingly. "Fully equipped. The biggest model." He transferred Janek's box to the other side, away from the agents, and kept a hand on it.

Abbott watched Bishop's movements with dread. He sighed, and gave up. "All right," he said. "A Winnebago." He held out his hand again.

Crease spoke up. "I've never taken my wife to Europe," he said.

"I'm sorry to hear it," Abbott said, losing patience. "Now—give—me—the—box."

"You will buy me two round-trip, first-class tickets to Lisbon," Crease said. "And Madrid, Athens and Scotland."

"Don't forget Tahiti," Bishop said.

"Tahiti's not in Europe!" Abbott said.

"Hey!" Carl said. "When you get the box, *then* you give us geography lessons. Until then, the man goes to Tahiti."

The Sneakers and Liz looked at Carl with new respect. Abbott screwed up his face in pain. "Fine," he said.

"Carl?" Bishop said obligingly.

Carl leaned toward Abbott and spoke low. "This girl with the shotgun?" he said, looking at the blond NSA agent. "Is she single?"

Everybody looked at him horrified—the Sneakers, Abbott, the other agents. "Think lovelier thoughts, Carl," Bishop said.

"I just want her phone number. Please." Carl said.

"Carl," Bishop said. "We've got this bozo over the biggest barrel in history. You can have anything you want."

"One date with the blonde," Carl said. "Please!"

Bishop realized he was serious. He shook his head, turned to Abbott. "Maybe a lunch," he said to the agent-in-charge. "You can chaperone."

"No," Abbott said. "I will *not* do this." The big man could not have looked more uncomfortable.

"Abbie, Abbie, the FBI'd get him twins!" Bishop said. He was beginning to enjoy this. Liz had to hide her smile behind her hand.

"No!" Abbott said, his face setting into a deeply lined scowl.

"Wait," the female agent said. They all turned and looked at her. She moved forward slightly and looked at Carl. She spoke carefully. "You could have anything you want, and yet . . . you asked for me?" she said.

Carl nodded. Their eyes locked. They were smitten.

"273-9164," she said, continuing to hold his eyes. Carl nodded again.

Abbott raised his eyes to heaven. The Sneakers melted. Even the other NSA agents smiled and shook their heads in amazement.

"I'm Carl," he said.

"I'm Mary," she said.

"I'm going to be sick," Abbott said. "Are we done here?

Can we get on with business?'' He stuck his hands in his coat pockets and emitted a growl of distemper.

"Not yet," Bishop said. "What about you, Whistler? What do you want?''

"Peace on earth, goodwill toward men," Whistler said, staring over Abbott's head.

Abbott looked at the other Sneakers and realized this was no joke. "Oh, this is ridiculous," he said.

"I want peace on earth, and goodwill toward men," Whistler said, shifting his sightless eyes downward and looking right at Abbott.

Abbott was genuinely disconcerted. "We're the United States Government!" he said angrily. "We don't *do* that sort of thing.''

"I want peace on earth, and goodwill toward men," Whistler repeated insistently.

"You'll just have to try," Bishop said to Abbott. Everyone on both sides except Abbott was hiding a smirk.

"All right!" Abbott said through gritted teeth. "I'll see what I can do.''

"That's all I ask," Whistler said serenely.

Abbott, a man at the end of his rope, threw his hands in the air. "*Now* may I have the box?" he said.

Bishop reached over, picked up Janek's precious box and handed it to Abbott. "By the way, it doesn't work," he said. "It never did.''

"That's not really your concern, is it?" Abbott said. "It's in good hands now. The important thing for all of you is: none of this ever happened. And this box . . . did not exist.''

"Never saw it before," Bishop said.

"Never saw it before," Whistler echoed. Mother guffawed.

"You'll remember that, all of you," Abbott said in his stern deep voice.

"Don't ever give us reason to forget it," Bishop said, standing squarely in front of Abbott, looking him in the eye.

Abbott nodded. He turned and strode toward his car. The other agents did the same. Except Mary. She and Carl were still looking at each other, fascinated. One of Mary's fellow agents clutched her arm and dragged her away toward the lead car.

The NSA contingent loaded up and drove off.

The Sneakers and Liz watched them go. Carl jumped for the van, found his little black notebook and hurriedly scribbled down the precious phone number.

The crew looked at each other in wonder.

Whistler leaned back against the railing and gazed up the Bay. Mother raised his hands in the air and walked around like Rocky.

Crease smiled, then laughed out loud and gave Liz a hug.

The light breeze off the water blew away the strain of the last frenzied days. The distant lights of San Francisco became visible through the wispy, ever-present fog.

"Marty, I don't mean to be naive or anything," Liz said, "but . . . can't they just hook it up and do awful things with it?"

"Nope," Bishop said, pulling from his pocket a large, shiny black chip—the master chip that powered Janek's box. He turned and flipped it over the parapet. They all watched it tumble and float on the way down, hit the water and sink out of sight, leaving a few momentary bubbles. A gull fluttered down to the spot, looking for the morsel—too late.

They managed a group high-five, getting their arms and legs more tangled up than necessary, laughing like twelve-year-olds.

They leaned again over the rail, peering at the floating gull marking the spot where Janek's chip disappeared. The gull took off and flew fast away from this polluted end of the Bay up toward his preferred fishing grounds around the Golden Gate. The Sneakers savored a rare sense of peace.

Bishop and Liz ambled along the promenade.

"Do you have any idea how attractive I find it when a man saves the world?" Liz said.

Bishop put his arm around her shoulders. "Why do you think I did all this?" he said.

"We're not getting back together, you know," she said with a serious look.

Bishop looked at her for a beat, then laughed it off. "Yeah, right," he said.

Liz smiled, put her arm around him, and they walked on.